GHOST OF
WHITE ISLAND

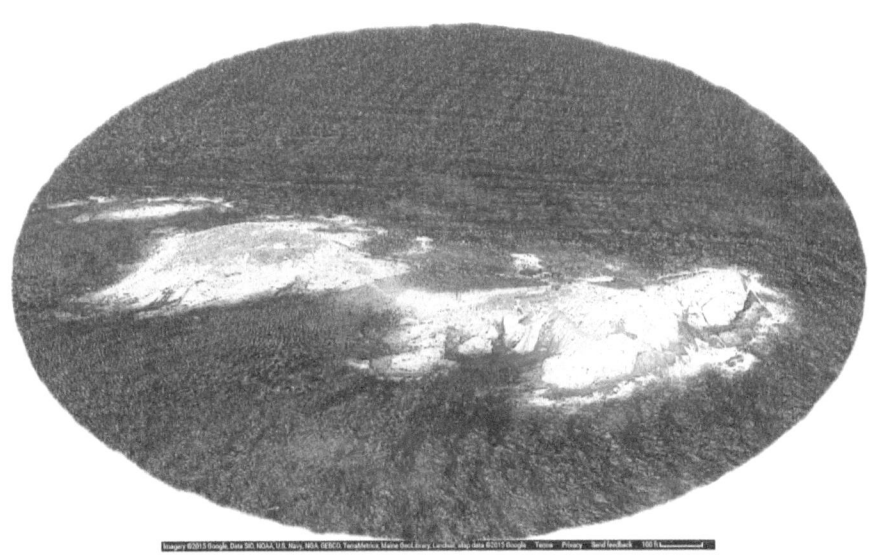

Jeff Lovell

TotalRecall Publications, Inc.
1103 Middlecreek
Friendswood, Texas 77546
281-992-3131 281-482-5390 Fax
www.totalrecallpress.com

Library of Congress Control Number: 2015951409

Printed in the United States of America with simultaneous printings in Australia, Canada, and United Kingdom.

FIRST EDITION
1 2 3 4 5 6 7 8 9 10

This book is dedicated to the memory of my grandparents, Wellborn and Marie Harrison. At their home I first found the book which fueled my imagination about pirates, *Doubloons* by Charles Driscoll. They did their best to encourage a young writer and to pave the way for his dreams.

Award Winning Author

is a native Chicagoan, with 3 degrees from the University of Illinois and an earned doctorate from Vanderbilt University. Jeff taught high school writing and literature for thirty three years and sponsored the school paper, Student Council and several other activities. He ran the drama program at two high schools, teaching and directing and designing sets, lighting and costumes. His specialty in his career focused on Shakespeare. Since he retired from education, Jeff has served as a theatre and film critic for a television station and appears frequently to review theatre and literature.

About the Book

Mickey Logan, a play director and theatrical from Chicago, finds himself accompanying his niece and her friend to search for the long lost treasure of the pirate Sandy Gordon. Not only do they struggle to find the treasure, but they must also contend with a terrorist organization also determined to located the loot to finance their terror activities.

A young woman's spirit walks in the moonlight, intent on preserving the lost treasures of a nation. Four young people make their way to the forbidding islands, trying to find and to put right an ancient secret and to liberate the soul of Martha Herring, forced into a marriage with a pirate as a young girl. Their quest, however, is being closely monitored by a team of terrorist fighter, believing that they can finance their evil with the lost pirate treasure.

Preface:

In 1715, a ship's carpenter tried to rape the 14 year old daughter of the captain of a British warship and was flogged almost to death. He mutinied and captured the ship, killing the captain and forcing his daughter into marriage. After falling in with Blackbeard, he abandoned his young wife on a cold, bitter rock called White Island, off the coast of New Hampshire. When he was caught and hanged by the British Navy, his treasure vanished into history. Many people believe that Martha, his reluctant wife, hid the treasure in the Isle of Shoals chain. This is the story of a search for those gold and jewels and treasure, protected by the Ghost of White Island.

Introduction

Four people join forces to locate the lost treasure of Sandy Gordon in the Isle of Shoals, off the coast of Maine and New Hampshire. According to the legends, a fabulous treasure lies hidden somewhere in the Islands. Mickey Logan, however, is seeking a greater treasure: the redemption of the soul of his great grandmother. Young Stephen Levin, meanwhile, is searching for the lost treasures of his nation.

PART I

CHAPTER 1

D on't go to White Island on a moonlight night especially if you are afraid of ghosts.

White Island rises with several other rocky islands above the North Atlantic, about ten miles out from Portsmouth, New Hampshire. Like the other rocks in the Isle of Shoals chain, White Island is cold and rocky, wind-swept and inhospitable much of the year.

A famous treasure, according to legend, lies hidden on the rock. But White Island is the subject of another, even more famous legend. A ghost story. The ghost of a young woman named Martha Herring walks there.

Many years ago—about three centuries, in fact--a mutineer whipped Martha's father with the cat-o-nine-tails before her eyes. He continued until he'd lashed all life out of the body of John Herring, the former captain of the small privateer known as *Porpoise*.

Sandy Gordon, the leader of the mutineers, forced the young woman to marry him. He turned *Porpoise* into a pirate ship and fell in with Edward Teach, the pirate known as Blackbeard. Later, Gordon imprisoned her, pregnant and terrified, on the miserable rock in the cold North Atlantic. He charged her with terrible oaths to protect his treasure.

A British man-of-war defeated and hanged the young woman's pirate husband. He never returned to his marooned young wife.

Martha's specter walks in the moonlight to a low spot on the island. She is dressed in a long dark blue coat, though her blood has not been chilled by an Atlantic nor'easter for 300 years. Her bones have lain in a grave on another island, many years since.

She stares out at the southeast horizon where she last saw her husband's ship, *The Flying Scot*, leaving her alone in a tiny cabin on top of the rock called White Island.

People who have seen her ghost say that she doesn't see them, but speaks in a soft, but audible voice. Over and over, she says, *He will return. He will return.*

Guests at the Retreat Center on nearby Star Island, the largest of the rocks in the Isle of Shoals chain, laugh when they hear the legend of the Ghost of White Island. Who can believe such a story? A ghost? Pirates? Absurd.

But they bid goodbye to others who are leaving for the mainland by repeating—in some cases laughing and mocking-- the young woman's cry of pain, loneliness and terror: *You will return. You will return.*

* * * * *

Another teenager named McKenna met the Ghost of White Island when grief had all but overwhelmed her.

McKenna's life fell apart one afternoon in January. The first semester of McKenna's freshman year in high school had just ended. The bus ride home from school after her last final exam found her giggling at everything her friends said.

As she left the school at 11:00 A.M., she buttoned up her

winter coat. The sun shone bright and the temperature hovered in the mid-40s. Though warm for January in the northern suburbs of Chicago, the weather that day didn't fool her. McKenna saw the storm clouds in the west. A big midwinter storm would hit the area soon. Thunder and lightning and drenching sleet would drive all activities indoors.

McKenna told her friends that she intended to go out to lunch with her mom, who had offered a celebration for McKenna's outstanding first semester in high school. Dad had gone out of town to Puerto Rico, entertaining some clients with four days of golf.

She walked up the long driveway to the house, listening to the sound of some winter birds in the large trees on their property. She felt enthusiastic about a few days off from school. She saw a flash of bright red and smiled to think about the lovely cardinals that frequented the wild bird feeder which she and her mom, Anna O'Neill, maintained.

The day fell apart as she walked in the front door, singing a greeting. Mom sat on the large leather couch in the living room. She rose as McKenna came in. "Honey," she said.

Mom wasn't crying but as soon as McKenna saw her mother, she knew that something big had happened. Her stomach fell.

"What is it?" McKenna said. Mom beckoned to her. She came over and Mom put a loving arm around her.

"Honey," Mom said, but then didn't speak for a few moments. "Honey, I just received a call from Mr. Denton," she said.

"Didn't he go with Daddy to Puerto Rico?"

"Yes, he did. He called me from the hotel in San Juan."

"Why would he call you? He isn't even. . ." McKenna stopped. "Daddy's. . . gone?" Mom hesitated. McKenna knew.

Mom told her that her father, Alan DiBiasi, died that morning of a heart attack on the golf course in Puerto Rico while entertaining his clients. McKenna's world seemed to collapse as Mom sketched in the details. The girl became all but inconsolable.

As she came down the steps a few mornings later, she saw Mom standing by the front door. Through the picture window, she saw a FedEx truck pulling down the long driveway.

"Did we just have something delivered?" she asked her mom. Mom pointed to several boxes on the porch. Together, they brought them in. One package contained her father's personal items such as his rings, watch, and wallet. Dad's suitcase and golf clubs had been sent by the hotel in Puerto Rico.

A small package, wrapped in brown paper, sat on the porch by the front door. "What about this one?" asked McKenna.

Mom put her arms around her daughter and pulled the girl's head against her shoulder. "Honey, said Mom. "The San Juan funeral home sent your father's ashes to us."

McKenna tried to be brave. "Oh Mommy," she whispered. Then the tears fell.

Mom stood embracing her daughter while McKenna wept the inconsolable tears of grief. "What shall we do with the ashes, Honey?" she asked in her gentle North Carolina accent.

McKenna thought for a few moments. She had to swallow and make an effort to say, "Door County." Mom nodded.

Mother and daughter packed up Dad's car, a magnificent BMW convertible. McKenna had always relished the rich smell of the leather upholstery and the feel of the breeze in her hair, giggling with the joy of the fine automobile. Today, though, they drove in silence across the Wisconsin border, then through Milwaukee on their way to the peninsula known as Door County.

They pulled into the driveway of their summer home just before the glacial winter darkness enveloped the beach. The weather, bitter cold with a howling west wind, slashed through their winter coats and blue jeans as they climbed from the car. The steel gray waves on Lake Michigan boomed on the shore, hurling an icy spray into the air.

"Can you go through with this?" asked Mom before they started down the path.

"Yes," McKenna nodded. "Let's do it."

McKenna and her mom, Anna, walked together to the beach, their hair whipping around their faces in the violent breeze. They opened the package and scattered the ashes on the shore of Lake Michigan. The powerful west wind blew the ashes out onto the lake where they vanished from sight.

Mother and daughter hugged while McKenna wept her goodbye to her father.

Anna took her to dinner at a restaurant though McKenna said she wasn't hungry. Some barbequed chicken and a baked potato raised her spirits, and she and Mom split a piece of Door County cherry pie.

In the darkness as they were driving home, however, McKenna turned to her mother. "You aren't as upset by daddy's death as I am," she said. The statement sounded like an accusation, harsher and nastier than she intended. She decided not to apologize, though.

Mom gave a little nod, not responding to the caustic tone in her daughter's voice. She didn't answer for several moments.

Mom's reaction confirmed McKenna's impression of the marriage her parents had lived with for eighteen years. McKenna had never thought her parents were in love, even though they stayed together. For example, Mom still went by her maiden name, Anna O'Neill.

Mom, though, didn't rise to the fight. She stared down the interstate. She took her left hand off the steering wheel and ran her fingers through her long copper-colored hair.

When Mom spoke, she didn't offer a direct response to her daughter's observation. "Honey," she said, choosing her words with care. "I know you're heartbroken. I'd like to keep you out of school for a few days and take you to the ocean."

McKenna was bewildered. "To the ocean?" said McKenna.

"Yes," said Mom. "Remember, I grew up by the Atlantic. I always went to the shore when I was sad. Like when my parents died, I drove over to the ocean. I'd watch the waves, and listen to the wind and the calls of the gulls. Being there, listening to the rhythm of the sea, breathing in the fresh salt air always restored my perspective."

"You want to go to North Carolina?" said McKenna, surprised. Mom had never once mentioned a desire to return to her home state. McKenna had never met her mother's stepsisters. Those women had never wanted any association with her mother.

"No, not North Carolina," said Mom. "I thought we might drive to New York and follow the coast to Maine. Say, Bar Harbor." McKenna thought about her mother's suggestion. Mom reached across the seat and stroked her daughter's hair, which so resembled her own. Her mother's gentle hands had always imparted comfort to her.

McKenna shrugged, but felt more excited than she allowed herself to show. A trip like this with Mom might be wonderful. "Okay," she said.

They left the next day. Mom took a beautiful route to the coast, driving back roads to let her daughter see the scenery across Indiana and Ohio. They stayed overnight in a bed-and-breakfast in the Amish country of southeast Pennsylvania. They reached the coast the next day and drove up to Boston. Late on the third afternoon, Mom stopped for the night at a hotel in Portsmouth, New Hampshire.

As they put their overnight bags in their room, Mom said, "Are you too tired for an ocean expedition after supper?"

McKenna shrugged. "No, that sounds great."

"Look," said Mom, holding out a brochure. "I picked this up downstairs. We can go with a local company on a nighttime trip to the Isle of Shoals."

"What's that?"

Mom read the folder. "It's a chain of islands about ten miles out from Portsmouth. It's going to be a beautiful night, with a full moon."

McKenna grinned and nodded, excited about a trip on the open ocean. Mom called the charter company.

Mom and McKenna, bundled up against the cold, were the only passengers that evening on a cabin cruiser with Sue McCatty, a longtime resident of the coastal town. The full moon illuminated the calm ocean.

Though McKenna's heart brimmed full of grief she nonetheless loved the trip across the ten miles of ocean. Despite the chill, she stood outside for several minutes, the wind whipping her hair. The spray felt wonderful and she breathed deep, embracing the solace that the ocean can bring to the heart. She went back into the cabin, where Mom hugged her and smiled as the cabin cruiser knifed through the swells.

Sue took them first to the largest island, Star Island, then to a couple of the others. As she went, she told them stories of the islands, some of which belong to the state of Maine and others which belong to New Hampshire. "Tell you what," said Sue. "Before we head back, let's go over to White Island. We'll look at the lighthouse and walk around the island. Maybe we'll meet Martha."

"Who?" said McKenna.

"A legend," said Sue, with a mysterious grin. The enigmatic reply took McKenna aback and she and Mom exchanged glances. Mom looked amused.

Sue anchored the boat in shallow water on the east side of White Island, and lowered a small rubber raft. They rowed to a small beach and clambered ashore.

Sue illuminated a path with a powerful flashlight as they scrabbled together to the top of the island. She pointed to the land bridge on the northern side. "It connects White Island to that other island when the tide is low," she said in her downeast twang. "It's called Seavey Island. Over there--" she pointed to a small rocky island a mile or so to the northeast—"is Sugar Island."

Sue told them about the efforts of local groups to save the famous lighthouse of White Island.

"I'm going to explore," said McKenna. Mom and Sue agreed, and walked off.

McKenna found a spot on the southeast side of the island and sat, staring out at the sea. She listened to the boom of the waves as they crashed on the rocks of the island, sounding like cannon fire from a pirate ship. The howl of the wind might have been the cry of lost souls begging surcease of their agony.

However, she did feel a peace descend on her, as Mom had said it would. She licked her lips, enjoying the salt taste from the ocean spray that dampened her face. Then she remembered.

Oh Daddy, why did you have to die?

McKenna let go and sobbed with her grief, the first death she'd ever experienced. As her tears fell, she fumbled in her jeans for a handkerchief. As she pulled it out of her pocket, a quarter fell out and rolled away. McKenna followed the coin, which came to rest behind a rock beside the path. She knelt and moved the rock a little—

And stared.

Her quarter lay on top of a shiny object, about an inch in diameter. McKenna picked it up. Even in the moonlight, she could see that she held a gold coin.

She couldn't make out the markings well. Still she knew it had to be valuable--

"He will return," said a whispery voice behind her.

Startled, McKenna gave a little scream and leapt to her feet. She turned to see a girl about her own age walking down the path toward her. "He will return," the girl said again. McKenna saw that the moonlight created an aura around the girl.

The girl, slim, about five feet tall, wore a long blue woolen coat against the cold of the evening. McKenna stared at the girl's beautiful red hair, which blew in the wind about her head. It looked a great deal like McKenna's own hair.

The girl reached up and tucked her hair behind her ear. She strolled down the path, slow and unhurried.

"I'm sorry I screamed. You startled me," said McKenna when her heart slowed a little. She managed a smile. "I didn't think anyone else was here on the island. . ."

But the girl didn't respond. She walked past McKenna and stared out to sea, looking to the southeast.

McKenna walked toward the girl. "Are you deaf?" she asked. When the girl didn't respond, McKenna reached out to tap her shoulder.

Her hand touched nothing. It went right through the girl.

Visceral terror seized McKenna. She shivered, near panic with eerie dread.

She turned and clambered up the path to the top of the island. "Mom!" she yelled as she ran.

Anna, perhaps twenty yards away, turned at her daughter's voice. She rushed to her daughter, followed by Sue. "What is it?" asked Mom, her soothing voice calming McKenna.

"A girl," said McKenna, pointing. "But she's—she's not there."

Sue turned and hurried to the top of the path. "No one is here, McKenna. It's all right."

Mom and McKenna joined Sue and looked down. Sue was right. The girl was nowhere to be seen. "What the. . ." said McKenna. She pointed, astonished. "She was standing right there."

"Did the girl say something?" asked Sue.

"Yes," said McKenna. "Twice she said, 'he will return.'"

Sue broke into a broad grin. "Congratulations," she said. "You've just met the most famous inhabitant of the island. I'm sorry she scared you."

"What?" said McKenna.

"Oh, yes. You've met the Ghost of White Island. Her name is—or was—Martha Herring."

McKenna, her heart still pounding, didn't know what to say. Looking down, she realized that she was still clutching her handkerchief and the two coins. "Oh!" she said. She held the gold coin out to Sue.

Sue shone a flashlight on it. "Where did you find this?"

McKenna pointed out the rock on the path where she'd found the coin. "Is it valuable?" she asked.

"Yes," said Sue. "I'm pretty sure it's a Spanish Doubloon from a pirate's treasure. See the cross? I imagine it was minted sometime around 1700 or so. They turn up once in a while on the beaches of the islands, but finding one on shore is unusual."

"How do you think it got here?" asked McKenna.

"I imagine that it's part of the treasure of a pirate named Sandy Gordon. He was Martha's husband. The British Navy hanged him. Gordon marooned Martha on White Island to guard his treasure."

"Why would she remain?" asked Mom.

"She made a promise," said Sue. "It's a legend. Come on. I'll tell you as we head back to Portsmouth."

They reached the inflatable. Sue turned to McKenna. "One other thing," she said.

"What?" asked McKenna, still shaken by the encounter with the Ghost of White Island.

"'You will return,'" said Sue.

CHAPTER 2
The Atlantic Ocean, 1715
The *Regent*

Rabbi Sholem Levin sat on the deck of the tiny ship *Regent* that was bearing him from his former home in Ireland to the new world. He still felt traces of the nausea of seasickness that had gripped him for the first few days of the voyage as the ship pitched up and down on the North Atlantic.

He was leaving his home in Ireland behind for good, but he felt no regret about it. The life of a Jew in England, in Scotland or in Ireland had been difficult.

Sholem sighed. His great-grandfather and his family and most of the Jews had been expelled from England. Vengeance had come upon them when Dr. Roderigo Lopez, a Spanish Jew, had been convicted—maybe by mistake--of trying to assassinate Queen Elizabeth in 1594, years before. Lopez was hanged and then drawn and quartered. The persecutions and expulsions of the Jews began, as if an entire race had been responsible.

Sholem hoped things would be better in the American colonies. Boston was the ship's destination, but Sholem would be happy to settle anywhere in the New World. Plantations and businesses were thriving. People told him that a man could find work in the largest cities. In addition to his work as a rabbi, he was a superb carpenter.

What mattered the most, though, were the family treasures that Sholem was carrying to the new world: two leather cases, one of which contained an ancient wooden staff and another that contained a translucent red rock. The value of the two treasures transcended reckoning.

According to legend, the rock was a channel to God. The staff was likewise famous. Both were assumed lost to the nation of Israel . . .

Yet there was no nation. Israel had not existed as a state for more than 1,600 years. The Romans destroyed the temple and crucified Jews until they ran out of wood. The remainder—the very few—had fled in the Diaspora to live in other parts of the world.

Jerusalem, the destroyed city that was the heart and soul of the nation, was lost to the Jews forever, to all evidence. Yet not forgotten. Every year the Passover feast concluded with the prayer, "Next year in Jerusalem."

The Fourth Night, Sholem believed, was coming.

The First Night was the night of creation. The Second Night was the giving of the covenant to Sholem's ancestor, Abraham, the father of many nations. The Third Night was the night of the Passover, when the great prophet Moses led the children of Israel out of Egypt.

The Fourth Night would see the return of Israel to the land. On that night, the Jews would climb Mount Moria to Jerusalem. The High Priest would again enter the temple, accompanied by the priest of the Lamb of God.

For Sholem and his fellow Jews held out the hope that some-day the temple would again rise on Mount Moria and that the holy city of Jerusalem would be rebuilt. On that day, David's songs would echo through the rebuilt temple; the fragrant smell of the burnt offerings would rise as the priests again sacrificed to the God of Abraham, Isaac and Jacob; the High Priest would again penetrate behind the veil on Yom Kippur, the Day of Atonement.

Many of the great treasures were lost, perhaps destroyed when Israel suffered invasions of pagan armies. Gone were the golden altar of incense, the golden candlesticks, and the greatest treasure, the Ark of the Covenant.

But two of the treasures had survived. Sholem grinned.

Sholem leaned against the rail on the quarterdeck and thought of the miserable first three days of journey. Never had he been so sick. Though he was a carpenter by trade, he often worked as a shipwright. *How ironic. Jews should never go to sea,* he thought. Well, this was his last trip—

A loud crash knocked him off his feet. Something slammed into the side of the ship and wood splinters flew everywhere. *Regent* rocked with the impact. Now, screams of terror rose from the passengers.

Sholem Levin struggled to his feet. He spied a monstrous ship off the port bow. The Jolly Roger flew from the mast of the huge ship. Flashes of fire burst from the cannon ports. Then he heard the din of a thousand thunderclaps.

Again cannonballs slammed into *Regent*. As it rocked and turned to flee, the little ship returned fire. Smoke and the smell of exploded gunpowder filled Sholem's nostril. He could see, however, that the defense of *Regent* would be to no avail. *Regent* surrendered within minutes.

Sholem ran down to his bunk and retrieved his treasures. He

slipped the leather case with the red stone into one pocket of his coat and his copy of the *Tanach* into the other. He clutched the staff to his chest and hurried back to the main deck.

When he emerged into the sunlight, the pirates had begun to swarm aboard. They covered the passengers and crew with cutlasses and pistols. The victims lined up with their hands raised. As they stood terrified, the pirate captain came aboard.

He had flaming red hair and was attired in an ill-fitting red uniform. Sholem watched the pirate smooth the uniform and his hair, the criminal's vulgar narcissism evident in every movement.

The murders began when the pirate crew lined up the passengers and crew of *Regent*. The captain and first officer died at once, thrown overboard to drown. Sholem felt his stomach knot at the nauseating brutality.

The pirate captain watched as his men stripped the ship and its passengers of anything of value. If a passenger or a crew man had nothing to give, two or three pirates would seize him and throw him overboard.

At last the pirate captain stood before Sholem. A pirate slammed a sword against Sholem's neck and forced him to empty his pockets. "What are these?" asked the captain, pointing to Sholem's treasures.

"Please. They have no value except to my people. You cannot use them. Nor can I. Yet they must not be lost. Please," Sholem begged the red-headed criminal.

The pirate regarded him for a few moments. "You're a Jew."

"Yes."

The captain sneered with contempt and gestured to the pirate behind Sholem. The man kicked Sholem behind his knees and he fell to the deck. The villain drew back his sword, ready to strike Sholem's head off.

"Wait," cried Sholem. "Please promise to protect the treasures, at least."

The pirate captain grunted. "You have more fear for these objects than for yourself."

"Yes, that's true. They are far more important than I am."

The captain nodded to the crewman, who sheathed his sword. The man leaned forward and took Sholem's treasures. As the man turned to go, Sholem's eyes filled with tears. He began to chant under his breath the words that had been the password of his people for millenia. "*Shema Yisrael, Adonai elohenu, Adonai echad.*"

"What are you saying?" demanded the pirate captain.

"It is called the *Shema*," Sholem said.

"What language?"

"Hebrew."

"What does it mean?"

Sholem gave the best translation he could. "'*Hear, O Israel, the Lord our God, the Lord is one.*'"

The captain grunted and waved his thumb at the crewman, who nodded and pulled the red stone from its leather case. He examined it, turning it this way and that. Then he held it to the sunlight.

A bolt of red light shot from the stone into the center of his chest. He turned toward the pirate leader. "Captain?" he said. His eyes rolled back into his head. He crashed face forward onto the deck, fingers still clutching the stone.

All movement on the ship stopped. The ship grew silent as a crypt. All eyes stared at the dead man, then at their captain.

The red-headed man stood with his mouth open, eyes wide.

He turned back to Sholem. "What did you do?"

"I did nothing. I cannot use the stone." Sholem walked to the corpse. He removed the stone from the dead fingers and returned it to its leather pouch.

"What is your trade?" asked the captain.

"I am a rabbi. That means teacher," Sholem explained, seeing the puzzled look on the Captain's face. "Also I support myself as a carpenter and shipwright."

The captain nodded to two of his men. "Watkins. Sturdevant. Tie him and bring him."

The two men, looking apprehensive, lashed Sholem and led him to the side of the ship. They tied a rope around his waist. The two pirates lifted him and threw him into the ocean.

Sholem, hands tied, dropped like a shot below the surface. Just as he began to panic he jerked to a stop. The rope jolted the breath out of him. He choked and inhaled water. In that moment he assumed he was dead. He focused his mind on the Eternal. *Shema Yisrael, Adonai elohenu, Adonai echad . . .*

* * * * *

Sholem began to regain consciousness, his head throbbing with pain. Though he was still tied up, he was lying flat on the deck of a ship. He choked again. He lifted his head and tried to sit up.

"No," said a female voice. "No, you must not move."

Sholem looked up at the voice. To his intense surprise, he saw the deep blue eyes of a pretty teenage girl with copper-colored hair who knelt beside him. Though she was several months pregnant, she had many bruises on her arms and face, including a black eye. She began untying his arms and legs.

Sholem, sensitive and kind, realized that the girl was frightened. Indeed, she lived in constant fear. He managed to smile.

"You will be all right," she said. "Do not try to speak yet."

Sholem took a deep breath. His lungs and ribs ached, and he coughed a few times. The girl laid a gentle hand on his forehead. "What ship is this?" he whispered.

"You are aboard *The Flying Scot*, under the command of Captain Gordon. The captain believes I am his wife."

"What do you mean?" Sholem asked her.

"I will explain another time. Be quiet if you want to live."

Sholem turned his head to the right and saw the two leather cases and his copy of *Tanach* sitting next to him. "Where are we going?"

"We are headed to White Island off the coast of New Hampshire."

"America?"

"Yes. White Island serves as his hideout."

"Why did not your—ah—the pirates kill me?"

"Gordon needs carpenters to repair the ship. It took a beating in a recent battle. The men are afraid of these objects," she said, pointing to the leather cases. "They hope to ransom you and the objects."

"But I have no friends in the New World."

"I see." Her brow wrinkled and she put a finger to her mouth. She regarded him for some time. "Who are you?"

"My name is Sholem Levin."

"How do you do?" she said, and shook his hand. "My name is Martha. I prefer to think of myself as Martha Herring."

"I understand," he said. Besides a potent intelligence, she had spirit and courage, he could see. She would not surrender to a forced marriage without a fight. Nor would the marriage be a pleasant one for the pirate captain. The captain, nothing more than a bullying, preening popinjay, resorted to beating her to destroy her spirit.

She pointed to the leather cases. "I will try to persuade him to let me have your treasures. Would you tell me what these objects are?"

He hesitated, unsure of her loyalty to the pirate captain despite the bruises on her face and arms. He didn't want to give the criminals more information than he had to.

She appeared to misunderstand his indecision and looked around. "No one is here. You can talk now."

He couldn't imagine that this young woman, though terrified, had an ounce of guile about her. He nodded. "Do you know anything about the Bible?"

"Only a little," she admitted. "I would love to learn, though."

He heard the note of eagerness in her voice. "Let me tell you about my ancestor, Moses."

Martha smiled and shifted her position, arranging her skirts around her. It was clear that she was thrilled to hear a story. He related how Moses and his brother Aaron had come to Pharaoh's palace to ask him to release the enslaved Hebrews. The king had refused. Aaron demonstrated the power of the staff.

Martha stared at Sholem, her eyes wide as he completed the story. "You mean Aaron turned this staff into a monster?"

He smiled at her innocence. "Not quite. The Eternal did the magic. But Aaron would become the High Priest of all Israel."

"Tell me another story," she said, her voice almost pleading. His heart broke as he sensed her appalling loneliness. He gave her hand a gentle squeeze as he began another story.

He related how Pharaoh had come to bathe in the waters of the Nile. Moses had come to him again. When Pharaoh refused to release the Hebrews, Aaron had touched the staff to the surface of the river. The Nile turned to blood.

The young woman stared at him in silence as Sholem finished telling the story.

"So this staff belonged to Moses?" she said, her voice hushed.

"Yes," he said, "and then to Aaron and all the High Priests until the time of Elijah. So did the Urim Stone," he nodded to the other leather case. "The high priests were able to use it to discern the will of The Eternal."

"Very well," she said. She sat up, looking inspired and confident. "Let me take the objects ashore with me at White Island. I can protect them there."

"Are you not afraid of the staff and the rock?"

"Yes. But I can touch them without harm coming to me."

Sholem's eyes widened in surprise. "I am surprised," he admitted, and chewed at a callous on his index finger, considering. "Perhaps only the iniquitous cannot touch these items," he mused.

She shrugged. "Try to be calm," she said, patting his arm. "We have several days to go until we see White Island. We can talk later."

Sholem spoke with Martha as often as he could during the trip to the Isle of Shoals. He spent hours rebuilding and repairing the ship. As he worked, she would sit with him. He told her story after story about the history of his people. Her curious mind and desire to learn all she could impressed him. They became fast friends.

One night, *The Flying Scot* stood in sight of land. Sholem saw the cold bleak rock known as White Island looming in the moonlight.

Martha came to Sholem in the darkness. "I have to go in the morning," she said as the crew dropped anchor. "I will take the staff and stone with me."

"Thank you," he said.

"Sholem," she said, "could I learn to use them?"

He shook his head. "I am all but certain you cannot. Only one person alive can use them, and I am not he. But please keep them safe. Please."

She smiled. "I will do my best," she agreed.

"No," he said and held out the *Tanach*. "This is vital. My family has watched over them for centuries. Please swear that you shall care for them."

She hesitated but then laid her hand on the testament. She said, "Sholem. I promise I shall make sure they are safe until the rightful owner comes for them." She put the Tanach into a pocket.

"Martha?" called the captain.

"I am here," she called back. "Just getting some air."

In the morning the pirates rowed Martha ashore. He saw the fear on her face, her terror at being marooned on this miserable rock. As Sholem waved goodbye, he felt hot tears in his eyes.

Martha, he was certain, would be true to her vow. He was also sure that he would miss the young woman. She was a ray of goodness and kindness on a ship of misery filled with murderers and criminals.

Sholem resumed his chores of repairing the damage to *the Flying Scot*.

CHAPTER 3
Two Weeks Later

On the fourth of March in 1715, Owen McClelland took his small boat out to fish off the coast of New Hampshire. He reveled in the uncharacteristic warmth of the day, the calm sea, and the expanse of blue sky. The cold spray from the waves made him laugh.

Since the death of his father two years ago, Owen had been earning a living in town as a carpenter and shipwright. He took care of his mother and two younger brothers. He supplemented his family's food by fishing in the Atlantic off the Isle of Shoals. His mother made no secret at how proud she was of him.

Owen headed his little skiff toward White Island, a rocky outcropping in the Isle of Shoals Chain, rejoicing in the pleasure of sailing.

As he sailed, he hauled in a few smaller fish, an ocean perch and a herring. They would make a sparse dinner that night.

He came within sight of White Island. Smoke rising from a small cabin constructed from rock with a metal roof surprised him. He didn't know that anybody lived out on White Island. Nor could he imagine why anyone would *want* a home on the barren rock.

As he stared at the cabin, his boat hit a submerged boulder. The boat pitched to the right, soaking him and all but capsizing the boat. He fought hard not to panic for a moment or two.

He seized a bucket and bailed as fast as he could. The late-winter ocean froze him to the bone.

He turned to the rear of the boat, and realized that he'd snapped the handle of the rudder on his little sailboat. Drenched with icy ocean water and freezing cold, he broke out the oars. He labored hard, feeling warmth spread through his muscles. In a few moments, he managed to come ashore in a small sheltered cove at White Island. He decided to go to the cabin and ask to borrow some tools to repair the handle of the rudder.

When he knocked, a young woman with bright red hair opened the door a crack and peered out at him, fear evident in her eyes. Owen, trying hard not to shiver, dragged his hat from his head and introduced himself. "Please excuse me," he said, his teeth chattering. "I had an accident in my skiff. May I--"

She opened the door wide for him. "Sir," she interrupted. "Please, you are wet. Yes, of course you must come in." Now he saw that she was several months pregnant.

Owen walked in and sat in a chair she drew up by the fire. She gave him a blanket to wrap around his shoulders. "I have some tea brewing now. It will warm you."

"Thank you," he said.

"My name is Martha Herring," she said. "I am married to a man named Sandy Gordon. He is not here, though I do expect him."

"May I wait for him, Mistress Gordon?" asked Owen, trying to keep his teeth from chattering. "I need. . ."

Her face flushed. "Please do not call me Mistress Gordon," she interrupted. "He forced me to marry him."

Owen blinked with surprise. "Forced?"

"Yes," she said, her eyes flashing with indignity. Then she drew a deep breath and cast her eyes down. "I apologize. You would not care about my life. . ."

"On the contrary," said Owen. "I should be honored to hear."

Martha looked up at him and studied his face for a time. At last, she seemed to make up her mind to tell him. "I am British. My father was the captain of a privateer bark called *Porpoise*. Last year he took me to sea with him."

"Why?" asked Owen. *The open sea is no place for a young woman*, he thought. She stared at the fire again. He could see her debating with herself about what to tell him. It occurred to him that he sat in the presence of the most beautiful woman he'd ever seen. Yet he could feel the appalling loneliness in her soul. And—what? Fear?

She tucked a wisp of hair behind her ear, an obvious habit. "My mother died of the fever, sir," she said at last. "I had no relatives with whom I could stay. I was but fourteen then. My father intended to go to the Barbary Coast to fight the Algerine pirates."

"So he brought you along." Owen couldn't believe the father had done such a thing.

"About three weeks into the voyage I met the carpenter's mate, Sandy Gordon."

Now Owen had warmed enough so that his mind cleared. He lifted a hand. "Sandy Gordon the pirate?"

"Yes," said Martha, rising and crossing to the fire. She took a pad and removed a kettle from the fire and added some tea.

Owen, now frightened, wished he could leave at once. Gordon ranked as one of the most feared brigands operating off the American Atlantic Coast. But Owen knew he had to wait until he dried off somewhat. If he went out into the cool air still drenched, he could catch pneumonia.

He also struggled not to curse her husband for leaving this young woman alone in the late winter weather on this bleak rock. *What sort of a monster would do such a thing? She must be terrified all the time. Storms ravage this rock and ferocious winds lash this cabin.* He sensed that holding on to sanity was a daily struggle for her.

Martha invited him to turn his chair to the small table. As she waited for the tea to steep, she told him where she was from, and a little about her father, John Herring.

"Sandy Gordon misunderstood my attempt to be friendly," said Martha. "He came to my cabin when my father was occupied with a matter of ship's discipline. He pushed his way in, and then tried to force himself on me.

"However, the first mate heard my screams and came to my aid. My father had Gordon dragged to a cannon. The bosun's mate lashed him seventy-two times."

"Seventy-two lashes!" said Owen, appalled. His fear began to subside in his compassion for his hostess. "And he survived?"

"Yes," she said. "He fell unconscious at the twentieth stroke. My father imprisoned him below decks for thirty days." She poured him a large mug of the heavy fragrant mixture and took a smaller one for herself.

They drank together for a few moments. The tea warmed him but he was still scared that Gordon might return.

"When he emerged, he was bitter and angry," Martha said. "He gathered around him other discontented men. They mutinied and captured my father. Those who were loyal to my father were thrown overboard." Owen shook his head in disbelief.

"Gordon's men dragged my father to the same cannon where my husband--" her face twisted with anger—"stripped him naked and whipped him to death." Her voice faltered and tears rose in her eyes as she relived the horror of the episode.

Owen murmured sympathy until Martha composed herself. "And you saw all this?" he asked.

"Yes," said Martha. "They forced me to watch." She dabbed a handkerchief at her eyes. "When my father was dead, Gordon nodded to three men who threw my father's body overboard."

Owen covered her hand with his and looked in her eyes. "And he came for you." Martha nodded.

They sipped the tea in silence for a few moments. "My husband turned *Porpoise* into a pirate ship," she said. "He captured several ships.

"Despite his success, he was not well liked by his men since he felt that he was entitled to all the loot for himself. He paid the men on the ship a salary."

"Salaries on a pirate ship? I always thought that they split any treasure they stole," said Owen. His mind was reeling at the young woman's story.

She shrugged. "They resented him within a few months. He became a tyrant. He had his closest allies throw anyone who questioned him overboard." Owen shuddered at the picture.

"At last the crew rebelled," said Martha. "At first I feared they would kill us both. They were merciful, I think, because of me. By then I was pregnant. The crew marooned us on the coast of Scotland, a mile or two from a small village." Martha rose and re-filled the cups.

"How did you survive?"

"Gordon had some money he'd hidden away. I tried to escape many times. He tied me to a bunk. On occasion he'd strike me."

"Your face is bruised, Martha," he said.

"Oh," she said, trying to dismiss the concern in his voice. "It is nothing."

"Did Gordon do that to you?"

"Please, Mr. McClelland, do not be concerned."

He grunted. *At least he didn't throw her overboard*, he thought. "How did you get here?" asked Owen.

"Captain Edward Teach found us in Scotland."

"Teach? Do you mean--"

"Yes. Blackbeard."

Owen felt his stomach tighten again. His hand trembled as he lifted the cup to his lips. Martha appeared lost in thought, her lips pursed, silent for a few moments. At last she took a sip and began to talk again. "We were taken aboard *Queen Anne's Revenge*, Teach's ship. Not many days later *Revenge* joined battle with a British warship named *Renown*. Gordon's ferocity in the battle impressed Teach. When the battle concluded, the pirates threw the British officers overboard."

"A novel way to treat helpless captives," said Owen, feeling disgust.

"Yes," she said, shrugging in agreement. "Gordon pressed the survivors into his crew, since he threatened to throw them overboard if they refused to join. Teach gave the ship over to my husband and he re-named it *The Flying Scot*. We parted company with *Revenge* and came to the island here."

"Why don't you leave?" asked Owen.

"They left me no boat. People sail by on occasion, but I have not been able to attract anyone's attention. Besides. . ." she bit her lip.

"Yes?" said Owen.

"I swore an oath to guard this chest and these items." She pointed to a large sea chest on the wall opposite to the door. Next to it was a leather case, well-worn and old, about four and one-half feet long. A small leather box sat on top of the chest.

"What are they?"

"The chest contains gold and jewelry stolen from several ships."

"Treasure?"

"Oh, yes."

"What of the two leather cases?"

"I can show them to you." She crossed the small room to the case and extracted a four-and-one-half-foot-long wooden pole, polished and well-worn. She handed it to Owen.

Owen examined the staff. "The wood is almond, if I am not mistaken. I do some carpentry. Almond tree stems grow very straight like this. Some letters are carved into it, but I don't know what they say. I don't even recognize them. It isn't English."

"Can you read?" asked Martha.

"Yes," said Owen. "My mother insisted that I learn. She taught me. I read the Scripture in our church services in the village." He blushed as she looked at him in some admiration. "I—er--seem to have some gift for language. I have studied Greek and Latin as well."

"I wish I could read," she said. "I have nothing to occupy my time. A friend gave me this Bible."

She reached to the Table next to her chair and handed him a small leather-bound book. He accepted it and began to leaf through it. He couldn't read the writing inside.

"I sleep with it," she went on. He glanced up and she returned his little grin. "It gives me much comfort. The nightmares are not so terrifying."

"This book does not seem to be a Bible. At least, it is not written in English. It appears to be valuable."

She knelt next to his chair and fumbled with the small jewelry box. Owen breathed in the fresh scent of her lovely copper colored hair. Her proximity felt wonderful. In that moment, he realized that he wanted this woman next to him for the rest of his life.

He lifted a hand, thinking to stroke the lovely hair. He'd seen the bruises on her face and knew how she'd gotten them. He wanted to say, *No one will ever hurt you again, Martha. I promise it.*

He shrugged the impulse away. She was another man's wife, even if she had been forced into the marriage. He could not allow himself to think of anything beyond that.

Oblivious to the effect she was having on him, she opened the small jewelry case. She handed Owen a small stone inscribed with letters similar to the ones he saw on the staff and in the book. Again he couldn't read the letters. The translucent stone seemed to be red crystal carved into an oval shape, bound with a band of gold. Owen held it up to the sunlight that streamed through the window.

"You can use the stone," Martha gasped.

Owen saw her staring at him. He looked down.

His entire body was radiant with a pure red light. He

extended his hand to her and she took it. The glow expanded to surround both young people. He felt soothing warmth as he held her hand. He studied her eyes, blue and deep. She gave him a smile of peace, as if she were experiencing the feeling for the first time.

"You and I belong together," he said to her. He felt sure in his soul that he was speaking the truth in the purest form that it could be expressed by a human being.

"I feel it too," she said. "It is so clear. You and I are supposed to spend our lives with each other."

He couldn't take his eyes from hers in the beautiful glow. He felt resolve. "Come with me. We must leave this place. I promise that I will hide you so that you are safe. You cannot live with a pirate."

"I see that as well," she said. Her voice trembled. He felt that she was afraid, but ready to take whatever steps were necessary. She put up her arms and he enfolded her. They kissed each other for a long time, with a gentle loving devotion.

For the next several years, the memory of that kiss would be one of the few things that would sustain Owen's heart.

At last they drew back and Owen lowered the stone and put it into his pocket. As the perfect light faded, he found that his clothes were dry and warm. He felt infused with courage, unafraid and confident. She smiled up into his eyes.

He swallowed, trying to calm down. "I must fix my boat before we can go," he managed, although he felt a desperate urge to resume the kiss. Do you have any tools, Martha?"

"Yes," she said. She stepped to the other side of the room and opened a small chest. She showed him hammers, augers, bits, nails and other tools. He selected a few.

"Pack some clothes," he told her. "We will hide in Portsmouth or go farther inland, or to Boston or New York. I can fix the rudder in no time."

Martha nodded. Her posture and attitude now reflected hope and newfound joy. She stepped forward and embraced him for a few seconds.

Owen felt a trace of dizziness at the girl's touch. Now he said, "No one will ever hurt you again, Martha. I pledge it." She lifted a gentle hand to stroke his face.

He slid the book and the stone into the pocket of his coat and ran to the boat. Within ten minutes he had repaired the rudder.

He ran back to the cabin and threw open the door. "Martha," he called. Owen gasped. He saw five men standing there in seaman's clothing. The red-headed leader wore an ill-fitting red uniform.

The leader came forward with his pistol drawn. "Who the hell are you?" asked the man, speaking with a severe Scottish brogue.

"My name is Owen McClelland," he said. "I came ashore to repair the rudder on my boat. Martha was kind enough to lend me these tools." He held them up.

"You were here alone with my wife?" said the man. Now, Owen understood the extremity of his situation. The man confronting him was Sandy Gordon, a vicious killer and pirate.

"For a few moments, yes. My boat hit a rock and almost capsized. I was soaked with sea water. Martha allowed me to dry my clothes and gave me hot tea."

"Did you take advantage of her?" asked the man, his face red and his eyes flaming with rage.

"Of course not," said Owen, his own anger now rising.

"No!" screamed Martha as the pirate placed the muzzle of the gun against Owen's forehead. Owen knew that Gordon would not hesitate to shoot him. He looked at Martha. Three men held the weeping young woman back.

Owen reached into his pocket and touched the mysterious stone. Nervousness and fear vanished. He smiled at Martha and nodded. She calmed a bit. He drew himself up to his full height, unafraid, and stared into the pirate's eyes.

Gordon lowered his eyes and his pistol. "What do you do?"

He spoke without thinking. "I work as a shipwright in Portsmouth."

Gordon nodded and smiled. "Dunbar, take him to the ship. I shall be there in a moment. I must see to my wife."

"Aye, sir," said the one named Dunbar. Two of the men released Martha. They bound and gagged Owen and dragged him down a path to a ship's boat.

Owen understood. Gordon planned to press him into his pirate crew.

The men rowed him out to a huge vessel. People on the ship threw down a rope, which the men in the boat tied around his waist. They hoisted Owen aboard.

Several men dragged him to a grate that was fastened to a mast. The pirates spread-eagled him and tied his hands and feet to the grate so that he was incapable of movement. A minute passed. Five minutes. An hour. The pirates ignored him. He was in distress, his arms leaden and aching, and his heart throbbing with horror over what that hideous human was doing to Martha.

CHAPTER 4

Martha Herring lay on her bed, flat on her back, motionless, hoping Gordon would not become aroused again. As always, he had been violent, one-sided, without concern for her. To her relief, Sandy Gordon rolled off the bed. He wiped himself down with a towel and began to dress.

"What are you going to do with him?" asked Martha, trying to keep her voice neutral.

"Who?" sneered Gordon, dragging on the red trousers.

"Mr. McClelland. He treated me with great kindness. He offered to take me to the mainland."

"What for?"

"I did not know when you were returning. My supplies are low. I intended to purchase some food and bring back some water," she lied. She'd had no intention of returning to the loathsome cabin on the dismal rock. But now, Owen's life was in jeopardy. Gordon wouldn't hesitate to throw Owen overboard if he suspected that they had planned to go ashore and hide from him.

"I will send more provisions and water over. I will be back in a few weeks. Meantime do not forget your promise."

He opened the door and strode away without closing the door behind him. He made his way down to the skiff that was waiting for him.

Martha stood and realized that she had changed. Not physically, but in every other way. She felt more confident, more determined, and now, she realized, she was not afraid.

She had not resisted Gordon, and not because she was afraid, but because she knew she couldn't overpower him. Now, she knew that her mind had expanded. She had become wiser, more mature—

And not by any means afraid any more.

It was the stone. The red light had enveloped her and in those moments, all fear, all anger, all resentment had vanished. She was no longer a scared girl. She had become a fearless, determined person.

She knew what to do. She had been afraid. She would be afraid no longer.

Martha dressed and walked along a path to the southeast nub of the island. In a few moments the boat's skiff returned, bringing supplies for her. She didn't return to the cabin but hid behind a boulder so that the pirates wouldn't see her. These men were terrified of Gordon but they hadn't been with a woman in months. Desperation might drive them to assault her, despite their fears.

When they returned to the ship, she emerged from behind the rock. She walked down a little path to the southeast side of the island and watched as *The Flying Scot* hoisted anchor and unfurled sail.

She wept, knowing what Gordon would do to Owen. The horror overwhelmed her and she fell to her knees. *Adonai*, she prayed as Sholem had taught her, *the God of Abraham, Isaac and Jacob, please protect him. Don't let him be destroyed.*

Owen heard voices and turned his head. He saw Gordon

approaching. "McClelland, is it?" said the pirate.

"Yes."

"When you speak to me, you will say, 'Aye Sir,'" said the man. "I am Captain Gordon." Gordon was dressed in the uniform of a captain of the Royal Guard. The red of his uniform exaggerated his red hair and ruddy complexion. The pirate removed his coat.

"You will address me as 'Sir', *do you understand!*"

"Yes—I mean aye, sir."

The Captain gestured to two of the men standing next to the grate. One produced a knife and cut a small hole in the back of Owen's shirt. Then he ripped the fabric from waist to neck and laid the skin bare.

"Count for me, Manning," said Gordon.

"Aye sir."

The force of the whip, a cat-o-nine-tails, slammed Owen against the grate. His knees buckled. The leather straps tore his skin and he shrieked with agony.

"One," droned Manning.

Owen tried to regain his feet, gasping for breath. The captain lashed him again. He screamed again.

"Two," said Manning.

Owen gave up trying to stand after the sixth lashing. He lost consciousness at the twelfth but Gordon lashed him twelve more times.

When he jerked back to consciousness, he was soaking wet, still hanging at the grate. Then the pirates threw cold sea water on his back. The fresh pain drew a new scream from his hoarse lungs. The salt sting was agony. They did it again. Owen collapsed again.

CHAPTER 5

Martha wept as she remembered her screams as her father died under Gordon's lash.

"Good-bye, Owen," she said aloud, standing at the top of White Island, watching *The Flying Scot* sailing away. "Why could you not have come to my prison yesterday?" she wondered.

The skiff tied in the cove on the eastern side of the island had to be Owen's. The pirates had come in from the west and hadn't seen it.

If only I knew how to sail, she thought, *I could be free and safe in a few hours. I could take enough money to hide. . .*

Martha pushed the notion aside. At that moment she felt a sharp pain in her abdomen.

Oh no, she thought. *The baby cannot come now. I do not know what to do.*

Terror seized her. She knew well that many babies died in childbirth. *She* could die.

To her relief, the abdominal pain eased and didn't recur. The panic receded as well, replaced by her new-found confidence. She had to get off the island. She made herself a quick promise to escape from her miserable prison. She spent the rest of the day gathering driftwood and hauling it to the top of the island.

Back at the cabin she fixed a meager dinner and went to bed early. She searched for Sholem's book, but then remembered that Owen had taken it with him.

Her dreams that night were terrifying. She relived her father's whipping and in the dream, her father became Owen. He looked at her, his eyes pleading.

In the morning she dug a pit in the sand at low tide.

Her husband had brought a load of treasure with him and dumped it into the chest. She loaded as much of the loot as she could carry into an improvised bag made of sailcloth, and then dragged it down the path to the beach. Her arms and legs ached, despite her effort to do the work with economy of effort.

A single doubloon fell from a tiny hole in the sack. It hit a small patch of sand, bounced and rolled behind a rock. In the stress of her effort, she didn't notice.

Martha retained a small sackful of coins behind the crude stove in the cabin. She would need them when she was rescued from the island.

At last she lowered the chest into the pit and filled it with the treasure. She covered the chest with sand and memorized the location of the loot.

Then she went to the southern tip of the island and built a fire. She sat next to the fire and waited. If a boat came by, she would be ready.

* * * * *

Consciousness returned to Owen in the dark. As his eyes adjusted, he saw that he was in the hold of a ship. He tried to stand but found that he was chained to the wall.

Now he felt the motion of the sea. The ship was under sail, leaving the island.

Owen's first thought was for his mother. Tears rose to his

eyes as he imagined how inconsolable she would be. Searching parties would go out. They would find his boat. They would assume that he had fallen overboard and drowned.

He groaned to think of the agony of his family at his death. They would never guess that he'd been pressed into the service of a pirate.

He was young and strong even if he was in crippling pain. He would desert at his first opportunity, he decided. Having grown up by the ocean, he could swim well, unlike most of the sailors of his time.

But it would be several days before he could move with the pain in his back, shoulders, and rump.

"You are awake, lad," said a voice in the darkness.

"Aye," he said. His throat ached with the hoarseness brought on by his screams.

"Drink this," said the voice. Owen felt a rough pewter cup pushed into his hands.

"What is it?"

"A mixture of rum and opium. It will dull the pain," said the voice. "Drink it at one draught."

Owen drank the foul mixture and handed the cup back. In moments the pain came closer to being bearable.

"Who are you?" he asked the voice.

"Levin," said the voice. "Sholem Levin."

"My name is Owen McClelland, from Portsmouth." The two men shook hands.

"Where are we?" Owen asked.

"In the hold of *The Flying Scot*, Captain Gordon. He ordered me to describe your duties on the ship."

Owen felt in his pocket and found the strange stone from the cabin on White Island. He showed it to Sholem.

"How did you get it?" asked Sholem.

Owen told him the story. Sholem nodded. "I gave it to Martha for safekeeping. I am glad she gave it to you. I can see that you are no thief."

As Owen's eyes had adjusted to the darkness, he saw a faint glow of sunlight through a crack in the deck above.

He held the stone to the light. The small cabin lit up with a red light.

"You can use the stone," said Sholem Levin, astonished.

"Yes," said Owen. He studied the man standing before him. The man named Sholem was perhaps a few years older than Owen. His eyes reflected gentle kindness. "You are no pirate," Owen remarked.

"I am a teacher," said Levin. "Gordon hijacked me from a ship a few weeks ago. I support myself as a shipwright. Gordon told me that is your trade as well."

"Yes," said Owen.

"Gordon is a good sailor, but he needed someone to repair his vessel after a battle. I have been doing so. You and I will work together."

"Aye. Where are we going?" Owen asked.

"I do not know," said Levin. Then he looked into the light and checked himself. "No. I do know. We are going into battle."

"This ship will be defeated," said Owen. "Gordon will die."

"You and I will survive though," said Levin.

"Yes. All else will die in battle or be hanged."

"Should we warn the captain?"

"No. This is inevitable." Owen and Levin nodded to each other. Owen put the stone away. The red light faded but he could still see Sholem's face, glowing with the soft red light. They sat and continued to talk.

"Sholem, are you Jewish?"

The other man laughed. "Oh yes."

Owen pulled the leather bound book from his coat pocket. He handed it to Levin and admitted that he didn't know what the book was. "Martha gave it to me to hold until we could escape the island. Her husband returned before we could get away."

Sholem gave him a little nod. "I gave it to Martha for safekeeping. You are welcome to it. It is a copy of the *Tanach*."

"The what?"

"You might call it the Jewish Bible."

"You mean the Old Testament?"

Levin chuckled. "I guess so. It's written in Hebrew."

"No wonder I could not read it."

Sholem chewed at a fingernail for a few moments, considering. "Would you like to learn?"

* * * * *

They agreed that Owen would begin his study of Hebrew at once. As they talked, Owen realized that his back didn't hurt. Sholem looked puzzled, but asked to examine him.

"Whatever he did to you, Owen," said Sholem, "you seem to be fine now. I see no trace of bleeding or welts."

The two men stared at each other, bewildered. "How can that be?" asked Owen.

"The stone," smiled Sholem. "I didn't realize its power, I guess."

CHAPTER 6

Two days later, *The Flying Scot* attacked a small passenger ship named *The Lark*. In the midst of the battle a British Man-of-War, HMS *Repulse* joined the fray. The two warships battled. In the end Gordon, a ferocious fighter, proved no match for the Royal Marines who boarded the ship and took prisoner all the pirates who survived the battle. The Marines took the captives aboard *Repulse* for trial.

Owen stood next to Sholem, their hands tied behind them. Owen's knees were weak with fear. He knew too well that the British navy hanged pirates without mercy. Although he reminded himself that the stone had predicted that he and Sholem would survive, he couldn't stop trembling.

The hangings began almost at once. The marines dragged five pirates, weeping and pleading with terror, to the main deck. Ropes were secured around their necks and the crew hoisted them to the yardarm. They strangled, swinging with the roll of the ship, high above the main deck.

Owen wrested his eyes away from the grim scene. He turned his attention to the small passenger ship, The *Lark*, which had just departed. The little ship was headed to America and would dock in Boston. Regret filled his heart. Boston wasn't far from his home in Portsmouth. Ten miles of ocean separated the Portsmouth harbor from White Island and the girl named Martha. He felt a tear trickle down his cheek.

The captain of *Repulse* reviewed the remaining prisoners, men who knew that they had seen their last sunrise. He stopped before Owen and Sholem and inspected the two young men. He appeared surprised to see a tear on the cheek of one of them. "Ringgold," he said to his first mate, "bring these two men to my cabin."

In the cabin, he spoke first to Sholem. "Who are you?" Levin told him his story. The captain looked dubious. "You have only been aboard a few weeks, Rabbi Levin?"

"Aye, sir," said Levin. "Gordon kidnapped me from a passenger ship and compelled me to repair his vessel."

"What about you, Lad?" asked the captain, turning to Owen.

Owen had to swallow before he could speak. "Gordon captured me two days ago, off White Island in the Isle of Shoals." Owen sketched out his story.

The captain looked back and forth between the two men. He crossed his arms and leaned back in his chair. "Can you prove this?"

Owen considered. "May I reach into my pocket?" he asked.

"Yes," nodded the Captain.

Owen extracted the stone. He held it to the cabin's candlelight. In the next moment he and Levin were surrounded with a glowing red luminosity. The captain's jaw dropped and his eyes widened. He sat up in his chair.

Owen spoke from the light. "Please, sir," he said. "Please send this stone to my mother in Portsmouth. It is precious beyond expression. I will write a letter to her to explain it. . ."

"You are not pirates," the captain said. "Very well. You both will join our crew."

Owen lowered the stone, his mind whirling. He struggled to

maintain his composure as he realized that the captain did not intend to hang him and his friend Sholem. His knees grew weak and he almost collapsed.

A sailor, seeing his weakness, clutched his arm and held him upright. "Courage," said the man, his voice kind. The Captain gestured and the man untied Owen, then Sholem.

Then Owen thought of his mother, and then of a beautiful red-haired girl marooned on an island. "Please, sir."

"Yes?" said the captain.

"Sir, please let me go home to Portsmouth. My mother is widowed and I am the sole support of her and my brothers. I fear they will take ill and die without me."

The captain looked at the young man, still glowing with the red fire of the stone.

"No, McClelland, I cannot," said the captain, not without kindness. "We are bound now for the Barbary Coast to hunt pirates there. We have been searching for Gordon and his men for almost two years, since his mutiny on *Porpoise*. We can try to send a message if we encounter another ship. We cannot go back and *Lark* is miles from here now. I am sorry, Lad."

The bosun's mate led Owen and Sholem to the crew quarters and assigned them a hammock. Owen fought back tears, thinking of his mother and his brothers.

And Martha. He tried to fill his mind with thoughts of her.

The Flying Scot, the vessel which had been profaned by Gordon, had been damaged beyond repair. The crew from *Repulse* stripped the black flag from its mainmast. The once-valiant ship, once again the warship *Renown*, sank beneath the waves, regaining some of its former pride as it bore its indignity to the grave.

The Royal Marines dragged the surviving pirates, one by one, before the captain of *Repulse* and his officers for summary court martial. The court sentenced the pirate crewmen to hang at once. Five at a time were hoisted by the neck to the yardarms where they hung for a half hour. Then their bodies were lowered and thrown overboard.

The captain of *The Flying Scot* died last of all. The marines dragged Sandy Gordon, blubbering and pleading, to the foredeck. The crew cut away and burned his stolen red uniform, which he had befouled as a pirate. He stood naked, begging for his life as his feet were placed in the chalked circle. A crewman put the black hood over Gordon's head and then the fatal rope. The hangman jerked the knot tight around his neck.

"My wife," he said, shouting over the drum roll. "She will die--" The rope cut off his words as five pairs of feet walked away, hauling the naked pirate to the yardarm by the neck.

Gordon, the last to die at the end of a rope, swung with the motion of the ship for the rest of the day, his body slamming again and again against the mainmast. His soul had been in Hell for several hours before the sailors lowered his body, cut the rope away, and threw his remains overboard. Nor did Gordon receive a funeral.

As the weeks passed, Owen and Levin integrated with the crew. When his physical and emotional anguish became extreme, Owen would take his secret glass and hold it to a light source. He would find himself bathed in a warm radiance of consolation, and the pain in his heart would abate. Owen's back had indeed healed without infection, though he would carry brutal scars for the rest of his life.

Having grown up by the ocean, Owen knew something

about sailing. When he could set aside the terrible pain of worry about his mother and brothers, he came to love the sea and the ship he was on. The men aboard *Repulse* respected him as a hard worker, a decent man, and a good friend.

When they were off watch, Levin taught him to read Hebrew. Sholem was a tireless teacher and Owen's mind was fertile and active. He proved to have a fine gift for the language. To occupy his mind, he began to memorize *Tehillim,* the Book of Psalms, in Hebrew. Then he would translate the texts into English and memorize them. Each day, he found that he could do more. His heart calmed and he always slept better when he worked with the scriptures.

* * * * *

Two days after the departure of *The Flying Scot,* Martha saw a fishing boat with two men aboard about a hundred yards from the island. She shouted to the two men and waved a pillowslip. They waved and steered to the shore.

"Who are you?" said the first man when they came ashore.

"I am Martha McClelland," she lied. She worried about using either the name Herring or Gordon. She didn't know if the men would have heard about the fate of her father's ship, The *Porpoise.*

"McClelland?" said the second man, surprised. "Do you have relatives in Portsmouth?"

"Yes, my husband's family. His aunt invited my husband and me to come and live with her," she recited her rehearsed speech. "We were coming to meet her and her family but we were captured by a pirate ship commanded by Captain Gordon. They killed my husband. The pirates marooned me here when they found that I was—" She stroked her bulging belly.

"Gordon, eh?" said one of the men. "I am surprised he did not just throw you overboard." Martha shuddered. The man grew flustered and offered to apologize for scaring her. Martha waved the apology aside.

"Please," she said. "Take me to Portsmouth to my aunt. I will pay you"

The men agreed without hesitation. "I need to bring some things, if you can wait a moment," she said. Martha hurried to the cabin. She seized the small bag filled with gold coins, then picked up the staff and tucked it under her arm. She called to the men. They carried her small trunk to their little boat.

The men opened their sail and tacked back to the mainland. The waves weren't high, but she'd lost her sea legs and felt nauseous during most of the journey.

At Portsmouth, the men took her to the main pier. She struggled up the ladder. One of the men introduced her to a man who would store her belongings for a time in his warehouse by the dock. Then she received directions to Widow McClelland's home. She gave each of them a gold coin, to their delight and gratitude.

The door opened after the first knock. A tall boy, perhaps ten years old and almost the image of Owen, stood there. His eyes widened with surprise. He managed a curious but polite smile. "Yes ma'am?"

"I am a friend of Owen's," said Martha.

The boy's eyebrows shut upward. "Do you know where he is? We are frantic. He has not been home--"

"Who is it, Charles?" said a woman's voice. Owen's mother, Grace McClelland, came forward. Her eyes were red with weeping and she clutched a handkerchief to her eyes.

"May I come in?" asked Martha.

A half hour later the sheriff sat in the small cottage listening as Martha related the story of Owen's kidnapping. "Gordon pressed Owen, eh?"

"Yes," Martha said.

"Well, Mrs. McClelland, this news gives us some hope. We assumed," he said, turning to Martha, "that Owen had drowned."

"No," Martha said. "I believe he is alive. He will try to escape, I know it."

When the sheriff had finished questioning her, he left. Mrs. McClelland thanked Martha for coming to the house. "But Owen was our source of income. I do not know how we will continue until he returns."

Martha stood. "May we talk in private?" She asked Mrs. McClelland.

"Yes, of course."

Martha took Mrs. McClelland outside and linked her arm with the older woman. Martha walked with her to the pier, a few streets away. Then she filled in what she had not told the sheriff. She told the story of her voyage on *Porpoise*. Gordon's mutiny. Her enforced marriage to the pirate. Sholem. Gordon marooning her on White Island. How Owen had found her. Their plans to escape together.

"Gordon entrusted me to protect his treasure," she said. She reached into her bag and extracted a gold coin. "If you will hide me and let me stay with you until the baby comes, I will pay you and help with the household."

"My dear," said Mrs. McClelland, her voice tender, "I would

let you stay with us for no charge at all. You are a friend of my son. I will never turn away anyone while I am able to help."

Martha began to cry and her new friend embraced the frightened young woman. Martha began to understand why she had perceived such great kindness in Owen and why she had confided in him with so little hesitation.

* * * * *

In the first week of May news reached the New Hampshire colony that Gordon's ship had been defeated. The ship he had been sacking, the *Lark*, had gone on to Boston and reported the sea battle between *The Flying Scot* and the British man-o-war *Repulse*.

Martha and Mrs. McClelland took a carriage to Boston. They found a man who had survived the battle. "Please," said Martha. "Do you have any news of a young man named McClelland?" She sketched Owen's story. "Or Levin?" she added.

"No," said the man. "The Captain of the British Warship assured us that he would hang all the pirates who were not killed in battle."

The pain was almost too much to bear as the two women returned to Portsmouth. Martha leaned on her new friend, weeping with grief and trying to console Mrs. McClelland. The British Navy had hanged Owen as a bloody pirate. *The love of my life*, she thought.

Also, her dear friend Sholem had asphyxiated at the end of a humiliating rope, his wisdom, kindness and knowledge lost forever.

The night they returned to Portsmouth, Martha's labor

began. The delivery was difficult and painful. But she gave birth to a beautiful baby boy.

Martha, overjoyed at the safe birth and her son's health, thought her son handsome beyond hope. She couldn't stop staring at the baby's copper red hair and startling green eyes.

A curious word stuck in her mind. *Faerae.*

"What is his name, dear daughter?" asked Grace McClelland, wiping Martha's forehead with a damp cloth.

Martha said, "I am naming him in honor of my father, but also, a man with whom I talked for less than an hour. My son's name is John Owen McClelland."

CHAPTER 7

Several months later *Repulse* engaged in a fierce battle off the coast of Algeria. No less than twelve small pirate vessels set upon the British warship.

The first volley of cannon fire killed the captain. The next broadside dismasted the ship.

Algerine pirates boarded. Owen and Sholem fought side by side. At one point, two pirates overpowered Sholem. One forced Sholem into a kneeling position and the other lifted a rusty curved sword to strike off Levin's head. Owen swung his sword twice. The two pirates fell with mortal wounds.

Before the battle ended, the pirates had killed most of the men. They captured Owen and Sholem and a few others. They loaded them aboard a filthy ship and brought them ashore.

Owen and Sholem were sold into slavery. They departed with their new masters.

Owen languished in slavery as months, then years passed. The head slave, a cruel thug named Ashan, beat him, starved him, and forced him to work sixteen-to-eighteen hour days. Still Owen labored every day to memorize and translate great portions of the *Tanach*. With his extraordinary gift of language, he managed to acquire more than a rudimentary knowledge of Arabic as well by listening to the other slaves.

One night, he realized it was the fifth anniversary of his captivity and sale into bondage. He took out his jewel, which along the *Tanach* were his only possessions and his only joy. He looked into the clear glass and saw the wavering shapes of beauty and peace. The firelight created a red glow that surrounded him in ruby light. He had noticed some time ago that when he did this, he didn't feel quite as hungry or as thirsty.

Ashan, the head slave, came out of the tent and caught the young American holding his jewel. "Give it to me," said the dull-witted brute.

Owen looked up, terrified of Ashan. He closed his hand over the stone.

All fear vanished. He scooped a handful of sand and stood up, confident and unafraid.

"No, I will not," said Owen in halting Arabic.

Ashan's face took on a sadistic grin of anticipation. He lashed at Owen with his whip. Owen dodged. He grabbed the lash and yanked Ashan off balance. Owen threw the handful of sand into the thug's face.

Ashan choked and stumbled, pawing at his eyes. Owen charged. He buried his shoulder in the thug's gut and drove him back onto the sand. Ashan landed hard, the breath driven from his lungs. He reached to his side and drew a long, double-edged knife. He struggled to his feet and Owen broke his wrist with a powerful kick. Ashan grunted as the knife flew out of his hand.

He rose to his feet, holding his wrist and still unsteady on his feet. He stepped forward, ready to fight, still trying to clear his eyes. Ashan, bigger and stronger than Owen, reached to snatch the jewel away.

Owen knew the thug wouldn't hesitate to kill him with his

bare hands. A torch on a long pole stood outside the entrance and Owen seized it. He placed his stone between the torch and Ashan.

A narrow beam of red light shot from the stone and hit Ashan in the forehead. He stood transfixed. A look of intense shock twisted his face and he screeched with terror. He clutched at his head as if trying to hold something inside. Then he crashed, face forward, to the ground.

Owen put the stone in his pocket. As he did so, two more servants came out of the tent. They screamed, "What happened?"

"I do not know," said Owen, replacing the torch. He wasn't lying. He hadn't the faintest idea what he had just done. "He threatened me and lashed at me with the whip. Then he got a strange expression on his face and fell over."

The other slaves summoned the master, who came out of the tent. He examined the dead body of Ashan.

The slaves rolled the body over. Fear contorted Ashan's face. His hands clutched his forehead as if someone were trying to tear his brain out. Still the body bore no other marks than the red blotch in the center of the forehead.

Owen stood aside, feeling no guilt or shame, but baffled by the stone's response to Ashan's attack. He began to comprehend that somehow the stone had protected him from the brute.

The master ordered the other slaves to search Owen but they found no weapon, only a piece of red glass. The master held it up, turned it this way and that, and threw it back to Owen. Owen and two other men dragged the body into the desert, dug a shallow grave, and dumped Ashan's body in.

Owen followed the other two slaves back to the camp.

Back at the tent the master called to Owen and demanded

water to wash his hands. He washed. Then again and again. "My hands are burning," he said to Owen. "What did you do?"

Owen replied in Arabic, "I did nothing. But I think I can ease the pain." The master nodded. Owen pulled the stone from his pouch and held it to the firelight.

In a few seconds the stone glowed in his hand. The aura spread to the master and the old sheik's hands shone with red light as well. Owen closed his hand on the stone and the glow faded. The master looked at his hands, and then showed them to Owen. They were smooth, ungnarled, and pain free.

Owen stared at the sheik, then the stone. *How did I know to do that?*

The sheik, just as amazed, turned to the young white man. He knew magic when he saw it and smiled at Owen for the first time. "Thank you, young man."

Owen gathered his wits and bowed. "I am glad I could serve you, sir."

"What is your name?" the sheik asked.

The next day, Owen's life began to change for the better. He took over running the desert sheik's household and began managing the man's business affairs. As Owen conducted the business of trading, the old sheik enjoyed unprecedented success.

To his delight, Owen learned that the sheik was not only able to read and write but was a prominent historian and scholar. When the sheik learned that Owen had a rich fertile mind, he taught the young man the Arabic language, some of the history of the region, the Islamic faith, and the life of the desert. He made it clear that he enjoyed engaging Owen in conversation.

One night, after a profitable day of trading, the master called Owen to his side. "Owen," he asked the young man, "how can you tell who is lying and who is not?"

Owen grinned. "What do you mean?"

"You seem to know what these other men are thinking—how low they will go, what they will accept. . ."

"It is a gift," said Owen, his hand stealing to the jewel in his pocket.

CHAPTER 8

Sholem Levin, languishing in slavery for several years, found himself in a caravan with a tribe of nomads who camped next to the Nile River. People from all over the region believed that the waters of the great river had life-giving and healing qualities. The slave master went to bathe in the river. He ordered Sholem to come along to guard him.

Sholem stood on the bank as the slave master entered the water. Out of the corner of his eye, Sholem saw movement. A crocodile entered the water not far from the slave master.

Without thinking, Sholem yelled a warning at the slave master and ran into the water, carrying a thick branch. The slave master turned, saw the crocodile and screamed with terror. He bolted for shore and had almost reached the bank as the crocodile lunged to attack.

Sholem leapt between the master and the crocodile. He struck the creature with the branch. The creature writhed and snarled and started for Sholem. Sholem lashed out at the creature again. The crocodile, roaring, turned aside. Again Sholem struck and the creature swam away.

Sholem hurried out of the water and approached the slave master, who stood panting, pale with fear. "Are you all right, Sir?" Sholem asked.

The master stared at him. "Why did you save me?" he asked. "I have not been kind to you."

"All life is precious, Master," Sholem shrugged. "You trusted me to protect you."

The master continued to stare at him. "Can you swim?" he asked when he had regained his breath.

"Yes, sir," Sholem answered, puzzled by the question.

"Then swim to the other bank," he said. "Hide until it is dark. A path lies on the other side. Follow it to the village two days that way. Go to the house of my cousin Elim. Mention my name and show him this amulet"—he removed a gold chain from around his neck—"he will help you get away."

Sholem protested. "No, sir," he said. "You would be in deep trouble for allowing me to escape."

"You are concerned about me?" the slave master asked.

"I do not wish for you to be punished," Sholem returned.

The slave master nodded, appreciating the point. "You are a noble man," he said. "It will be all right. I will say you gave your life to save me from the crocodile."

Sholem embraced him and ran into the river. He swam to the other bank, terrified that he would be attacked, but made it in safety. Some bulrushes grew along the river and he hid in them.

He emerged from hiding at night and ran along the path the slave master had indicated. He came to the village late the next day.

After making a few inquiries, Sholem managed to find Elim, the slave master's cousin, who took Sholem with him in a boat. They followed the Nile to the Mediterranean. Sholem found a Dutch trading ship anchored in the bay and persuaded the captain to take him along.

Sholem voyaged with the Dutch ship to Portugal, where he

worked at his trade for some months. Then he took passage on a ship coming to America.

* * * * *

In Grace McClelland's home in Portsmouth, Martha's son John demonstrated a unique gift that far transcended ordinary sensitivity. One morning when he was five years old, he came to his mother's side in the small house and found her weeping. "What is it, Mama?" Martha saw the concern on her son's face. She managed a smile of consolation.

"I had a strange dream, John," she said. "I cannot remember it, but I dreamed of someone I have not seen in years."

The boy knelt on the settee next to his mother and took her face in his little hands. He stared into her eyes and said, "Do not be scared."

Martha felt pleasant warmth in her mind. New colors and sounds and smells swirled and cleared. Then, to her complete amazement she saw the dream again.

She found herself sitting outside a tent under some strange looking trees, gazing into the depths of the inscrutable red stone. Torchlight illuminated the area. A huge man emerged from the tent and stood over her. Martha comprehended that the man was a brutal thug and she was afraid. The ruffian spoke in a strange language, but Martha somehow understood what he said. "Give it to me."

"No," she said in the same language. "I will not." She fought with the thug, then held the red stone before a torch, not comprehending why she did such a thing.

A beam of light shot out and hit the man in the forehead. He fell forward.

Then she was back in the small home which she and her son shared with Owen's mother and his brothers.

"Owen," she gasped and clutched her son to her.

"Who, Mama?" said the little boy.

"Owen is the man for whom you are named. He is alive." She knew that Owen had survived, and that he still had the strange stone.

The stone had communicated with her. She couldn't imagine why she knew this.

Martha, dumbfounded, felt the most extreme emotions flood over her. She went from joy to despair to fear to peace. "What do I do?" she said aloud.

At that moment someone knocked on the front door to the cottage. Martha rose, trying to calm her heart. She crossed to the door and opened it.

The man who stood there recognized her at once. His face broke into a wide grin. "Martha," he cried, overjoyed.

She also knew his face at once, but she was so taken aback to see him that it took a few seconds to respond. Then she giggled with delight and threw her arms around the man. "Sholem," she laughed.

"Martha," said the man, returning her embrace. "I found you. Are you all right?"

"Yes," she said. "Oh, yes. The staff is here, as I promised."

"Wonderful," he said. "And the stone is safe with Owen."

"It is true then," she said.

"What?" he asked.

"We heard that the British Navy hanged you and Owen with Gordon," Martha said. "But I dreamed of Owen last night. And here you are."

"Owen is alive, or was so when I saw him last," Sholem said, and grasped her hand between his. "But we were both captured more than five years ago and sold into slavery in North Africa."

"Slavery!" said Martha. Her right hand stole to her mouth. All these years, Owen had been a slave deep in the desert.

Sholem told his story to the family that night. When he reached the part about his escape, he said with a smile, "So, I hid in the bulrushes. Not unlike my ancestor Moses."

"I know the story of Moses," young John piped. "Momma read it to me. Moses' momma made a little boat and hid him in bulrushes."

Sholem turned to Martha, who saw his delight. "You have learned to read, Martha?"

"Yes," Martha blushed. "Grace taught me," she said, taking the hand of her dear friend Mrs. McClelland.

* * * * *

The family welcomed Sholem into their home. With his carpentry skills he had no difficulty gaining employment on the docks. He took delight in teaching young John to read and do mathematics. At night his stories of his years in slavery and his escape from captivity, as well as his expert telling of Bible stories, made him a welcome guest in the McClelland home.

Martha wrote a letter to her uncle in England. A few months later he welcomed her aboard a sturdy ocean-going yacht. John and Sholem went aboard with her.

CHAPTER 9

Deep in the desert, Owen settled into a routine of study, work, and sleep. The household of the sheik thrived under his leadership.

One night, Owen served the evening meal to the master. He bowed and began to leave, but the master stopped him with a gesture.

"Owen," said the sheik. He indicated a cushion opposite him.

"Sir," said Owen, sitting on the cushion.

"Have you ever been in love?"

Owen hesitated, puzzled by the personal question. "I thought so once."

"What happened?"

"I learned that the woman was married. Then her husband died, but I was too far away to return to her. I imagine she has re-married by now." His stomach tightened with pain at the thought of Martha with another man.

The sheik clucked his tongue. "Your father did not find another girl for you?" He took a sip of water and handed Owen a fig.

"No," said Owen, struggling not to betray his amusement. "My father died when I was young, right after the birth of my youngest brother." He bit a little of the fig and thanked the sheik.

"How old were you when your father died?"

"Sixteen. I became the support of my mother and brothers."

"Was this girl wealthy?"

"Oh yes. She had a pirate's treasure," Owen told him. "May I know why you ask?"

The old sheik's eyes lit up but not with greed. More like intense interest. "Tell me the story," he said. To Owen's great surprise, the sheik invited him to eat some of the meat at the table.

While Owen talked, the old sheik listened with rapt attention. As the days went by, the old sheik wrote the story down, noting names of people, locations and so forth.

* * * * *

One morning, Owen was supervising the slaves in their work and giving out the daily assignments. The master summoned him to his tent. Owen walked in to find two sunburned white men standing before the sheik. The master gave evidence of great distress. Tears stood in the old man's eyes and his lips trembled. "Owen," said the sheik. "Go with these men. They have purchased you."

When he recovered from the shock of the news enough to speak, Owen said, "But, Master--"

"No," said the old Sheik. "I have prospered because of you. I cannot bring myself to forbid your release."

One of the men spoke to him in English. His tone was gentle and kind. "Come, Lad. You are free and safe now. We have many miles to go before night and we must be off. Do you have belongings?"

It had been so long since Owen had heard English that he had to translate the words in his mind for a few moments. "I have only two things to take." He touched the stone in his pocket. He went to his sleeping mat and retrieved his *Tanach*.

The men had a horse waiting for him outside the sheik's tent. Owen begged the men to wait for a brief moment. He returned to the tent of the old sheik and found the man still weeping. "Owen," said the sheik.

Owen withdrew his glass and held it to the light. The red glow surrounded Owen with a warm peace and comfort. He took the outstretched hands of the old Sheik and the glow enveloped both men.

After a few moments, Owen covered the glass. The sheik embraced him and kissed him on each cheek. "Go with God, Boy. I shall miss you."

Owen returned the embrace. With a similar blessing he left the tent. The men helped him onto the horse and they rode toward the sea.

When they had ridden out of sight of the oasis, he asked the men who they were. "My name is Lawrence," said the tall blond man. "This is Fillmore." Owen shook their hands. "A woman has been looking for you. She has spent considerable money to locate you and now to purchase you."

"Who is she?" he asked, dumbfounded.

"We have not met her. Her uncle, whose name is Stott, hired us to find you. He seemed to know where you were. I do not know how."

Owen, baffled, couldn't remember ever meeting someone named Stott.

They rode late into the night and camped at a small oasis in the desert. Late the next day they came to the Nile River.

Within a week he arrived at the Mediterranean. A rowboat

waited at the pier, and two men rowed him out to a small yacht.

"Welcome aboard, lad," said the captain as Owen stepped onto the deck. "My name is Isaiah Stott."

Owen saluted the man and shook his hand. "How do you do, sir?"

"Come. I have someone who will want to see you at once." Stott turned and walked to the back of the ship. Owen had to jog to keep up.

His heart pounding, Owen climbed down a ladder to the main cabin of the yacht. Stott knocked and a female voice said, "Come in."

Stott winked at Owen and placed him to the side of the door. He made a motion for him to stay back and opened the door.

"I have someone to see you, Niece." He beckoned to Owen.

Owen walked into the room. A tall, poised woman rose to her feet with her arm around the shoulders of a young boy to whom she had been reading. She put her hands to her mouth with a little cry and ran to his arms.

"Martha," he said, too overjoyed to speak well.

"Yes," she said, drawing back a little and indicating the boy. "This is my son John. His middle name is Owen." The boy crossed the room to him and held out a small hand. Owen took the boy's hand, noticing that the boy had deep green eyes and copper red hair.

"How do you do, Sir?" said the boy.

"Uncle," said Martha. "Will you please take John on deck with you for a few moments?"

The boy stood looking up at Owen, his namesake. He spoke in a calm firm voice. "Uncle, I will come to you in a moment."

"Very well, John." Stott grinned at Owen. He squeezed

Owen's shoulder in encouragement and left.

The boy again took the right hand of the emaciated, frightened man before him. "You are scared, Sir," said the boy. "You have been scared for a long time."

Owen felt tears start. Young John's compassion touched him to the depths of his soul. "Yes," he said. "I have been a slave for many years."

The boy squeezed his hand and looked into Owen's eyes. Owen couldn't look away from the compelling deep green eyes of the boy.

Peace and joy spilled over him. Owen hadn't cried in several years. Now tears fell as he realized that his capacity to feel love and grace had not departed, burned out of him for good. Someone embraced him.

"Are you all right, sir?" asked the boy.

Owen wiped his eyes. "Yes, John. I have not felt this well in many years. Since the last time I saw your mother, I believe."

The boy smiled at Owen and left to join his great-uncle on deck.

"Martha," Owen said. She came to his arms and they embraced. Martha let him cry, speaking soothing, gentle words to him. In a moment they both leaned back.

Owen kissed her, long, deep, and with a passion he didn't know he possessed. She returned the kiss with love and reassurance. The kiss continued for some moments.

"You came for me," he said, embracing her. "You came from America to save me."

"Yes," she said. "I would have come for you sooner, but I learned that you were still alive less than a year ago." She stepped to a small table, opened the cabin door and rang a bell.

A man knocked and entered. Owen gaped. "Sholem. Is it you?"

"Yes, Owen," said Sholem Levin. The two men shook hands, then embraced, pounding one another on the back, laughing with joy.

Sholem sketched out his escape from slavery and how he found Martha. She had become determined to find him and bring him home. "About a month ago Young John said he knew where you were," said Sholem. "We came. Captain Stott went ashore. He hired Lawrence and Fillmore to go into the desert in search of you. They've been gone about two weeks."

The three friends chatted for some time, catching up on years of separation. After about an hour Martha turned and smiled at Levin, who saw the meaning of that smile: Martha wanted to be alone with Owen. "Oh yes," he said. "Yes, of course. Excuse me, Owen, we will talk later." He left and shut the door.

"We have only a little time," said Martha. "John does not like to be out of my sight very long."

"Martha," Owen said, still amazed, feeling this must be a very pleasant dream. "You came to look for me?"

"Yes. With Gordon's death, then Sholem's arrival, I no longer felt bound by my promise to Gordon. I spent a great deal of the treasure to buy this yacht and look for you."

"How did you know where to look for me?"

She gave him a strange smile, her brow creased. "I dreamed of you in the desert. Someone had tried to take the red stone. The message was very clear."

Owen remembered the night the Stone delivered him from Ashan's clutches. He rose and crossed to her. He knelt before her and took Martha's hands. "I have thought about you for years. I am," he said with complete sincerity and honesty, "and will be forever, your servant to command as you wish."

Martha, her cheeks wet with tears of joy, smiled. "Very well," she said. "I now give you your first command."

Sholem, brimming with joy, married Owen and Martha that evening. That night for the first time, Owen held his new wife, afraid that if he slept, she might vanish.

At morning light, though, she was still there, smiling at him. They lay side by side, talking. She told him about her life with Grace, and his brothers and sister.

"They will be so glad to see you," she said. "As I was."

Something had been of concern to him since the previous afternoon. "Your son," he said. "He did something to me yesterday."

"Ah, yes. He does it to me on occasion."

"What can he do with the gift?"

"I do not know the extent of his ability. My grandmother had red hair and emerald green eyes like his. Being around my grandmother comforted me."

"But he seemed to be able to see into my mind."

"I know," she said. "My grandmother used the word 'Cymreig'."

"I see."

"Were you frightened?"

"Of course not. The boy is gentle, kind and loving."

"Yes, he is. But many children are afraid of him in Portsmouth." They turned the conversation to Owen's slavery and his life since she had seen him on the bleak rock called White Island.

* * * * *

The ocean crossing to America took several days. At last, the yacht stood off of White Island.

Martha held Owen's his left hand while his new son grasped his right hand. "We must come back here after we see your family," she said.

"I understand," he agreed.

Owen's homecoming overjoyed the community of Portsmouth. His family wept with joy at his return. His mother couldn't stop smiling, then crying with joy, thrilled that her son was safe and alive, and that her beloved young friend Martha had become her new daughter-in-law.

A week later Owen and Martha took Sholem back to what was left of Martha's cottage prison on White Island. The three worked together to hide the treasures.

Owen's knowledge of the Hebrew canon amazed the pastor of their church in Portsmouth. The young man had a fine grasp of the Hebrew language. Though he was weak in speaking the language, he had far more than an expert grasp of the written language. The pastor was astonished that Owen had memorized and translated great portions of the Old Testament.

One day, the pastor told Owen that he had written a letter to the chancellor of Harvard College. In the letter, the pastor explained that he had a young man in his congregation who was already a significant scholar in the sacred texts. He was fluent in Hebrew and Arabic and had reading knowledge of Latin as well as Greek. The chancellor wrote to invite Owen to come to Boston. Owen and Martha traveled to Boston and found a small house.

Two months later Owen McClelland entered Harvard

College in Boston where he studied in the Seminary for several years. He graduated and the church ordained him. He taught Old Testament Theology at Harvard for years. When he was old enough, Young John, Owen's adopted son, enrolled at Harvard.

Despite the joy in his life, and the stimulation of his studies, the horror of slavery was a long time departing from his soul. Even in the arms of his wife, he would find his thoughts and dreams haunted by memories of terror and forced labor and hunger.

In 1735 Owen buried his beloved wife on Star Island. His lifelong friend Sholem stood at his side, sharing his grief, his arm around Owen's shoulders.

The treasure of Sandy Gordon passed into legend.

Sometime later, another legend was born. People recounted seeing a young woman standing on White Island, looking off to sea, as if watching a ship sailing off into the distance. The people whispered the legend of the Ghost of White Island.

Part II

CHAPTER 10
The Love of a Lifetime

McClelland Logan couldn't say his first name when he was little. It came out Mickey, and that became the name by which he would be known for the rest of his life.

A lot of people, even his own parents, seemed to dislike him, fear him, and mistrust him, even when he was a small boy.

He looked different from most of the rest of the family. He inherited from his grandfather McClelland vivid green eyes and copper colored hair.

Mickey became aware early in his life that he could do things that others could not: Strange things, things which frightened others, things which he didn't understand himself.

One day, when Mickey was about four years old, he was in a shopping mall with his mother. An old woman, who might once have been a radiant beauty, sat on a bench resting after a day of shopping. Mickey saw that her white hair still had some copper streaks and her eyes were emerald green like his. She wore heavy, clunky shoes, a white shawl and a long dress that might once have been a brilliant green.

She saw him holding his mother's hand and smiled. "Hello, little Faerae," she said. The old woman offered him her hand and looked into his eyes. Mickey took her hand . . .

In the next instant he was sitting on the back of a silver horse that was prancing toward a girl with blond hair and blue eyes who was about his age. He felt delighted to see her, as if she were his best friend.

He reached down to the little girl and she grasped his hand. She leapt up and sat behind him on the horse, her arms around his waist.

They rode fast, the horse's silver hooves striking sparks on a cobblestone street. The two children giggled, unafraid, confident somehow that the horse had a special magic which wouldn't allow them to fall off. The horse stopped before a beautiful lady in a flowing green gown and green shoes. Her copper hair fell around her shoulders and stirred in the mild breeze. Her emerald eyes flashed joy and happiness as she greeted them and lifted them down from the horse.

The woman handed each of them a silver apple to give to the horse. The huge animal stamped his hooves as he ate the apples from their outstretched palms. The horse leaned forward and touched Mickey's chest with his nose. Warm liquid joy spread over Mickey and a tender red glow surrounded the little girl and him.

The lovely woman pointed to a shining golden gate, which swung open before them. People came through the gate, waving and laughing, welcoming the two children and the lovely woman. On the other side of the gate they saw a magical fair and carnival. The little girl and Mickey giggled in anticipation of a day in this magnificent amusement park.

The girl and Mickey held the woman's hands as they walked into the magic world. They laughed and played for what seemed like hours.

At the end of the day, the sun went down in a spectacular sunset: reds, greens, gold, silver, and other colors for which Mickey had no words. Just before the sun went down, a beautiful green glow flashed at the top of the vanishing orb.

The woman led him and the blue-eyed girl to a petting zoo in the carnival. A bright red giraffe leaned his head to them and let them pet him. A rhinoceros, whose coat was metallic blue, came over. He spoke to them and gave them a ride on his back.

A bear, golden with silver polka dots all over, stood on his hind legs. He came forward and gripped their hands. Absurd calliope music began to play, and music of flutes and guitars and yodeling voices joined the sound. The bear danced silly dances with them.

Then they heard a crack of thunder. Lightning flashed around them.

The little girl and Mickey hugged in fear.

"He's coming," said the woman. "Nehushtan. He knows you are here. You are not ready to fight him. We must go back . . ."

* * * * *

Then Mickey was back in the shopping mall holding the hand of the smiling old woman. Her gentle emerald eyes warmed him and they laughed together. Mickey felt as if many hours had passed at first. He turned and looked at his mother, who hadn't moved. The music over the loudspeakers in the mall was the same as it had been when the dream started. Mickey realized that no time at all had elapsed.

The old woman gripped his shoulder and gave him an

affectionate squeeze. "Remember, little Faerae," she said. She looked back into his eyes and colors and wind and beautiful sounds again surrounded him.

The woman and Mickey stood together on the side of a large cliff. "Where are we?" the little boy asked.

"This is the cliff of Dover, overlooking the English Channel. Over there--" she pointed toward a rising sun—"is the coast of France."

"Why did you bring me here?"

"You needed to be taught about who you are, little Faerae."

"Why do you call me Fairy?"

"Because you are a Fair One, little Green Eyes. The blood of Faerae flows in your veins. England is the land of the Old Ones. You have inherited their ability to look into the minds of others, to see what they see, to feel and experience what they experience. Has no one spoken to you of this?"

"No. My parents seem to be—er—"

"Afraid of you?"

"Yes, Ma'am. Anyway, angry at me all the time."

She shook her head, an expression of sadness turning the corner of her mouth down. "Yes, little Faerae. You will face this from others all your life. Use the ability with wisdom. Do not use it to scare others, to hurt others, to embarrass others."

"I promise," said Mickey. "But I don't know anyone who is like me, except for you."

"Some more time will elapse, little Faerae, before you meet others who can do as you can. Be wise."

"Will I see you again?" Mickey asked.

"I think not," she began. Again thunder crashed and lightning flashed. A rainstorm waited to strike. The old woman looked frightened and peered around. "It begins, I see."

"What begins?" asked the boy.

"The attack. I worry that Nehushtan may already know about you, dear one."

"Who?"

"Nehushtan. The enemy. He knows us and fears us and all who share the gift of the Cymreig."

"I. . ." the little boy stumbled.

"Nehushtan is fear, little Faerae. He is anger, jealousy. All things that scare you or dismay you are part of Nehushtan."

"My parents hate me, don't they," he said.

She looked into his mind. "No. That is not true. They live in fear of you, but also in jealousy. Go to your grandfather. He must teach you."

Then, Mickey found himself in the mall again.

His mother's eyes hardened and her mouth curved down in anger. Mickey saw that she had no idea what had happened. Her face transformed into a mask of fury.

Mother reached out and grasped the old woman's hand. She removed the hand from Mickey's shoulder. "Take your hands off--"

The old woman turned and looked in her eyes.

A moment later his mother smiled. "Say good-bye to the nice lady, Mickey. We have to be going." Mickey gave the woman a wave and walked away, holding his mother's hand. The old woman waved goodbye. As she predicted, Mickey never saw her again.

Mother, to his surprise, was nice to him, loving and kind, for several days afterward. Then, as if something wore off, she resumed her aloof, almost hostile attitude toward him.

The old woman, Mickey knew, had looked into his mind and knew his thoughts and his dreams. Then she had— Bewitched?--his mother.

The old woman had seen that he had the same strange ability as she did. She was right: Mickey came to realize that he could change other's thoughts, make them feel different, allow them to see things that have never happened or things that have or might occur in the future.

Yet the old woman was correct about the cost of having the talent. Mickey's talent with his eyes always alienated others when he was a child. His mother and father, his brother James, and his sister Abigail would scream at him to stay out of their minds. His little sister Nicole picked up on their fear of him and avoided him.

His parents forbid him to use his eyes to look into their minds, to change how they were feeling, to give them visions and dreams. Mother said it was a dirty, nasty habit Mickey had to learn to overcome.

And the terror came upon him.

Nehushtan began to visit his dreams.

The first nightmare came the night just after Mickey met the old woman in the shopping mall. He'd just started sleeping in a big boy bed.

He rolled over and saw a huge snake rising by the side of his bed. It was mud-colored, far bigger than him, with hideous fangs and piercing red eyes.

The snake spoke to him. "Hello, little Mickey. I found you. Now I'm going to hurt you. You will die in terrible fear and pain. Then you will belong to me forever." Three old women came into his room. They surrounded his bed and chanted horrible things, describing how they would torture him and kill him, burning him in hideous red flames.

When his mother woke him, Mickey was screaming and terrified. She was angry with him for waking the house with his screams. The dream came again the next night. When the dreams became regular occurrences, his parents and siblings told him that Mickey needed to learn to deal with the dreams.

"Just tell yourself that you're dreaming and wake up," said his mother in exasperation. "That's what everyone in the world does."

Mickey never remembered her comforting him.

His Grandfather McClelland, whom Mickey called "Papa", died when Mickey was little. He, of all his relatives, took a serious view of the nightmares. When Mickey would sleep at Papa's house and have one of the hideous dreams, Papa was the only one who would hold him and comfort him. Papa would murmur that strange name.

Nehushtan.

Mickey began to realize that the rest of his family regarded Papa as a freak. Like Mickey, he had green eyes and copper hair. Papa could reach into his mind, as Mickey could with others. Papa worked with Mickey, teaching him how to deal with the terror.

As Papa neared the end, he asked his daughter to bring Mickey to the hospital. Mickey didn't understand about death, but he felt terrified when his mother brought him to Papa's bedside.

Papa, not even able to sit up, took his hand. The others in the room fell back. "Dear little Green Eyes," said Papa. "I'm so sorry I won't be here to teach you. But I have a present for you."

"A present," Mickey said, and managed to smile, not understanding the extremity of the situation.

"Yes," said Papa and he motioned to a book on the bedside table.

Mickey picked up the book. "What is this?"

"It is called the *Tanach*," said Papa. "It is very old and very important. Someday a letter inside will tell you what to do." Papa opened the book to the inside cover and showed him a name inscribed there. "This man is your great-great-grand-father. His name was Owen McClelland." The date read 1715.

Papa's hands trembled as he caressed Mickey's face and looked deep into his eyes.

His parents told Mickey later that an expression of fear crossed his face for a moment. Then they said that a gentle smile replaced the terror. Papa released his face, and Mickey beamed up at him. Mickey spoke a name: "Miranda."

"Yes, that's her name," Papa said. "Find her and treasure her always."

"I promise, Papa," Mickey said.

"And I promise that we will see each other again when the time is right, little Green Eyes," Papa said.

Mickey began to cry as he realized what Papa was saying. Mickey wasn't going to see him again for a long time.

Then his parents guided him from the room with firm hands. Later that day, as they were driving home, his mother asked him, "Who is Miranda?"

Mickey stared at her, perplexed. "Miranda? I don't know anyone named Miranda."

"But you said that name," she said. "And what did you promise Papa?"

Mickey looked up at his mother. He knew that tone. He was in for it. He tried hard, but finally had to say, "I don't know."

"You promised something to Papa."

"I did?" Mickey said. Baffled, he began to stammer, as he sometimes did when he was upset. He wracked his brain. Whatever he'd promised, he had no memory of it.

"What happened?" Mickey asked.

"Don't you remember?" asked his mother. Her expression changed to anger, which was always just hesitating to surface when she spoke to him. "He gave you this book." She took it from his hand.

"Oh. Yes, I remember that he gave me the book. But I don't remember making any promise."

Mother lost her temper. She threw her hands in the air and shook her head, muttering and irritated. She gave Mickey her silent treatment the rest of the day to punish him.

Papa died that night. His father said Mickey was too young to go to the funeral.

Mickey acquired the habit of sleeping with the *Tanach* under his pillow. Some nights he cuddled it like a teddy bear. After a while, Mickey noticed that when he hugged the book, the dream of the Snake came less often. Once or twice a year he paged through it. But it was written in a language he didn't understand. He saw notes scrawled in the margin, but he couldn't read them either.

Nonetheless, the book became his most prized possession. He held on to it through a move to New Hampshire. When Mickey was fourteen and ready to enter high school, his family moved to a suburb of Chicago. Mickey carried the book in his hands to the new house.

CHAPTER 11

Mickey's Aunt Melinda let him come and stay with her during summer breaks. She gave him J. R. R. Tolkein's *The Fellowship of the Ring* when Mickey was ten. Though he was a voracious reader, Mickey struggled for the first fifty pages. Then she had a hard time getting him to do anything but read Tolkein. Mickey read the rest of *The Lord of the Rings* trilogy. Those books led him to the *Chronicles of Narnia* by C. S. Lewis, then as he got older, into such books as Robert Heinlein's *Stranger in a Strange Land* and Murray Leinster's short story *First Contact*.

He learned that reading leads to dreams, and dreams are the closest thing to magic most people ever experience.

In one recurring dream, a girl with blond hair and sapphire eyes came to him and stood guard over his bed. The dream girl became his best friend. Mickey cherished his time with her.

Still they often found themselves in horrifying situations. They'd find themselves fighting armed men in a cave. Then, they would come under attack in an alley. Mickey would dream of being crushed by a huge machine, or being electrocuted, or beaten by anonymous foes. In these ghastly nightmares, the girl would come to his aid.

The dreams would begin as occasions of joy. They would be excited to see one another. In most of the dreams, though, the joy would vanish when would hear the sounds of a terrifying thunderstorm with high winds and vivid, omnipresent lightning and driving rain. When the storm lashed at them with its fury, they knew they were in for a fight.

When Mickey reached his teens, the dream of the girl with blue eyes came more often. Mickey could never remember much detail from the dreams except for the Snake and the hideous women, and the lovely blond haired girl. When he was awake he couldn't remember her name or what she looked like. Yet when he saw her in the dreams, he knew her at once. She had a strange name in the dreams. So did he.

* * * * *

He did good work in school until high school, when he became a superb student. There he met Jack Curry and Pauline Douglas, two teachers who understood unicorns and encouraged them. Through them Mickey met the romantic poets: Blake, Keats, Byron. Through a college professor named Brian Wilkie, he met Shakespeare.

The first time Mickey saw a live production of Shakespeare's *Tempest*, he was entranced. The play took Mickey to an enchanted island where he flew with Ariel and romanced the lovely Miranda. That play helped him begin to take back what was his.

To most people, magic was a myth. To Mickey, his parents and many others had tried to get him to bury it in the sea, like Prospero. Unlike Prospero, Mickey didn't bury his magic. He accepted it.

As he did, he learned to turn his back on those who sought to hold him back. He left home, not only in a physical sense, but with his emotions.

His life became much happier, to his surprise. When Mickey embraced his magic, people began to think he was brilliant. He learned to fly with the unicorns. He began to walk in beauty like the night of cloudless climes and starry skies. He saw that in beauty there was truth, and that was indeed all he needed to know.

* * * * *

In college, Mickey majored in English and took a minor in history. He became fascinated by studies of the Middle East in particular.

One time Mickey was reading a book about the history of Christianity in America and ran across the story of a man who had a powerful influence on the theology of the early colonies in the 1720's and 1730's. His name was Owen McClelland. This pastor was famous for his efforts to fashion a reunification between Judaism and Christianity. Owen McClelland's best friend, according to the text, was a Jewish rabbi.

Mickey recognized the name. The pastor was Mickey's ancestor. Mickey spent two weeks reading all he could find about McClelland, including a moving biography.

After Mickey graduated, he taught a few years of high school. Mickey took a master's from The University of Chicago in Mideast History and toyed with becoming ordained, but got interested in theatre. A couple of years later Mickey took another master's degree and then a doctorate in theatre from the University of Illinois.

In May, about two years after Mickey graduated with the doctorate, Mark Silber, a professor at the University of Wisconsin, shocked him with a telephone call. Silber had accepted a position as head of the theatre department. They had completed their dissertations at about the same time and worked together on a lot of shows.

"What're you doing for the next fifteen months?" Mark asked after some small talk and catching up.

"What do you mean?"

"One of our professors in the theatre department has been diagnosed with cancer. No, it isn't fatal, but bad enough to keep her out for a year. You want a teaching gig for a year?"

Mickey accepted at once. He agreed to start in the summer term and stay for the next year. He'd leave in August when the next summer term ended.

He arrived on campus and set up an office. Mark gave him three course syllabi. Two days later Mickey taught his first class, a graduate level survey of world theatre history.

He tried hard to make ancient theatre history as interesting as possible. He figured that he must have done a good job because the whole class stayed awake. Mickey even got a few laughs.

As the students trooped out, Mickey gathered up his books and notes. "Excuse me," said a voice. Mickey looked into the sapphire blue eyes of a tall blond woman, about his age, who smiled at him. "Can I talk to you for a few moments?"

"Sure," Mickey said. He shot a quick glance at her left hand. No ring. "Miss. . ."

"Fixx," she said. "But you can call me Rand. That's short for Miranda. My parents liked unusual names."

"I'll call you Rand if you call me Mickey," he said. In graduate school, teachers and students operate on a first name basis.

She smiled and agreed. "Okay, Mickey. I just wanted your

opinion. It seems to me that ancient theatre is intertwined with the religions of the country in which they're produced."

"Interesting observation," Mickey said.

She asked him some intricate questions about concepts that exceeded the normal scope of a master's degree student. She already knew a lot about the subject. Mickey didn't want the conversation to end, so he suggested that they go to lunch. She beamed acceptance and they walked to a campus restaurant.

They wound up chatting for about three hours. They talked about theatre, the university and her life. Mickey asked what had brought her to the school.

"I'm just here for the summer," she said, staring with rapture at a piece of cheesecake on her fork. Mickey had the feeling this pastry was a lifelong weakness of hers. "I teach high school in Whitewater, not far from here."

"Theatre classes?"

"My primary assignment is English, but that includes theatre and acting classes." She smiled as Mickey told her that he'd had a similar assignment when he taught high school. "I direct two of the school plays each year."

"I'm directing the first play here this summer," Mickey said. "Tryouts start this afternoon."

"What are you doing?"

"Shakespeare's *Much Ado about Nothing*."

"Sounds like fun."

"You plan to audition?"

"I just got to campus last night."

"Come on. What have you got to lose?" She considered, and then shrugged with a nervous little smile.

CHAPTER 12

They walked back to the theatre department. Mickey led her to the audition room. They found the room full of people wanting to try out.

Rand waited for her turn, scanning a copy of the script. Once Mickey heard her read, he hadn't the slightest doubt that she was the best actress in the room.

He cast Rand as Beatrice, the romantic lead. In view of Rand's talent, he reorganized his concept of the show to take advantage of her natural wit and excellent stage presence.

Rand responded well to direction. She played opposite a doctoral candidate, Leo Graham, as Benedick. They had exceptional chemistry on stage.

Over the next three weeks Rand and Mickey were separated only when they slept and for her other classes.

He went backstage on opening night and visited with the cast to ask how they were doing. Mickey calmed jitters, reinforced egos, and reminded people of notes he'd given in dress rehearsal. As Mickey came to the women's dressing room, Rand came over to him wearing a robe. She had just finished makeup and Mickey had a hard time recognizing her. He chuckled at her, but she didn't laugh back.

"Mickey," she said. Her face was drawn and she was biting her lip.

"Yeah," Mickey said, growing a little concerned. "What's wrong with you?"

"I don't think I can go on. I can't remember any of my lines."

"Oh, cut it out," he said with a teasing grin. "You've got stage fright. Breathe deep a few times. You'll be okay."

"No, you don't understand. I've never done this big a role. I've never had this many lines. I'm afraid--"

"Of course you're afraid," he smiled. "If you aren't scared, you aren't approaching the role with enough concern."

She bit her lip. She took his hand. Her hand was trembling. "Come on," Mickey said. "They're going to love you."

It didn't help. Well, Mickey thought, no sense in having her in panic. Mickey squeezed her hand, and with his free hand he turned her face to look into his. He went into her mind.

"Where are we?" she said. She looked around at the lovely countryside to which he'd brought her. The hills were purple and green, with stalks of yellow grain. They could see vineyards all around them. The sky was blue. They were the only people around.

"We're in Tuscany," Mickey said. "I brought you here to rehearse. Ready?"

"Aren't we going to miss the show?"

"Nope. You'll be fine. Ready?"

"I. . ."

"Come on. *I wonder that you will still...*"

"*I wonder that you will still be talking, Signior Benedick. Nobody marks you.*"

"*What, my dear lady Disdain! Are you yet living?*"

"*Is it possible. . .*" and so on. They ran the entire scene. She

giggled at his reading of some of the lines. She corrected him a couple of times.

"Better?" Mickey asked at last.

"The best," she affirmed.

"That's more like it," he said, and slipped away from her mind, sealing the memory.

They stood again outside the women's dressing room. She looked around as Tuscany faded.

"Logan?" she said. "What happened?"

"What do you mean?"

"I. . ." she mumbled. "I don't know what I mean."

"Feel okay?"

"Never better," she said. She put her arms up around his neck and gave him the first hug she'd ever given him.

"Kill 'em, Tiger," Mickey said. "If you do, I'll buy the cheesecake."

Most of the time, the mere mention of cheesecake made Rand's knees go weak. "What flavor?" she demanded.

"Any one you want," Mickey promised.

"With chocolate sauce?"

"Goes without saying. White or dark, your choice."

"They're at my mercy," she said, and walked back into the dressing room.

* * * * *

Rand stole the show. The audiences loved her.

Mickey stood at the back of the theatre for each of the performances. He found his cheeks burning with pride as he watched his friend perform the difficult role with grace and humor. To his amusement he felt jealous of Leo in the kissing scenes.

When the run of the play ended, Mickey and Rand continued to spend a great deal of time together with class, meals, and going to movies and parties. Rand was the best student in his class. Nor was there any hint of jealousy about her being teacher's pet. The class respected her work and sought her out for help.

"Hey," he said to her one day. "Look, have you thought that you might pursue your Ph. D.?"

She smiled. "A doctorate?"

"Sure, you'd be great."

She promised to think it over.

They discovered that they had a mutual interest in golf. She loved the sport and played well. They golfed together often.

Rand and Mickey continued to spend almost every evening together while Mickey planned lectures and she studied. They ate lunch and dinner together and deepened their friendship. Mickey continued to avoid physical intimacy.

But Mickey began to sense something was wrong. He was tempted to go into her mind and find out what was wrong. She'd been enthusiastic and fun at the beginning of the summer, but as the summer progressed, Mickey became aware that she wasn't quite as happy as she had been.

One night just before finals, she stood up and said, "That's it. I'm going home. I can't even see the page any more. Logan, this theatre history stuff is a big bore, and you know it."

"Ah, shove it," he teased. "You're the one who's doing the pledging. You asked for it. Deal with it."

She giggled, and Mickey walked her to her car. She unlocked

it and turned back to him.

At that moment, they heard the crack of thunder in the distance. Rand turned pale.

"What's the matter?" he asked.

"A thunderstorm," she said. "Er…"

"You're afraid of thunderstorms?"

She nodded. "Since I was a little girl."

"Why?"

She started to answer, but thunder cracked and lightning struck nearby.

She gave a little scream. She took one step and was in his arms.

He hugged her and she returned it. He went into her mind.

They were in a canoe on the Avon River in Stratford, Ontario, near the Festival Theatre on a magnificent day. Beautiful swans swam nearby as Mickey rowed the canoe with gentle strokes. The swans came to the canoe, and Rand handed them pieces of bread. Mickey and Rand laughed together at a bunch of little cygnets paddling hard to keep up with their parents.

They reached an island and went ashore. They spread a blanket and ate a picnic lunch, laughing and giggling at one another's jokes.

Then lunch was over. The day was warm and they were alone on the island. "Mickey," she said.

"Yes?" he said.

"Make love to me."

"Now? Here in public?"

"No one is around. We're alone."

"Yes, but--"

"Do you have a better plan?"

"No. I've never heard a better plan."

She came to his arms and they began to kiss. They relaxed into the kiss and lay back on the blanket.

Then Mickey released her, sealing the memory as he did. She was still in his arms in the driveway of the house he was renting for the year. Mickey looked into her eyes. He lowered his lips to hers. Her eyes closed and she smiled in anticipation of the kiss.

As their lips touched he drew back.

She opened her eyes, puzzled. "What?" she said.

He swallowed. She had no idea what drawing back from kissing her cost him. "It just can't. . ." he stammered. He cleared his throat. "It isn't really kosher for me to make love to my students, Rand."

"Ah," she said, with a mischievous smile. "Thanks for the hug, then. I hope you don't get fired."

He regained a bit of composure. "I think I'm allowed to comfort frightened students," he reassured her. She giggled and climbed into the car.

She drove away. Mickey was aching. *Idiot*, Mickey said to himself. *You should have kissed her. You're an idiot.*

For the next several years, that moment would haunt him. He would wonder if things might have turned out better if he'd kissed her that night. They might have gone back into the house and made love, he knew it, and their lives might have changed forever.

CHAPTER 13

At the end of the summer term Mickey sat in his office, struggling through some final exams. Rand rapped on the door and came in.

"Hi, Mickey," she said. She looked distracted.

"Hey, Blondie," Mickey said with a grin, grateful for the interruption in the tedium of reading the examinations. They chatted about little things for a moment or two.

"All right," he said. "What's really going on here?"

She cleared her throat and inspected the nails on her right hand. "I think I want to stay this year," she said. Mickey felt the room grow brighter. "I'd like to finish up my master's," she said.

"No kidding?" Mickey asked. "Why the change of heart? I thought you were leaving tomorrow. I figured I'd never see you again." He didn't mention that he had nightmares about that very eventuality.

"I know," she nodded. "But some things have just changed in my life."

"I see," Mickey said, trying not to betray his elation.

"There's just one problem." she paused. "I don't know how I can. . .er. . ."

"How you can pay for it?" Mickey guessed.

She nodded.

"Come with me," Mickey stood and led her down the hall to Mark Silber's office. "Rand wants to stay and finish her master's," Mickey told him.

"That's great," said Mark. He held up a piece of paper. "As a matter of fact, one of the guys we accepted just found out his wife is pregnant, so he's not coming. We just got his letter."

"Something else," said Mickey. Mark turned toward him with a raised eyebrow. "Rand tells me she needs some financial assistance, though."

"I see," said Mark, and gave Mickey a mischievous grin and wink. "Well, Rand," he said. "Would you be willing to take on a half-time assistantship?" he asked Rand. "That's what we had this guy down for." He waved the letter.

"I imagine so," she replied, surprised and pleased. "What would be involved?" she asked. Mark told her that she would have to work twenty hours a week for the department, perhaps in the scene or prop or costume shop, or maybe teach an undergrad class or two.

"In return we'll waive tuition and pay you a stipend." Silber named the figure, which wasn't lavish but would keep her in food and housing.

She nodded. Then she began to grin with excitement. "Oh," she managed. "I didn't think. . .I mean, I didn't know it would be that easy. . ."

Mark shook her hand. "Welcome back," he said. Grateful for the interruption in marking the papers, Mickey took her to lunch. They hugged good-bye, looking forward to the end of August when the next semester would begin.

When the fall term started, they resumed their platonic friendship.

At Thanksgiving break Rand surprised him with an invitation to her aunt and uncle's home in southern Wisconsin.

Mickey accepted. Thanksgiving and most holidays were times of loneliness for him. His family has always been distant and unwelcoming, as if they were embarrassed about him. Except for his little sister Nicole, Mickey hadn't stayed in touch with them much.

Rand's aunt and uncle, however, welcomed him as if he were a son. Mickey proclaimed the dinner fabulous. Rand raved about one of the desserts, a white chocolate cheesecake.

On Friday, it snowed a few inches and Rand and Mickey took a long walk in the woods near her aunt and uncle's home. She linked her arm through his as they strolled. She told him about her brother Casey and two kid sisters who lived in Illinois. Her brother, a year or so older than she, was raising his sisters since the death of their parents. Casey had taken the girls to Florida for a couple of days. The devotion she expressed for her sisters and brother impressed Mickey.

When they returned to the university, Rand and Mickey continued to pass up physical intimacy. That changed for a moment just before the winter break. She came to his office early in the afternoon to say good-bye. Mickey was going home to Chicago.

She sat across the desk from him. Her face was drawn, and the normal sparkle was gone from her eyes.

"I didn't sleep much last night," she said. "Nightmares."

"Strange. Neither did I." He'd had a terrible dream of the three old women. The fantasy girl had been with him at first, but then she'd disappeared, swallowed up by something Mickey couldn't see. The terror and the loneliness of having to let the dream girl go had haunted him all day. "Must've been those tacos we had for dinner."

She shrugged with a little smile.

He switched the subject. "Ready to go?" he said.

"Yeah," she smiled, "I'm on my way to Los Angeles."

"Have a great time." Mickey came around the desk to shake her hand.

She put her arms around his neck and kissed him.

The kiss ended, Mickey continued to embrace her. He heard a ringing in his ears. He couldn't breathe for a few moments.

"Mickey." Her eyes had regained their normal sparkle. "I wasn't planning on doing that. I'm sorry."

"Don't be sorry."

"I have to go," she whispered, lingering in the hug.

"No, you don't," Mickey said.

"What?" she asked, looking into his eyes.

"Stay with me." Mickey stroked her blond hair. "Stay for good. We'll get married this afternoon."

"Oh Mickey," she said, pulling back. The tears rose in her eyes. She clutched at a Kleenex on his desk and turned away.

He released the hug. Her lips quivered and tears glistened on her cheek. "I have to go. . ."

"Wait," he said. "I'm sorry, now. I never should have. . ."

"No," she said. "Don't you dare apologize. You've just paid me the greatest compliment of my life."

"But. . ." She backed away and hurried through the door.

He stood there for a long time. Mickey picked up a pencil on his desk and read the name. BT MASTERBRAND. What happened here? He asked the pencil.

At last he retrieved his coat from the hook on the back of the door and walked out into the winter air. Mickey drove home to Chicago.

CHAPTER 14

After the winter break, she came back to campus, looking tanned and happy. They kept things between them professional and, by some tacit agreement he never understood, never once mentioned the kiss or the awkward proposal. When spring showed up, they played several rounds of golf and continued an amicable rivalry. If Mickey had to attend a function with the department, she came with him. The department regarded them as a couple.

The last week of the semester came far too soon. On the night before commencement, he'd had terrible dreams again. The Snake came again, surrounded by the three old women, threatening to kill him. The blond girl didn't come to help or comfort him.

About 5:30 that morning, Mickey realized that any attempt at further sleep would be futile. He was too nervous about the day. He decided to go to the office and start closing things up for the semester. Rand would come in, he knew, at some time or other that morning. Mickey rehearsed his speech over and over.

He was going to ask her to marry him.

About 10:00, Rand came to his office. Mickey stood up, the huge oak desk separating them. He tried to think of something appropriate to say.

"I'm leaving in a few minutes," she said.

"Aren't you staying for graduation?" he stalled for time.

"Dr. Silber will mail my diploma to me."

They stood in silence for a while. "I'm sorry to see you leave," Mickey managed.

"I brought you a bottle of wine." She handed him a pleasant vintage of merlot, his favorite red.

"Thank you," he said, touched. Then, he took a deep breath. Feeling like a high school freshman trying to summon up the nerve to ask a girl on a date, Mickey managed to say, "I need to say something."

"No," she said in a voice so soft Mickey had to struggle to hear her. "Don't say anything. I've been an idiot." She walked to the window.

He opened his mouth, shut it, and tried to speak. "What are you talking about?"

After an awkward pause, she said, "Mickey, I owe you an apology." She wiped at tears on her cheek.

"You have nothing to apologize for," Mickey said. "You've been a great friend, the best I've ever had."

"I feel the same way about you." Her voice was only just audible.

She turned away from the window and came back to the desk. She sat in the chair opposite him, and blew her nose. She tried to say something, but then closed her mouth. At last, she said in that quiet voice, "I'm getting married. I'm moving to live in Los Angeles. "

He stared for a second. Then, his mouth opened as he tried to say something. A pain in the middle of his chest expanded to his entire torso. "Oh. I . . . see," Mickey said, the words coming with difficulty.

"I met Larry here when we were undergraduates. We started

dating. He moved to Los Angeles when I started here last June. That's one of the reasons I stayed last fall. I thought I'd miss him so much."

"I see," Mickey mumbled. He put his hands over his face and drew the fingers down. Mickey rubbed his fingertips together, trying to clear his thoughts.

"I missed him a lot less because you were my friend."

"Ah," Mickey said, staring at the top of his desk.

"Larry's a graphic artist. Very talented. You saw some of his paintings when you came to my apartment. The one above the couch . . ." She went on for a few moments describing how talented her fiancé was. He worked for a big graphic arts agency in Los Angeles.

"Rand," Mickey interrupted, his stomach hollow, "why are you telling me this now? Why didn't you let me know from the beginning?"

"I know you're angry. I don't blame you. You have every right to be infuriated with me. I led you on and I feel terrible."

"Have you been engaged all this time?" Now Mickey felt the anger beginning. His Irish temper made his face burn. Mickey felt his eyes narrowing.

She shook her head. "No. Larry and I decided to get married at Easter. I should have told you right away. But I couldn't. I loved being friends with you."

"Yeah," Mickey said.

"You've been such a wonderful friend. . ."

He stopped listening. Mickey took a deep breath to calm himself, and swiveled the chair to the right. By the oak tree that stood just outside his window, Mickey saw an attractive young couple walking together, holding hands. The couple strolled across the quad.

He realized she had stopped talking. For several moments, Mickey struggled, trying hard to be gracious. He turned back. She stood in front of his desk, staring at the carpet, not looking at him. "Okay," he said, using his formal teacher voice. "Thanks for coming in today."

"Will we stay in touch?"

Mickey's heart wanted him to say, *Sure, of course we will. You bet. Here's my Chicago address and phone number.* He instead said, "No. We won't. It's better if we don't."

She bit her lip, nodding. She extended her hand. Mickey, angry and bitter, turned away without taking it.

"Would . . .would you like to open the wine now?" she asked. "I hoped we could share it. . ."

He snapped. "No. Take the damn thing with you. I'll buy my own after you've gotten the hell out of my life."

His tone had been harsh, nasty. Now tears started down her cheek, her face showing the pain of the encounter.

The tears melted his anger. Mickey now felt terrible for her. He knew what it had cost her to come to him that morning. She couldn't have slept for days. His heart melted and he came around the desk with his arms open. "I'm sorry, Honey," he said.

"I understand," she said.

"Come here," he said.

"It would be better if you don't hug me," she said, as she crossed to him.

"Okay," Mickey said and hugged her. She put her arms around his neck. The embrace tightened, and became almost frantic. He felt her trembling with grief.

She looked up at him. "Don't kiss me," she said.

"Okay," Mickey said. Mickey leaned to her and their lips met. The kiss became passionate.

Then she broke away. She put her hand to her mouth, as if sealing the feel of the kiss. "Goodbye, Mickey. . ." She began. Then she turned and ran to the door. She pulled it open and sped down the hall. A chunk of his heart followed her.

CHAPTER 15

When the summer term started, Mickey found other people with whom to play golf. He started dating a couple of professors, one in the social science department and one who was a nurse at the university hospital.

A couple of weeks before the end of the summer term, Mark Silber came to his office. Mickey was alone, reading a couple of papers that his graduate students had turned in. "Hi, Mickey," he said. He took a chair across the desk. Mickey noticed that he wasn't making eye contact. Nor was he smiling. Unusual.

Mickey gave him a grin. "What's up?"

Mark held up a greeting card. "We—uh—we received this in the office just now. It's addressed to the department."

"Yes?"

Mark flipped the card to him. It was a wedding announcement. Rand had married someone named Larry Connor the previous Saturday.

"You okay?" Mark said. "You look pale." Mickey realized that he must look awful. His stomach hurt with new pain. He'd been thinking that someday, he'd look up and she'd come through the door of his office, sapphire eyes sparkling with joy.

"Yeah," said Mickey, his voice husky. "I'll be okay. Thanks, Mark." Mickey tossed him the card. He gave him a smile.

"Don't take it too hard, pal," Mark said. "There'll be others." Mickey nodded as his friend left.

Mickey looked out the window and let the tears fall. The tears didn't ease the pain.

The end of the summer term arrived. The department had a going away picnic for him. Mickey packed and cleaned out his office.

Mickey began loading his car, a ten-year-old Crown Victoria.

The day was overcast and rainy, with thunder rumbling and lightning flashing, typical of a storm in the Midwest in late August. Most people were inside.

It was a perfect day for a murder.

* * * * *

Two men sat in a rental car watching Mickey load his car with boxes of assorted books and papers from the office.

The men climbed out of the car. One of them, a tall blond man, slipped on a pair of brass knuckles as the other man slipped around behind their target. The blond man walked over to Mickey, who was puffing a little under the weight of a box full of heavy books. "You Mickey Logan?" the tall man asked.

"Yeah," Mickey said, looking for a brief moment into the face of the blond man. "Give me a second to set this down." Mickey walked toward the car trunk with the box in his arms.

The guy slammed his fist with the brass knuckles into Mickey's gut.

Mickey doubled over and dropped the box. His books spilled out onto the sidewalk.

The second man caught him from behind and pinned his arms. The first guy picked up Mickey's copy of Barney Hewitt's *Theatre U. S. A.* and hit Mickey across the face with it. Then he backhanded him with it.

The thug holding his arms twisted his right arm up into his back and kicked his spine. Mickey screamed and collapsed to the ground. The thugs kicked him into insensibility. The blond man found a bottle of wine in the trunk of the Crown Vic and smashed it. He held the neck and advanced on the broken man lying in the gutter.

"Don't bother with cutting his throat," said the man who had held Mickey from behind. "He's done for."

"You sure? He's still breathing."

"It's better if it looks like a mugging. Let's go."

The two men drove away. The blond man said, "Where now?"

"Drive down toward Chicago. We'll go to O'Hare and head back."

* * * * *

Mickey found himself lying on a bed in a cave, with delicious odors, comfortable warmth and lovely sounds like music. He looked around and saw a man standing next to the bed.

"Hello, Mickey," he said.

"Am I dead?" Mickey asked.

"No," said the man. "No, not quite. You are still in danger, though, if you don't fight."

"But the pain--"

"I know, Son. You will suffer much for some time. Yet Nehushtan cannot take you yet. We will need you."

"'We?' Who is 'we'?"

"You will learn that when the time is right. Nehushtan knows this. Do not give up, Son."

"Can't I please just sleep, Master?" Mickey said, sensing that this was the right name to call him.

"Yes, sleep. But you must not die. Do you understand?"

"I'll do my best," Mickey said.

"You must survive."

"Will I remember this dream?"

"It is not a dream, Son. But you will not remember it for some time."

"Who are you, Master?"

"My name is Myrthynne."

"Merlin?"

"That's what I am called in your time. But you will not come to me yet."

"But, Master. . ."

"No, not now," said the man. "Ask me no more questions. Go back. Remember these commands: Be at peace. Rest and gain strength."

Mickey Logan woke up in a hospital room. Mark Silber stood there with his wife, Liz.

He tried to say hello but his jaw wouldn't move. Mickey realized it was wired shut. He had a serious concussion and couldn't even nod.

Liz had tears in her eyes. "Oh Mickey," she said. She wiped his forehead with a cool cloth.

"Good to see you open your eyes," said Mark.

"What happened?" Mickey managed. He knew it didn't sound like it was supposed to, but Mark understood.

"You were mugged," Mark said. "The police haven't caught the guys who attacked you. Two of your students found you.

Your wallet was next to you, but the cash was gone."

"Unh. . ."

"Did you have a lot of cash in the wallet?" asked Liz.

Mickey shook his head a little. He knew that he had to rest, to gain strength, and be at peace. He tried to say, "Tell Rand," but the words wouldn't form.

It was a couple of weeks before Mickey could talk and a month until he could eat. Everything hurt.

The old women came to his dreams every time he fell asleep, tormenting, threatening as always. Laughing at him, mocking him. The blonde girl didn't come to him.

The police talked to him and showed him some mug shots, but Mickey couldn't identify the punks who attacked him. All Mickey could remember was that one of them had short blond hair. Mickey never saw the second guy. They seemed to be ordinary muggers.

According to the police theory, the muggers beat him until Mickey looked like he was dead. The detectives found the bottle of wine Rand had given him smashed next to his body. The police figured the thugs were planning to cut his throat with the bottle, but decided not to when they thought Mickey was dead.

When the hospital released him, Mickey drove to Illinois to recuperate at home. The physical hurts healed. His heart didn't.

He bought another bottle of merlot. But he knew he couldn't replace the one that the muggers had smashed.

CHAPTER 16

While three years passed, Mickey met other women, dated some of them, and continued to direct plays. Mickey heard about Rand once in a while from mutual friends at the University of Wisconsin. Still, Mickey never called her or wrote to her.

Then, Brody Herndon, a buddy in his doctoral program, called him from the west coast. He said, after the usual greetings, "I'm a prof in the department of theatre at UCLA."

"Not bad," Mickey said. "So what's going on?"

"Want to come out here for a year?"

"What do you mean?"

"I called Mark Silber. He said you did a stretch for him as a visiting prof. We'll offer the same deal. One of our professors is going to Saudi Arabia with her husband. She's willing to let you rent their house and car if you want. What do you say?"

Two weeks later Brody picked him up at LAX.

Mickey's year in Los Angeles proceeded well. He learned to surf, directed *A Midsummer Night's Dream* and taught some great kids. He had so much fun that he considered relocating to the west coast.

He toyed with the idea of trying to find Rand, but decided that would be inappropriate. Mickey didn't remember her married name anyhow. Besides, her husband might not appreciate him trying to contact her. *I don't need a punch in the nose*, Mickey decided.

Melt Shop, Cleveland Steel Corporation
South Chicago Works, IL
March

The two men watched Albert Thomas from a distance. The hulking thug sat on a bench outside the melt shop. A little light leaked out of the mill, but the night was dark. It was three A. M. on the midnight shift and they shivered in a cold wind. They made sure no one else was around.

As they watched, Albert stared at his peanut butter sandwich. He chewed with a slow deliberation as if that would make his half hour lunch break last longer.

"You ready?" said the shorter of the two men.

"Yeah. What're our names again?"

"I'm Tom, you're Roger. No screwups this time, right?"

In a moment they stood next to the man. "Hey, Albert," said Tom. "Can we join you?"

Albert looked up. Tom saw a glimmer of recognition in his eyes, but Albert didn't know their names. "Sure, siddown," he rumbled.

The men sat on either side of Albert on a makeshift bench behind a rail car outside the Melt Shop at the large mill.

"I'm Tom," said the first man. "This is Roger." They shook hands though Albert's heart wasn't in it. Tom was tall, perhaps a few inches taller than six feet. Roger was an inch or two taller, though thinner, with blond tipped hair.

A roar from inside the mill attracted the attention of Roger and Tom. "Whoa!" said Tom. The three men watched a huge overhead crane pour tons of molten iron into a furnace. Sparks shot everywhere.

"What's the big deal?" sneered Albert. "You've seen them do it once, you seen it all."

"We ain't been here as long as you, old pal," said Roger.

Albert grunted. "Say," Tom said, "want a little something to make the evening go faster?"

Tom handed Albert a glass bottle containing what looked like iced tea. He wore his work gloves so he wouldn't touch the glass.

"What is it?" said Albert.

"Taste and see," Tom said.

Albert sniffed. He liked what he smelled. "Foreman catches you with that, you're out the gate."

Tom laughed. "How's he gonna know?"

"Smell your breath?"

"That's why I carry this," said Tom, pulling out a pack of Beeman's.

Albert took a long pull at the bottle. "Nice," he nodded. "Real smooth."

"Mr. Daniels knows how to distill his stuff," agreed Tom. Albert took another long swallow.

In a few moments, Tom saw that Albert realized something was wrong. Albert's eyes took on an expression of fear.

"Albert," said Tom. "You're a dead man. Think hard. Do you remember me now?"

Albert looked up into Tom's face. His eyes widened and he mouthed a name, but it was too late to speak out loud. "Right, you miserable bastard," Tom sneered. "Enjoy hell."

Albert passed out a moment or two later. Tom took the jar to a water fountain and dumped the drugged whiskey out. Then he rinsed out the bottle, and then poured a small amount of whiskey into it. He sloshed that around, dumped it out, and again put in a little whiskey.

He looked around, scouting. No one was around. He looked back and nodded at Roger.

The one called Roger hoisted Albert onto his shoulders and started up the stairs to the crane loft.

A half hour later, they were in their car, leaving the mill. It was pitch dark, and no one had noticed their exit.

"Let's go to New York," said Roger.

"Now?"

"Yeah. My sister wants to see you."

"It's been quite a while since I've seen her."

Roger pulled out his wallet. Watching the road with one eye, he found the picture he wanted in the billfold.

"Yow," said Tom.

* * * * *

State Policeman Rusty Ivers climbed up the stairs to the crane catwalk. Ivers and the two other policemen with him had been fitted with safety glasses and hardhats.

Rusty tried to repress a yawn. He'd been dragged out of bed at about 4:00 A. M. It had taken him about a half hour to get to the mill.

Two men in white shirts and ties waved the policemen over.

"I'm Ted Van Lier, the Mill Superintendent," the first man said. Rusty shook hands with him.

"Jack Schultz," said the other man. "I'm the melt shop superintendent." He pointed at the crushed body that lay on the crane track.

"My God," said Rusty, taken aback by the scene. "What do

you figure happened?"

"Albert never was very smart," said Schultz. "He must've climbed up here where no one could see him. So he could hit this," he said. He held up a glass bottle with a vegetable drink label on it. A small amount of a clear brown liquid remained in the bottom.

Rusty sniffed. "Gack. Old Rattrap, huh?"

"I'd guess he got so loaded he couldn't move when the crane came along," said Van Lier.

The two men looked down at the floor. A large red stain had accumulated forty feet below. "How long you think he's been dead?" asked Rusty.

"Jimmy Broglio, the pusher on the yard crew, said he missed Albert after lunch break, around 3:30," said Schultz. "One of his crew found the puddle of blood a few minutes later. Jimmy ran up here and found the body. He got sick over there." He pointed to a corner. "When he calmed down, he called me, and I called you."

Rusty nodded. His men fanned out around the area, looking for any other evidence.

Van Lier sighed. "If you don't need me, Lieutenant, I need to call the main office. Poor stupid Albert, damn it. No lost time accidents for months. Main office won't be happy that they broke the streak with a death, that's for sure." The men shook hands.

Later, Rusty called Albert's mother, who lived in a nursing facility in San Antonio. The news devastated the poor woman.

Lieutenant Ivers called her again, a month later. He told her that they regarded the incident as an accident. Again he passed on his condolences.

She told him that she had the body of her son cremated. The mill mailed the insurance check to her.

"A strange thing happened, though," she said.

"Yes?"

"A few days after I got the insurance settlement, I got another check from another insurance company. It was very generous. I didn't know about this policy."

"You didn't?" Ivers said, a little surprised.

"Well, no I didn't," she said. "I was baffled, but I cashed the check."

She told him the amount of the check. He almost choked when she told him the amount.

He didn't tell her, but the settlement flabbergasted him. He'd never heard of a laborer having a life insurance policy that large.

CHAPTER 17

A group of people, most of them young but with anger seething in their eyes, sat in the lounge of a lovely yacht on the Pacific Ocean. The leader, Mohammed Awad, nodded to a man sitting across the room.

"Will we be able to strike as the heroes did on Holy Tuesday, Baal?" said the man, who was codenamed Dagon. Awad had taken the code name of Baal, the terror of Philistines.

All of Awad's followers had taken names from the Hebrew canon. The names had struck fear into the hearts of the Jews centuries ago. Now they would again.

"Holy Tuesday," said Awad, pointing a finger at the young man, "is called 9/11 in America. Try to learn to think of it in those terms."

"We will do better than the heroes did," said Milcom, another of the young men.

"We will exceed their effort," asserted Astarte, one of the two female members of the group.

"Agreed," said Awad. "Many of our brothers have died because of Bin Laden's bungling. The Americans have recovered to wreak havoc on our brothers in Arab lands. The Taliban has fallen in Afghanistan and the terror has come upon Iraq. American puppets now lead the people."

The group murmured, turning to look at one another and sneer in disgust. Awad went on. "We must have funds. The US and other countries have worked to stop donations to the freedom fighters of Palestine and other Arab countries. So we must act. We must find our own treasure."

"We know all this. How do we acquire these funds?" said Milcom, curling his lip.

"An ancestor of mine was a scholar, a sheik who lived in Egypt and Libya," Awad said. "He owned an American slave, who told him a tale of fabulous wealth hidden on an island off the northern Atlantic coast of America. My ancestor recorded the location of this island and his writings tell where we may find it."

The group appeared dubious. "Buried treasure?" said Astarte, narrowing her eyes in a frown of disbelief.

"Yes. I have researched the tale. The treasure has never been found. It still exists."

"If we locate such a fortune, we will see the last Jew driven from the Mideast," said Astarte.

"That is certain. We will also preside over the destruction of the infidel culture that threatens the lives of those who serve Allah, may peace be with him," said Awad.

The group muttered assent and even applauded a little. Awad held up his hand for silence. "We must destroy the young Jew as well."

"After we get the information," said Milcom.

"How can we do that?" said Asherah.

"My cousin Astarte"—he pointed to Astarte, a beautiful woman with red hair—"and I have found people who will help us," said Awad. Astarte grinned.

CHAPTER 18

Brody dropped by Mickey's office toward the middle of March. Mickey was finishing up a conference with a grad student when Brody knocked on his door. Mickey waved him in and the three of them chatted and joked until the student excused himself.

"What can I do for you, Brody?"

"Mick, would you like to serve on a dissertation committee for a defense next week?"

"Sure," said Mickey, pleased. He asked what would be involved.

"Oh, read the paper, make some comments, come in and ask questions when the candidate defends," Brody said. "Wouldn't take long."

"I could do that, but don't you want someone who knows the student and his work? I mean I'd be coming in pretty late, wouldn't I?"

Brody shook his head. "Not to worry," he said. "The dissertation matches your course work pretty well. Besides, the student asked for you by name."

"For me?"

"I guess you've earned a heavy rep among the doctoral candidates."

"Heavy rep," Mickey grinned. "Right out of *The Warriors* by George Hill."

They chuckled and Mickey agreed to help. Brody and Mickey chatted about the dissertation for a bit. Brody left him a copy of the dissertation, written by someone named Miranda Connor. Mickey took it home that evening.

The paper was brilliant: clear, well researched, and well written. This Miranda Connor was as sharp as a fishhook. Mickey was flattered when he saw that she had referenced some of his own writing and his dissertation.

*　*　*　*　*

On the day of the defense Mickey arrived at the conference room about an hour early and met with the rest of the committee. The chair, Janice Watts, had dated Mickey on occasion for dinner and movies. Nothing serious, but fun. Two other professors completed the committee.

After they all agreed the dissertation was a winner, they reminisced about their own defenses. Mickey told them his had lasted for two hours but seemed like twenty-four. "I wore a tan suit," he chuckled. "I sweated right through. I could never wear the thing again."

The committee members laughed in sympathy and related their own experiences. Defenses were no fun.

At about one o'clock, the department secretary knocked on the door. She told them Mrs. Connor had arrived. Janice told her to show her in. The secretary stepped aside.

Rand Fixx walked in, chewing her lower lip, a common facial expression when she was nervous.

Mickey was so surprised he didn't stand up with the rest of the committee. She managed a little laugh at his facial expression.

"Nice to see you again, Professor Logan," she said. She looked just as Mickey remembered her, except that she was huge with pregnancy. Mickey came around the table to her, and leaned forward to hug her around her enormous midsection. They released the hug and then explained to the rest of the committee how they knew each other.

Mickey held her hand as he pulled the chair out for her. Her smile of thanks didn't reach her eyes. Her hand trembled a little as she put her briefcase on the table.

He squeezed her hand and looked into her eyes.

The two of them stood on a lonely beach on a cool autumn afternoon. Gentle waves splashed on the shore and seagulls called.

"Mickey," she said, looking around. She was still pregnant. She held his hand as she asked, "Where are we?"

He'd brought them to a place where he felt comfortable. "That's Lake Michigan," he pointed. "We're on a beach in Michigan City, Indiana. Bus stop 12 on the beach road. My grandparents used to live in that house up there." Mickey pointed past the little dune covered with waving beach grass to a cottage nestled between two larger houses.

"How did we get here?"

"I brought you here to relax you."

They walked hand in hand to the water's edge. As they did, he kicked at the sand. It made a squeaking sound.

"This is one of the few places in the world with sand that squeaks when you walk through it," he told her.

They walked along the water's edge. She took his arm and he felt the trembling ease. He showed her how to skip rocks in the water.

"Are you ready?" he said.

"You've done this to me before. I'd forgotten about it. We were in a canoe, we had a picnic. Did we make love? I forget."

"No, we didn't. You're going to forget this, too, though."

"Do I have to?"

"It's best if you do." Then he said, "There's something I want you to know."

"What?" she said.

"I'm afraid that I still love you."

She nodded. "I thought so," she said.

Before he released her, Mickey sealed the memory away. When he brought her back to the committee, she had no memory of what he'd done.

She thanked him as Mickey helped her with her chair. Her smile was no longer tense. The eyes sparkled with good humor.

"Be tough," Mickey whispered. "The paper is a winner. You're going to kill this thing."

"Thank you," she whispered back.

After a few pleasantries, the committee got down to business. The professors explored some minor points of research, questioned her conclusions, asked about some sources. Rand explained her position and agreed to make their suggested revisions which were minimal. Throughout the meeting, she appeared cool, unruffled and poised.

After about ninety minutes Janice Watts looked around. They all nodded. Rand's smile faded. Her eyes roved around the committee, trying to figure out what they were thinking. Mickey saw her hand tense into a ball.

Having been there, Mickey knew what she was thinking. Was this committee going to sentence her to another year of revision? Re-write? Delay? "Professor Logan," Janice said, her voice formal. "Would you care to do the honors?"

He stood up, creasing his face into a scowl, and walked around the table. Rand looked at him and then at the rest of the committee. Mickey stood in front of her and paused long enough to heighten the tension. Then he said, "Congratulations, Dr. Connor. Welcome to the club."

Her mouth fell open and her eyes widened. Mickey took her hands and helped her to her feet.

She whispered, "Did I do it?"

"You sure did," Mickey said, and gave her a huge grin.

She looked at the rest of the committee, trying to absorb the idea that the defense was over. She snuffled. "Oh, damn," she said and fumbled for a Kleenex. "I promised myself I wasn't going to cry." She put her arms around his neck. The committee applauded and came around the table to congratulate her. In a moment they were all laughing.

They took Rand to the faculty club and ordered champagne to toast the new doctor. Rand, pleading her pregnancy, sipped just a little champagne. She ordered orange juice and the committee took turns toasting her.

Mickey expected her husband to show up. He was looking forward to meeting him. When Mickey asked Rand where her husband was, Janice Watts kicked him under the table.

When Mickey saw Rand bite her lip, her face twisting as if in pain, he realized how stupid he was to ask. This was a difficult moment with her husband not showing up. "Well," she said. Mickey saw her make an effort to smile. Again, the eyes lacked the sparkle of her genuine smile. "He wanted to come, but he had a business trip to New York. He had a big deal he was trying to close…" She stopped. Mickey thought she looked a bit angry.

He started to mumble an apology, but she waved it off and said, "No big deal."

Mickey thought to himself, *Earning a doctorate ranks as a major accomplishment in a person's life, and he couldn't arrange to come and support her?* Mickey was angry at her husband but also at himself for bringing it up.

CHAPTER 19
Manhattan, New York City
Room 1215

The man who called himself Tom lay back on his pillow, breathing hard. Sex with this woman had become the most erotic thing that had ever happened to him.

"You seemed to enjoy yourself," laughed the woman.

"I'll say," he agreed.

"He told me about your plan," she said, leaning on his chest.

Tom came alert at once. "What?"

"Oh don't worry," she said, giving his chest a little slap and giggling. "No one will hear it about it from me."

"Yeah?"

"No. In fact, I think I can be of help."

Tom thought about that for a moment. "You want to?"

"Yes. I have a perfect target for the next effort."

"Who?"

"Do you remember a thug called Frank Capriatti?"

"Huh. Yeah, I do. A little squirt with a big mouth and a crummy attitude. Married—what was her name?"

"Her name was Paula."

"Yeah," he said. "She was a knockout in high school. I never understood what she saw in that creep."

"I think I know what we can do about her husband." She

began to tell him her plan. He grinned as she laid it out.

"It'll take several months to set up, you know."

"Yes," she grinned. "No rush."

* * * * *

After a couple of hours the party at the faculty club broke up but Rand and Mickey stayed to catch up. He told her he was thrilled for her about the baby.

"Thanks," she said. "He's due anytime. I'm glad that he waited. I thought for sure I'd go into labor about the same time the defense started. Good boy," she said, speaking to her gigantic belly.

They talked about their lives. Mickey surmised from her comments that things were very far from happy in her marriage.

He went into her mind and checked it out.

"Larry?"

"Hunh?" He didn't look up from the TV. He was unshaven, his feet on an ottoman, a bowl of chips at his side.

"I have some news." She handed him a little plastic stick.

"What's this?"

"It's a home pregnancy test. It's positive."

"You're pregnant?"

She nodded. He muttered a bitter curse. "I didn't want kids. You know that."

"These things happen, Larry." She was starting to get annoyed.

Larry's face reddened. He threw the television guide across the room, and stood. "Damn it. How in hell could you be so careless? Yeah, this is your fault. Of all the stupid. . ."

"How dare you?" she said.

"How can I be sure the baby is mine?" he sneered.

Now Rand snapped. She slapped his face hard and turned to leave the living room.

"Okay, wait," he said. "Look, how much would an abortion cost?"

"An abortion?" said Rand. "We're not even going to discuss that."

Mickey didn't want to see any more. He backed out of her mind.

He found himself wondering why she stayed with such a jerk. Mickey realized that Rand was not the type to divorce someone without making a serious effort to save the marriage. She also would be worried about the baby.

Now Mickey knew the truth. Rand was in a miserable, unloving marriage. She had started on the doctorate because her husband was more concerned about money and the job than her. He didn't care about the child or the doctorate his wife had just earned.

There was something else. Larry Connor looked *familiar*. Mickey decided he must have seen him at Wisconsin, maybe at one of the performances.

"I'm so sorry, Mickey," Rand said, "but I have to get home. I've got quite a drive ahead of me."

He checked his watch. Six o'clock. "Why don't we have dinner first?"

"I'd love to but I really have a way to go. . ." she didn't finish the sentence.

He shrugged and smiled. "Where do you live?"

"Just north of La Jolla. Larry's graphics arts business is located there. He and his partner have several employees."

"How did you do this work on the dissertation by commuting?" Mickey asked.

"I finished most of the coursework a year ago. My topic lent itself to commuting only about once every two weeks."

"I never saw you on campus."

"I know," she said. "It was my fault." Now she dropped her eyes and took his hand. She gave it a little squeeze. "I was afraid that it would be too easy to fall back into things between the two of us again."

"Not with you that pregnant," Mickey said, trying to make a joke.

She smiled. They agreed that they'd try to stay in touch. Mickey knew they wouldn't.

He walked her to her car. Mickey kept trying to say the right thing and kept saying the wrong thing. She gave him reassuring little smiles and an occasional thump on the arm.

Mickey hugged her and gave her a peck on the cheek. He offered to drive her home.

"Are you trying to pick me up, Dr. Logan?"

"No. I can't imagine how you're going to fit behind the wheel."

She giggled, hugged him, and kissed his cheek. Mickey wanted to kiss her so much he couldn't stand it, but he stepped back and opened the door for her. She slid in and started the car. "We always seem to be saying good-bye," she said. Her mouth twisted to one side and she bit her lower lip.

"I know," Mickey said. He remembered how he felt the first

time they said goodbye. The same pain in his stomach and chest. His voice grew husky.

"We can't stay in touch, can we?" Now a tear leaked out of her eye. She brushed it away.

"No, we can't," Mickey agreed. She said something but Mickey didn't answer. She drove off. "Goodbye, Rand," Mickey said to himself. He felt like crying, too.

A week later Janice Watts told him that Rand had given birth to a son. Janice went with him to a department store and helped him pick out an outfit as a gift for the baby. Mickey also bought a copy of E. B. Harrison's *Complete Works of Shakespeare*. He found a beautiful bookmark and put it in the book at *Much Ado about Nothing*. He had the gifts wrapped and mailed them to the address Janice gave him. He wrote a neutral note to Rand: "Congratulations on the doctorate and the new baby." He signed it, "Best wishes, Dr. McClelland Logan."

CHAPTER 20
Harlan, Illinois
January

"There he is," said the woman. She pointed at a man sitting on a stool. The man, whose name was Frankie Capriatti, had a beer in front of him. From the looks of things, it wasn't his first of the day. Tom nodded.

Frankie Capriatti, a short, wiry man, had a vile temper and not an atom of patience. He didn't have much time to live, even though he didn't know that.

"Say, Frankie?" said Tom, standing at his elbow.

Frankie Capriatti looked up at the man who'd just spoken to him. "Yeah?" He asked in a tone that suggested that whatever the hell the man wanted, it couldn't be worth interrupting him. The bartender put a beer on the counter in front of this man. The man flipped a dollar onto the counter as a tip.

"You mean you don't recognize me?"

Capriatti, having put away a few beers already, wasn't at his best. He tried to unfog. Then he remembered.

"Yeah," he grunted. "It's been a while."

"Yeah. Since high school," said Tom.

"What are you doing in this hole?"

"Drinking a beer, just like you." Tom nodded at the glass full of beer in his hand.

Frankie lifted his glass, and the man tapped his glass to it.

"How about this snow?" said the man, his tone dispirited. "Must be two, three inches on the ground already. We're supposed to get a ton more."

"Yeah," snorted Frankie, then took a swallow, disinterested.

"You look a little down tonight," said the man.

"Ah, rough day at work. The boss was on my keester all day." The door opened and two people came in. Someone walked up behind him, but Frankie didn't turn around. A tall man with blond tipped hair strolled to the other end of the bar and sat on a stool. Frankie noted the man out of the corner of his eye, but he didn't pay any attention.

Tom smiled to himself as Frankie, supposing he had a sympathetic ear, continued to yak about his crummy day. Not much different from the others in his mundane life. Nowhere job, debts out the wazoo, nagging wife and all the trappings of failure. He was going nowhere in life.

"You still married to Paula?" Tom interrupted when Frankie took a breath.

Frankie snorted. "Yeah, but I dint feel like listening to no nagging tonight."

"Say, let me introduce you to someone."

"Who?" asked Frankie.

The man introduced Frankie to a woman who stood behind him.

Tom had to suppress a laugh as he saw Frankie Capriatti's reaction to the woman. She was, Tom knew, one of the most beautiful women Frankie had ever seen. She was a bit shorter than Frankie, about 5'-6", in exotic high heels. She was wearing a leather miniskirt and a blue mohair sweater. She had red hair, and her smile showed brilliant white teeth.

Frankie struggled to say, "Won't you sit down?"

The woman assented with a smile. She took her time climbing up on the bar stool on the other side of Frankie, letting him enjoy an extended look at her legs.

It was about the last thing Frankie would ever enjoy.

"Buy me a Coke?" she said. Tom smiled, listening to her affect the breathy vocal quality that drove men crazy. Frankie wasn't immune.

"Sure," said Frankie. "You want some Captain Morgan in it, maybe?"

She shook her head. She set her purse on the bar and opened it. It was Tom's cue. The bartender was occupied at the other end of the bar helping the man with the blond tipped hair.

"Hey, Frankie," said Tom, "let me show you something else. You'll get a kick out of this." Displaying little enthusiasm, Frankie turned to his left, where Tom stood. The man showed Frankie the butt of a large pistol shoved into his waistband.

Tom saw at Frankie's eyes widen with terror. Capriatti stared at the pistol, unable to look away, eyes riveted. While he was occupied, the woman dumped something from a small packet into his beer. The powder dissolved.

Two months later
Near Kankakee, Illinois

State Police Lieutenant Rusty Ivers stood with the farmer in an obscure corner of the farmer's field, staring at a mangled corpse. The farmer had called the state police when his son found the body which, to all evidence, had been in the cornfield for some time. It appeared that a hunter had stumbled and discharged his shotgun. The blast had blown a fair bit of the hunter's head off.

Rusty telephoned the county medical examiner's office. They dispatched a crew to the field. While Rusty waited for the ME, he asked the farmer, "You give this guy permission to hunt this field?"

"Nope. Never seen him before."

Rusty knelt next to the corpse. "Must have shaken your boy up, huh?" said Rusty, drawing on plastic gloves.

"You ain't kidding," said the farmer. "Poor kid's a mess, scared, sick. He threw up over there." Ted pointed to the nearby tree line.

Rusty patted the body and found a wallet in the hip pocket. The deceased, dressed in hunting clothes, had a valid hunter's license. The man's right hand still clutched a rusty Remington shotgun. Rusty examined the weapon and found that it had been fired once.

"Nice gun," said Rusty.

"Damn fine rifle," agreed the farmer. "Remington Model 1100, Sporting 12."

"Any idea what it's worth?"

"Close to a grand, I'd guess," said the farmer.

Rusty grunted and looked through the dead man's wallet. He found a driver's license. Rusty inspected it, noticing that the man had lived in a town that was a considerable distance from the field where the body lay. "Why would he come this far to hunt?" Rusty asked. "Lots of fields around his home town." Ted shrugged.

Rusty slogged through the mud back to his cruiser. He radioed headquarters and learned that the man, Frankie

Capriatti, had been missing for several weeks. His wife had reported him missing the night of a big snowfall.

A few hours later, the medical examiner removed the body. The state police secured the crime scene. Rusty drove to Harlan, Illinois, to the house of the dead man.

"Mrs. Capriatti?" he asked the woman who opened the door.

"Yes," she said, her face going white.

He introduced himself and showed her his badge. "May I come in?"

"Yes, please." She led him into a small but immaculate living room. Rusty saw her struggling to be hospitable. She managed to say, "Would you like some, ah, coffee? It would take just a few minutes. . ."

"No thank you," he said.

"Frank's dead, isn't he," she said. It wasn't a question.

"I think he is, yes," said Rusty, trying to be gentle. "I do hate to ask this. Would you be able to come and identify the body? Or does he have a father, a brother--"

"No, I'll come. Er. . .now?" She stared into her eyes. He had a bit of difficulty dragging his eyes away from hers. In his heart, he realized that staring into those brown eyes had changed his life.

"Yes, please," he said. She agreed and asked permission to change into some other clothes.

On the way to the office of the medical examiner, he tried to prepare her for what she was going to see. She nodded, trying hard to retain her composure.

Rusty found that he had to struggle not to stare at Frankie Capriatti's widow. She was about five-six, with long brown hair and an attractive figure. Her deep brown eyes were compelling. She had a mild, quiet way about her. Her voice was composed.

When Paula saw the body, she turned to Rusty, her mouth trembling. He put a comforting hand on her elbow. She nodded up to him. "That's Frank," she said. The tears began and he led her to a waiting room.

A few days later, he called Paula to request a list of Frank's friends and the places he frequented. After some chat, she told him that she had arranged a memorial service for her late husband. Rusty offered to drive her and asked how he could help, even though that was out of his normal scope of duty to a widow. At her request, he escorted her to the memorial service.

Paula seemed to be dealing well with her grief. She gave him a list of Frank's haunts and all the friends she knew about.

Rusty tried to investigate the death of Frankie Capriatti. He hit nothing but dead ends. A bartender at a saloon called Rocky's Lounge remembered that Frankie had come in several weeks before, but he couldn't remember if Frankie had been alone, or with anyone.

Rusty noticed that he was seeing Paula a great deal, calling her when he had any excuse to do so.

The police found Frankie's car off the dirt road in a culvert not far from the field, and towed it to the municipal pound. They found no fingerprints other than those of Frankie and his wife.

Rusty returned the car to Paula Capriatti. He also gave her the rifle. He didn't tell her how much he'd wanted to see her again.

"What's this?" Paula asked. Her mouth was open, her eyes wide with surprise.

"Excuse me?" he said, bewildered.

"What's this gun?" she asked.

"It's your husband's shotgun," said Rusty.

"Now where did he get this?" she asked.

"Don't you know?" he asked. "It's expensive."

She shook her head. She seemed to be struggling to frame a question. "He never owned a gun. He must have borrowed it from someone. But you say it's valuable?" she asked.

"Yes. It's a fine rifle."

"Is there any way to trace the owner?"

"I did. Frankie's name is registered for it."

"W-w-what!" she stammered. He shrugged. "I...guess I should clean away the mud and rust, shouldn't I?" she asked, turning her wide eyes to his. Rusty stared into those eyes.

"If you want to," he mumbled.

He gave her directions for cleaning the rifle. She looked baffled. He offered to help. She agreed.

Rusty drove to a nearby sporting goods store and purchased materials to clean the gun. He also purchased some wood and metal cleaner, as well as some steel wool and other supplies. Then he returned to Mrs. Capriatti. He spread some newspaper on the kitchen table and got to work.

The cleaning of the rifle took Rusty some time longer than it should have. Rusty was very particular.

When they finished, the rifle looked as good as new. They'd had a pleasant conversation.

Rusty decided he had to ask. He felt like a seventh grader, his stomach aching, his hands trembling. "Mrs. Capriatti," he began.

"Trooper Ivers?" she said, her eyes dancing.

"Can I call you Paula?"

"Not unless I can call you Rusty," she giggled. He relaxed.

"Paula, then."

"Yes?" she teased.

"Could I please see you again?"

"I'd like that, Rusty," she said, her face was glowing with pleasure. Rusty felt his face breaking into an idiotic grin.

They began seeing each other on a regular basis. At first, they saw each other a few times a week, though they talked on the phone almost daily. Then they began to see each other every day, moving with moderate speed into a sexual relationship. He let her dictate the pace of the intimacy, careful not to press her into something for which she wasn't ready.

In late April, as they were leaving a restaurant, she took his hand as they walked to the car. Then, their first kiss came about a month later. He would remember the soft, lovely press of her lips against his.

One night in early June, he brought her home from a movie and dinner. She invited him in for coffee. The weather had turned raw, rainy and chilly.

He kindled a fire in the fireplace while she brewed some coffee. They sipped at the coffee together, watching a fire in the fireplace and listening to the wind howl outside. She snuggled into him and they chatted in whispers, as if afraid to disturb the atmosphere in the room.

"Well," he said at length.

"Well?" she said.

"I need to go."

"It's miserable outside."

"I know. But I drive for a living."

She hesitated. "Rusty. . ."

"Yes?"

Silence.

"Rusty?" she said.

"Still here."

"I don't want you to go home tonight."

"Oh. I see."

"Would you like to stay?"

Now he heard a roaring in his ears. "Er. . ."

"I have a toothbrush you can use."

"You mean, the guest bedroom?"

"You know," she said. "I always thought the police were trained to follow clues."

"We are. I . . ." He stopped. "Oh," he managed.

She took his empty coffee cup and set it on the table. "Come on," she said. She stood and took his hand. "Unless you want another cup of coffee."

He laughed. "Maybe later," he said. She giggled and led him to her bedroom.

The intimacy served to cement their developing love for one another. The nights they spent together became the highlight of his life.

One day, she paged him. He called back with the speed of light.

"Hi, Honey," he said.

"Rusty. Are you coming by today?"

"I'm on a case now. But I'll swing by at about six, if that's okay. Let's go out for a bite."

"I guess so. It's just. . ." her voice trailed off.

"Are you okay?"

"Yes," she said. "I'm a little shaken. I just got a check from an insurance company."

"What, a life insurance check for Frankie's death?"

"Yes," she said.

"So what's the problem?"

"Well, it's huge."

"How much?"

She told him. He almost drove off the road. "What?" he said. She repeated it.

"Well, that's terrific, Honey. Just great."

"Please come as soon as you can, Rusty."

"Sure," he said.

"Rusty?"

"Yeah?"

"I didn't know anything about this policy."

"He must have bought it on his own, Honey."

"Yes, but, see, I always took care of the bills. I never wrote a check to this company."

He chatted with her for a few moments. She calmed down a little. A few moments later, they said good-bye and hung up.

Rusty continued down the interstate for a few miles, happy for the woman that he—

"I love her," he said aloud. "I really love her."

He grinned.

Then he thought. *Wait a minute. This guy Frankie was a laborer at a mill, not a millionaire. They had a hard time making ends meet. How could he have afforded an insurance policy this huge?*

On Christmas Eve, Rusty gave Paula an exquisite diamond ring that he had saved for months to purchase. He knelt and begged her to marry him. She accepted with tears of delight.

CHAPTER 21
The Pacific Ocean
Off LaJolla, California

Tom saw the man named Vali awaken. The Arab man shivered, since he was wearing only swim trunks and an orange life preserver. Tom saw that Vali felt nauseous with seasickness. The man lay tied up on plastic sheeting on the deck of a small cabin cruiser. The boat rocked from side to side in a moderate swell.

The Arab turned on his side and wretched.

"Damn it!" cried a coarse voice.

Tom looked up. Roger, a tall man with black hair tipped with blond stood over Vali, fury on his face. The man gave Vali a vicious kick in the ribs.

"What the difference?" said Tom. "The whole thing's going over the side in a few minutes anyhow."

"Stinks like hell, that's what," said the first man.

Now Vali's legs jerked as he felt a tickling sensation on his legs. He looked down. A beautiful woman was stroking him with a paintbrush. She was painting him with—

The Arab's eyes widened as he realized what she was painting him with.

Blood.

"What are you going to do to me?" he asked her.

"We're going to kill you, Vali," the woman said. He cried out in fear. She smiled. "This is cow's blood. We obtained it from a slaughterhouse today."

"Why?" stammered Vali. "What have I done to you?"

"Nothing," said another voice. He was about five-nine, built like Vali. Indeed, Tom thought, he could be Vali's brother. "But I have very good news for you," said the man. "You are going to die for the sake of *jihad*."

"Yes," said the woman. "And the grace and mercy of Allah is better than any treasure, Vali."

"What do you mean, *jihad*?" asked Vali.

"We must drive the infidels from the Mideast," asserted the man. "I need your identification. So when you are dead I will take your place. But I promise that you will be honored as one of the heroes of *jihad*."

"But. . ." stammered Vali, trying to think, "my wife--"

"You have no wife, Vali," said the man. "That is why you were so receptive to the attention of my cousin here." He indicated the beautiful woman.

Tom had watched her as she strolled into Vali's store that afternoon as he was about to close up. She had flirted with him, speaking impeccable Arabic. He led her to his car. As he was opening the door, Roger smashed a length of pipe into his head.

"You in turn will take my place," said the Arabic man. "I am honored that one so brave will bear my name to the grave."

The woman smiled. "You have relatives, yes, but not in this country," she said. "When we are successful, be sure that we will tell them that you are one of the great heroes of *jihad*."

Tom started the engines and turned from the controls of the cabin cruiser.

"Let's get it over with," said Tom.

"He's right," said the other American from the back of the boat. "They're going nuts," he said, pointing to the ocean. "Here guys. Enjoy yourselves." He poured a substantial quantity of blood from a large bucket over the side. As Vali lay tied up on the plastic sheeting, the American had been chumming for sharks.

"Please," said Vali. But the three men seized him and held him upright. The woman untied his hands which had been bound with ropes over a substantial amount of terry cloth. No bruising. Vali began screaming.

The woman went back to the cabin and engaged the engines. The men lifted the struggling man and hurled his blood-soaked body into the ocean.

The boat left the area as Vali's screams faded.

Tom and Roger placed two construction blocks in the center of the plastic sheeting. They washed the deck with heavy bleach. They tossed the mops and buckets into the center of the sheet. They tied shut the plastic sheeting, then pushed it over the side. It sank into the Pacific Ocean.

The Arab man pulled out a cell phone. His hysterical phone call to the coast guard made the others laugh. "My sailboat had hit a floating log," he wailed in a stereotypical Arab accent. "The boat is sinking."

The man completed the phone call and threw the cell phone into the ocean. The woman turned the boat and headed full throttle back to Los Angeles where they had rented the boat.

Tom smiled at Roger. They each opened a beer to celebrate. They were about to be very rich with insurance money. Vali had died with no idea of how much he was worth.

LaJolla, California
Later That Evening

Rand Connor knew a storm lingered behind the mild breeze off the Pacific Ocean. She had lived there too long to be fooled by the façade of delightful weather. Rain, lightning, thunder and mammoth waves would arrive soon.

She felt the beginnings of the visceral fear of thunderstorms that had always haunted her. She wished she could sleep. If I could sleep, she thought, maybe I'd have one of the good dreams.

She always felt better when she had one of those dreams. There were three or four of them, and they were dreams of places she'd never been. One place, she was sure, was Tuscany. Another was Stratford, Ontario. Yet another was a beach in Northern Indiana on the shore of Lake Michigan. In each of the dreams, she would be nervous at first, but then she would relax.

In these dreams she would find herself with a person she really loved. Someone she hadn't seen for years.

Rand Connor sat on the glider on the front porch of the little house she shared with Larry and their son Joey. As she sipped a glass of wine, she noticed that her hand trembled a little. She took a few deep breaths, trying to calm her anger. Her watch read 11:00. Yet Larry hadn't come home.

She had to admit that Larry's excuse this time had been novel. Going sailing. Sure. She believed that even less than she believed in the future of her troubled marriage. She had not the slightest doubt that Larry had spent the evening with some bimbo. Maybe the stunning redhead she'd seen him with at the office party. She guessed that Larry would be gone all night.

Rand grimaced as she thought about the shambles her

marriage had become. She struggled to remember why she had married Larry in the first place. Cowardice came closest to the truth, she admitted to herself.

Rand, a creative and energetic person, found the artistic man named Larry attractive when they first met at the University of Wisconsin. He surprised her when he invited her to a dance at his fraternity house. They had a good time together, and began to see each other on a regular basis. Then a daily basis.

Then, they began sleeping together several times a week. She hadn't intended to make love to anyone except her husband, but something told her that it was okay with this artist.

The sex had been less than sensational, she now admitted. He was, when they got married, the only man with whom she'd made love.

Then he went to the west coast, a year or two after they'd graduated. She promised to follow. And then, she met the right man.

After knowing this guy with strange green eyes and unmanageable red hair for a few days, she knew that he was the right person. But she couldn't bring herself to break her promise to Larry. *That's rich*, she thought. *I didn't want to hurt him.*

The phone ringing in the living room startled her. She knew who it was. Mitch again. He always called when Larry wouldn't be coming home.

She resisted the urge to go in and look at the Caller I.D. She'd let her machine answer. But the caller didn't leave a message. He never did.

In that moment, Rand felt dirty, incomplete, and ashamed. She shuddered.

She knew why Mitch was calling. He wanted to start things

up again. Not a chance, Rand asserted to herself. The affair had demoralized and humiliated her. Sex with Mitch had been a Band-Aid for a wound, but the pain of the affair, her shame, the lying—

She told herself again and again that she wasn't a liar. The affair with Mitch had been an aberration. That's all. The sex had been ferine, unconventional, and even kinky sometimes. She would tremble in anticipation of seeing him and of experiencing the things he liked to do to her. Yet she always felt empty and unfulfilled when the sex ended.

Larry lost interest in her about the time they conceived Joey. Sex became infrequent, if not rare.

She met Mitch at Larry's company picnic. He worked with Larry at his office.

He was several years younger than she, tall, handsome, flat-stomached, with well-toned muscles and short black hair with blond tips. His handsome face had more than a hint of Arabic features.

When the conversation turned flirtatious, she found herself enjoying it, and even amused. Mitch said, "I've seen how Larry treats you. It's not right."

"That's kind of you to notice, Mitch."

"So can I see you again?"

Rand's antennae went up. "Mitch," she said. "Are you attempting to pick me up?" But she was still amused. Even interested.

"I don't want to be pushy or force you into something. Maybe we can be friends?"

"I think you'd better excuse me," she said and walked away. But she was flattered and she did think about him. A great deal.

Rand's ego was at an all-time low. She enjoyed knowing that a man still found her attractive.

She began to notice that she ran into Mitch with some frequency and in some surprising places. The grocery store. Her son's swimming lessons. Once or twice at a gas station. One day, she ran into a McDonald's for a sandwich. To her surprise, Mitch joined her at her little café table. He was in the neighborhood, he said, and saw her go into the restaurant. She was always polite and tried not to encourage him.

On the night of Larry's office Christmas party, she went to quite a bit of trouble to look good. She put on a short, slinky black skirt, black hose with provocative high heels, and a dazzling red-and-green Christmas sweater with sequins and sparkly fake jewels. With her hair done up in a twist, her makeup and nails perfect, she knew looked terrific.

She wanted Larry to notice and appreciate her, of course, and she wanted to impress his partners and clients. But if she was honest with herself, she wanted to stun Mitch too.

All the men at the party noticed except her husband. Larry had driven to the party in a separate car, mumbling something about maybe needing to stay in town.

Her feelings hurt by the churlish behavior of her husband, she ordered a cocktail. Rand never drank much. A glass of wine or a cocktail put her right at her limit. She found herself exchanging surreptitious glances with Mitch all evening.

She sat off to the side of the party, drinking her vodka gimlet. Then she drank another. She was working on a third when one of the young women came up to her.

"Mrs. Connor. This may be none of my business, but your husband just went into his private office with Marisa."

"Who?"

"You know, the fake redhead."

Rand stood, fury starting in her chest. She stormed to the door of Larry's office, intending to bang through the door and demand an explanation.

She wrenched the handle. The door was locked. No lights showed under the door. Maybe she could talk Carlos into giving her the key. She looked around for Larry's partner, and spotted him in a large group of people, laughing.

Then she thought better of it. Rand didn't want a scene in the office. She'd had too much to drink. Pushing a confrontation right then wouldn't be wise. She felt woozy and didn't trust her judgment.

Emotions high, struggling not to cry, she retrieved her purse and shawl and went downstairs to the first floor. Then she thought, *I can't drive. I've had too much to drink.*

Mitch came up behind her. He had followed her downstairs. "You look like a woman who could use some help. Can I drive you home?"

She felt weak in her legs and stomach. She started to refuse. Then she gazed up into the eyes of the attractive young man standing in front of her. She thought about Larry locked in his office with the gorgeous client with the dyed hair. She smiled and nodded. "Thank you, Mitch. That would be very nice."

He reached for her hands. He brought them to his lips and kissed her fingers.

The months of frustration fell in on her. She heard herself saying, "Oh, Mitch. . ."

He put his arms around her. Her arms encircled his neck and drew his lips to hers.

The first kiss began slow and gentle, then became almost violent. It was the most romantic thing that had happened to her in ages.

She thought about the indifference of Larry, his disinterest in the stress of writing her dissertation, his lack of cooperation in Joey's birth, and the redheaded client. She felt herself surrendering, her will slipping away.

Mitch led her to his office on the first floor of the office building far away from the noise of the rest of the party. The sex on his couch was wild and unrestrained.

He drove her home. At her house she asked Mitch to wait in the car for a few moments. Rand paid off the babysitter, who lived just next door. She watched the girl run home across the yard. A message on the answering machine told her that Larry was going to spend the night in town. Rand ran out to get Mitch. Her legs felt unsteady as she led him in, holding his hand.

Mitch left about five o'clock the next morning before Joey woke up.

* * * * *

Rand shrugged away the memory, wishing she could shut out the persistent guilt and depression that thinking about the affair always engendered. Not to mention the fear.

Thank heaven she hadn't gotten pregnant.

Over the ocean Rand saw flashes of lightning. Faint sounds of thunder reached her ears moments later. The fear began to knot her stomach.

She saw a car turn onto her block. When it passed under the streetlight, she saw it was Larry's car.

He parked the car, shut off the engine and got out. He saw his wife sitting on the glider and paused. Then he sauntered to the porch. His face was grim.

"Where have you been?" asked Rand.

"Is your kid asleep?" he asked.

She gritted her teeth. "Of course he's asleep. It's the middle of the night. You didn't answer my question."

"You'd better come to the park with me," he said.

"I can't leave Joey here alone. Don't be ridiculous."

"This won't take much time," he said. "I don't think you want take the chance of him hearing this."

Rand hesitated, then rose and went inside for a sweater. When she came out, Larry was halfway down the block. She strode after him, anger driving every step.

He stopped at a bench and sat down. He stared straight ahead of him.

"Well?" she said, standing before him, arms folded.

He pulled out a small tape recorder from the pocket of his suit coat. He removed a manila-envelop from another pocket. "This showed up in the mail this afternoon." He removed a small cassette from the envelope and popped it into the recorder.

"What is this?" she asked.

"You'd better just listen for a while." He pressed the play button.

A male voice said, *"You look terrific tonight."*

She recognized the voice at once. Mitch.

"Thank you." Rand was startled to hear her voice.

"Seems a shame to take that outfit off," said Mitch.

Rand remembered the night. About a month ago. She had

just about decided she couldn't live with the duplicity any longer. Then she'd seen Mitch. He looked good. She couldn't bring herself to go through with the breakup just then.

Mitch made a tape? He was that angry? She couldn't believe it. Did he tape the other times?

"*Come on in*," Mitch said on the tape.

"All right," Rand said to Larry. "You can turn it off."

"Oh no," he said. "Sit down. It gets better."

The tape went on. Tears of humiliation flowed down her cheeks. Larry made her listen to it all. The foreplay. The undressing. Mitch's comments. The coupling. She felt as if it would never end.

At last Larry turned it off.

"Well?"

"Well what?"

"You deny that's you?"

"Of course not," she said. Anyone who knew her would recognize her voice at once.

"Okay. Then here's what's going to happen."

CHAPTER 22

When Mickey's dad died, he bequeathed his property to Mickey's siblings, excluding Mickey. The meanness of the omission was far from unexpected, but it did hurt Mickey a great deal. However, Mickey learned that his parents had kept an inheritance in trust for him for many years.

Grandfather McClelland, he learned, had left him some real estate in Pennsylvania. Nobody in the family cared or wanted it.

He drove to Pennsylvania to visit his legacy. It was rocky clay soil, worthless for agriculture and too far from any cities to build on. The land had some trees on it but they were valueless as timber.

In a remarkable twist of irony, the property made Mickey a rich man. About a year after he inherited it, the state built an interchange off an interstate not too far from the property. The little town where the land was located became a bedroom community for a couple of cities. All of a sudden the land became valuable. Mickey sold some of it, kept the rest and became rich. Not dazzling rich, but comfortable.

Almost as if Grandfather had known something, Mickey thought.

He left teaching, but stayed busy writing articles, working in professional theatre, directing commercials and acting in a few local productions. Mickey dated once in a while, and even got engaged, but the engagement fell apart.

One night, Mickey was directing a show with a small theatre group when he had an attack of appendicitis. Two of the actors drove him to the emergency room at Northwestern Hospital in the Gold Coast area of Chicago. The doctors operated.

He was laid up about three weeks. The group brought in another director who finished the show. By the time Mickey got back on his feet, the show was ready to open. At the opening the producer introduced him to the director, whose name was Casey Fixx.

Mickey had never met the man but when he saw Casey, he knew. They chatted for a while and found that they had similar backgrounds. Like Mickey, Casey had received his doctorate from the University of Illinois, though they hadn't known one another.

After the chitchat, Mickey asked, "Rand's your sister, isn't she?"

"Yeah," Fixx said, with a surprised grin. "Do you know her?"

"I sure do. I haven't seen her for five years or more, though." Mickey told him about meeting Rand at the University of Wisconsin and serving on her defense committee at UCLA.

"I remember now that she mentioned you," Casey said with a warm smile.

"How's she doing?" Mickey asked, trying to sound casual, though his stomach was aching.

"Not good. She's in the middle of a divorce."

"Ouch," Mickey said. His knees felt a little weak.

"Yeah. Her husband Larry the Creep initiated it."

"Larry the Creep?" Mickey asked, amused.

"Yeah. '*Dost know this water fly?*'" he said quoting Hamlet.

"'*No my good lord,*'" Mickey responded.

"'*Thy state is the more gracious, for 'tis a vice to know him,*'" Casey said. "I brought her and Joey, her six-year-old, back here to live with me for a while, until she can get on her feet."

"Could I. . ." Mickey stammered. "Could I see her?"

Casey paused for just a moment or two. Then he nodded. Mickey gave him a business card. Casey smiled and promised he'd give it to her.

* * * * *

Two days after Mickey met Casey Fixx, Rand called. That morning, Mickey had lifted some weights, stretched, and was getting ready to go out for a run along the Fox River. It was a gorgeous day. The phone rang as Mickey was hooking up Bogey, his white shepherd mutt. "Hello, this is Logan."

"Hi, Mickey."

It took a second for Mickey to register who was calling. Then Mickey recognized her voice. She sounded terrible, lacking the spirit Mickey remembered. "Rand?" he asked.

"Casey told me you wanted to talk to me."

"Could we have lunch?" Mickey asked. "Some cheesecake?" That worked almost all the time.

"I don't know," she said.

"Chocolate sauce. White or dark."

She chuckled a little. "I'd like to but. . ."

"How about some golf?"

"Golf?" she said.

He could hear the smile in her voice. "What about this morning?"

She hesitated for a moment. "Sure," she said.

They agreed to meet at a local course around ten o'clock that morning.

At 9:30 Mickey strolled into the pro shop at Redtail, the course he'd suggested. Mickey paid the green fees, signed up for a cart and went out to the putting green.

Just before 10:00 A. M., Mickey saw an old Buick pull into the parking lot. The car at one time had been grand, but now looked dilapidated and worn out. A tall woman wearing a short tan golf skirt emerged from the car. The woman walked to the putting green.

When she walked up the little hill on the side of the practice green, Mickey recognized her. He dropped the putter and hurried over to her.

Rand looked awful. Her face was drawn, her hair was askew, and her makeup wasn't applied in the expert fashion Mickey expected of Rand. She'd lost a lot of weight. Mickey extended his hand and she took it.

She managed a little smile. "Hi, Mickey," she said, the lovely smoky voice distorted just a little with a note of sadness. She looked in his eyes and they both started to grin. The smile he'd missed so much remained lovely and welcoming as always.

He felt as if he were melting into the ground, like the wicked witch in *The Wizard of Oz*, when Dorothy threw the water on her. "Hello, Rand," Mickey stammered. Her smile widened as she looked at his golf outfit of jeans, open collared shirt, white golf glove. The eyes began to take on the sparkle Mickey remembered.

She let go of his hand and crossed her arms under her breasts, looking him over. "You need a haircut," she said, and the smile became teasing.

He laughed. Without warning she yelled, "Oh Mickey!" and threw her arms around him.

He lost his balance and they tumbled to the ground. They were shrieking with silly laughter, rolling over and over down the little hill. *The height of dignified behavior between two civilized, educated people,* he thought.

She wound up on top. "My back. My back," Mickey groaned in a very stagy voice.

"Don't tell me you're still stealing other people's acts. That's Jack Lemmon in *The Odd Couple*," she said with mock contempt.

"Helluva tackle, though," he said.

"Thank you," she said, with becoming modesty.

Mickey remembered they were in public. "Dignity," Mickey said. "Always dignity."

"Gene Kelly in *Singin' in the Rain*," she said. They got to their feet, being formal in case other golfers were watching. Brushed away grass clippings.

They hugged again. She leaned back, arms still around him. Mickey saw tears in her eyes. He kissed her on the cheek. Then on the lips. She kissed him back for a long time.

"So," Mickey managed. "Are you okay?"

"No," she said, and the tears flowed. "I'm just so glad to see you."

He gave her his handkerchief and stroked her hair while she cried.

At last she wiped her eyes and blew her nose on his handkerchief. "You know I'm divorced?" she asked.

"Casey told me you were in the process."

"It's over now. I received the papers yesterday."

Mickey decided not to push her to talk about it. He said,

"How about we load up your clubs?" She nodded. They hopped in the cart and drove to her beat-up Buick in the parking lot. Mickey opened the trunk and lifted out her clubs.

"Need any golf balls?" Mickey asked.

She shrugged. "I'm sure I have a few, but I don't know if they're any good."

"I'll get a dozen. I could use some myself." While she changed into her golf shoes, Mickey went into the pro shop and bought a dozen Titleists. Mickey came back and gave her a sleeve of three.

"I've got more if you need them," Mickey said.

"Why would I need more than one golf ball?" she said, trying to bring off indignation, but failing. They giggled and arranged for the stakes for the match.

They teed off. She was a little listless at first but her competitive nature soon emerged. Her handicap had never been much higher than his. The old skill came back about midway through the second hole. Mickey, as always, had fun just watching her swing the golf club.

A tremendous rainstorm hit the course when they were on the twelfth green. They ran to the cart and Mickey sped toward a shelter. They pulled in as the rain came down in bucketfuls. "Want to go in?"

"With you winning?" she sneered.

"Okay. We'll wait."

"Hungry?" she asked. She pulled two tuna fish salad-on-wheat sandwiches and a couple of apples out of her golf bag.

They ate in silence for a while, watching the rain. At last Mickey asked, "Want to tell me?"

She chewed her sandwich a few moments with her shoes

propped on the front of the cart. Her tan golf skirt settled a little north of mid-thigh. She seemed oblivious to the effect her legs were having on him.

Finishing her sandwich, she began to caress a grass stain on her Titleist golf ball with her thumb and chewed her lip. She started to speak, then stopped. Looking up, she said, "The divorce is my fault."

He put an arm around her shoulders. She moved closer and leaned against him.

"You have custody of your son?" Mickey asked.

"Yes," she nodded. "Larry didn't want him. He said he was never sure the boy was his anyway."

Mickey's mouth dropped open. He started to speak and couldn't, trying to digest this dreadful calumny. "What!" was all he could say in his outrage.

"I don't blame him," she said.

"Why would you let him say such an awful thing?"

She paused for quite a while, stroking the grass stain. It wasn't going away. When she spoke her voice cracked. "I had an affair."

"Oh," said Mickey.

"It didn't last very long. Larry found out." She rubbed the grass stain. It wasn't budging.

They didn't speak for several moments. The rain was unremitting. Mickey resumed staring at her legs.

She spoke in a quiet voice. She left out the intimate details, but Mickey understood that the brief affair had been passionate, if unsatisfactory.

She told him how Larry asked for the divorce that night in the park. "He said if I agreed to a minimal settlement and a quick divorce, he wouldn't tell Joey what a whore his mother is. So I got nothing."

"I see," Mickey said, and hugged her tighter. Mickey stroked her damp hair away from her eyes.

"He let me keep my clothes and books and some personal things. I gave back the diamond we picked out when we got married. I took Joey's clothes, the photo albums—stuff that had no value to him."

"Like your golf clubs?"

She smiled a little.

"I called Casey and he sent me the money to come back here to live with him," she said.

They were silent for several moments. "Why didn't you call me?" he asked.

"I don't know. It's been so long. I figured you must've gotten married."

Tears ran down Rand's cheek. She rubbed at the enigmatic grass stain on the golf ball. It wasn't budging.

She used his handkerchief to wipe her eyes and blow her nose. "Joey's a great kid. You'd like him."

"I can't wait to meet him," Mickey said.

She turned to look in his eyes. "You want to meet him?"

"If that's okay with you."

"Of course it's okay," she said. She looked at the golf ball. The stain was still there. "So that means you want to see me again too?"

"What on earth did you think?" Mickey said with a smile.

Tears again filled her eyes. "You still want to be friends with me?" she said.

"Why wouldn't I?" Mickey said.

"I guess I figured that once you knew about . . . things, we'd never see each other again." The defeat in her voice made him realize how profound her heartache had been for the last couple of years.

"You're my friend," Mickey said. Mickey took the golf ball from her hand and rubbed away the grass stain.

She sat watching the rain for a few moments, and then turned to him. She put her arms around his neck and they kissed for some time, the only people on the rain-soaked golf course.

When the kiss ended, she asked if they could talk about him. They chatted about what he'd been doing with his life until the rain stopped and the sun came out. "Want to finish the round?" Mickey asked.

She wiped her eyes and cheeks. She took a deep breath and expelled it. Then she managed a smile. "If you don't mind losing your money," she said. Mickey laughed.

That afternoon she won five bucks from him. She spent it in the clubhouse on a pitcher of beer for the two of them. They took it out on the porch and sat at a picnic table.

They were talking about a play Mickey was reading when she shushed him and pointed to the golf course.

He turned and saw a foursome on the tenth tee about thirty yards from them. One member of the group was teeing off. He was dressed in an aqua-and-orange shirt with orange shorts and socks, greenish golf shoes, sporting a green tam.

The man brandished a $600 graphite-shafted driver with a club head just a bit smaller than a bowling ball. He looked at the ball. He looked at the fairway. Ball again. Fairway again. Ball. Fairway. Ball. Fairway. He stepped back, shook his muscles loose, and consulted his scorecard. He looked at the green some four hundred yards away. He reset his feet, stamping up and down. He looked at the ball. Then the fairway. He waggled the club head. He waggled his tush.

He drew the club over his head with calculated speed. He leaned forward toward the fairway, shifting his weight onto his left foot. His right foot came a few inches off the ground. He struck a dramatic pose with the club pointing straight up. Then he whaled away with sickening violence, as if walloping a loathsome serpent that was menacing him.

To Mickey's amazement, the golfer hit the ball. His right foot came down. His left foot came up. His body pivoted so that he was facing 180 degrees away from the tee.

To judge by his friends' reaction, his shot would have signaled the end of the career of Tiger Woods, Phil Mickelsen, and many other top pros. The despondent pros would weep bitter tears of envy and start looking for a job. The ball wobbled maybe seventy-five yards down the fairway, then hit and rolled another ten feet. His pals continued to congratulate him for the way he'd smoked it.

"Well," Mickey said, "at least he hit it farther than he could throw it."

Rand looked at him and giggled. "Not bad, considering the lie he had," Mickey added.

She snorted at the ancient joke, her hand over her mouth. Mickey felt a laugh welling up within him. They turned their heads away from the course and their shoulders shook with repressed laughter. She started to cough and took a sip of her beer to recover her composure.

The foursome waved to Rand as they drove by. Calling on

years of theatrical experience, she waved back without betraying her amusement with the swing.

After the golfers were gone, Mickey and Rand laughed out loud, wiping tears from their eyes. She stretched her legs in front of her and turned her face to the warmth of the sun.

As they chatted further, the pain started to descend on her again. Mickey took her hand and looked in her mind. He gave her a vision of color and brightness. Then Mickey released her and they came back to the table.

Her face relaxed. Her hand unclenched, and she shook back her hair with a wide smile. "I feel better," she said.

"Why don't you bring the boy along tonight?"

"Tonight?"

"Yeah, I'm going to take you to one of my favorite restaurants. 7:00 okay?"

She nodded, smiling, and gave him directions to her brother's house. They separated in the parking lot, where Mickey kissed her goodbye.

He pulled into the driveway of the Fixx home about 6:45 P.M. *Not that I'm too eager*, he smiled to himself.

Casey Fixx met him at the door. He invited Mickey to sit down.

"Is that you, Mickey?" Rand yelled from upstairs.

"Yeah, take your time. I'm a little early."

"Okay. We had a bit of an emergency here," she said.

"Nothing real bad," Casey grinned, speaking so Rand couldn't hear. "She thinks her good dress is too big on her. She's lost some weight."

"I could see that," Mickey said. "She didn't have a lot to spare."

"You're right," Casey said, his face becoming a bit grim. "I can't believe that creep dumped her. She insists on taking all the blame," he said, his voice bitter.

"I know," Mickey said.

At that moment a woman with long brown hair came downstairs. Perhaps twenty-five years old, she was a few inches shorter than Rand and just as beautiful. A man came in from the kitchen and took her hand. They crossed to him. "Hi," she said. "I'm Cheyenne, Rand and Casey's sister. This is my husband Derek."

"Glad to meet you," Mickey said. The Fixx family resemblance was remarkable. Mickey chatted with the young couple and Casey until Rand made her appearance, fluttering her hands, her face showing her anxiety. She began apologizing for being late when she saw him. Mickey hastened to tell her that she had no reason to be sorry.

She looked much better than she had that morning. The smile was radiant. She'd put her hair up. The short black dress flattered her lovely figure.

"Do I look okay?" she asked.

"Breathtaking," Mickey said. She smiled, gratified, and relaxed a little. A boy sped downstairs a moment later. He was wearing his good suit with a white shirt and a clip-on tie. To Mickey's surprise the boy walked up to him without hesitation or shyness and put out his hand. He gave him a good grip. "How do you do, Dr. Logan? I'm Joey."

"I'm glad to meet you, Joey. But listen. I'm a good friend of your mom. She calls me Mickey and so do most of my friends. I'd like you to call me Mickey, too." The boy looked at his mom. Rand nodded.

"Okay, Mickey." The boy shook Mickey's hand again.

He tried not to laugh at the little guy's eagerness. "What kind of food do you like?" Mickey asked.

"Everything," the boy said with a shrug. This time Mickey did laugh and Rand grinned.

Mickey shook hands all around and took Rand and Joey to his car. He drove to a place called the Tornado Café which specialized in barbecue dishes.

Rand and Mickey each had a martini and Joey a root beer. Joey yakked about football, his new friends, his new school, his teacher, his favorite holiday (Christmas) and what he wanted, his room at Uncle Casey's house, how he wanted to join a soccer team, his baseball team in California, and his swimming lessons. Mickey saw Rand watching her son with a gentle smile, which he returned when he had to take a breath.

Mickey enjoyed Joey a great deal. He was polite, well-mannered, and had a good sense of humor. *Why would a guy want to get rid of a son like this one? He wondered. What a great kid.*

They returned to Casey's house about 9:30 and Rand invited him in. Mickey waited while she put Joey to bed. Then she joined him on the couch in the family room. She poured a little scotch for each of them.

"Did you have a good time tonight?" Mickey asked.

"Sure did," she said.

"Was this your first date? Since the divorce, I mean?"

"Yes it is. Unless you count how I cleaned your clock at the golf course this afternoon."

They laughed and chatted like old friends about old times. At last Mickey looked at his watch. It was one A. M., Mickey told her. She looked surprised.

"Can I see you again?" Mickey said.

"When?"

"First thing in the morning?" Mickey said.

"Okay," she said.

"Want to neck for a while before I go?"

"As a matter of fact, I do."

CHAPTER 23

Two weeks later, Mickey took Rand downtown to see a play. She loved it. Mickey saw some of her old spirit coming back.

At intermission Mickey asked how long she'd been out of theatre. "Since Joey was born," she said. "I was doing a little teaching at the community college and acting with a local group when I got pregnant."

"Miss it?" Mickey asked.

"Of course. You never get it out of your system, do you?"

"No, you never do."

After the show, they went to a late supper at The Goose Island Brewing Company. Mickey asked her how she was doing.

"Discouraged today," she admitted. "I've been trying to get interviews for jobs at high schools and at the community college. Teaching jobs are hard to come by with my degrees. Casey isn't charging me rent despite my protests."

"How's Joey doing?"

"Pretty good. He's sort of adopted Casey and Derek as his fathers. He doesn't mention Larry at all."

He agreed that it was strange. "It's been my experience in teaching that kids seldom do well after divorce, you know."

"I know what you mean. That's been a worry."

"Did you ever consider divorcing Larry?"

She shrugged. "Once about three years ago, when Larry was withholding intimacy. So I confronted him."

"How?" Mickey asked.

"I asked him flat out if there was another woman," she shrugged. "He denied it. I know Larry was with other women but I didn't have a shred of proof."

"What made you think that?"

"Sex was very important to him. Then it stopped between us. Let's not talk about him."

He agreed. His stomach hurt, thinking about Rand making love to Larry. He rushed to change the subject. "There is something I've wanted to ask you."

"Yes?"

He reached into his pocket and withdrew a little box covered with white satin. She stopped chewing her hamburger. She stared at him without saying anything for a few seconds. Then she chewed, swallowed and took a sip of water.

"Open it, please," Mickey said.

She did. The ring had a blue sapphire flanked by diamond chips in a white gold setting.

"What is this?" she asked.

"It's a ring," Mickey grinned. "The stone is a sapphire. It's the same color as your eyes. That's why I like it."

"What does it mean?"

"I was wondering if you'd consent to marry me."

She regarded him over the top of her water glass. After a long pause, Mickey decided he had to ask. "Have your feelings for me gone away?" Mickey asked, studying his fork, afraid of what she'd say.

"No. Never. I've always loved you. I also know you love me."

"You do?"

"Of course. I've known you were in love with me since the first time we met at Wisconsin."

"I see."

"But I don't know if I can marry you," she said.

"Why not?"

"For one thing, I'm not sure it's been long enough since Larry dumped me."

"In what sense?"

"It's been an emotional roller-coaster the last few years," she said. "Most of the ride has been downhill."

"I'm sure that's true," Mickey said.

After a sip of wine she shrugged. She took a bite of her hamburger. "There's something else too."

"What?"

She put down her hamburger and sipped at her water. After a few false starts she said, "I don't know that you'd ever be able to believe my vows."

"Why wouldn't I?"

"I'd try not to lie or deceive you, ever. But I'm not sure what our vows would be based on. I took those vows with Larry. But when things got rough with us, I found another man."

"Would you do that to me?"

"I don't know. I didn't think I could ever sleep with anyone else before I did it. It went against everything I believed and wanted."

"So you've made some mistakes. Remember when I had to correct you when you crossed the stage the wrong way in *Much Ado*?"

"I remember," she said.

"I never saw you make the same mistake twice."

She pushed her food around her plate for a few moments. "What about Joey?" she said.

"He's a marvelous kid," Mickey told her. "Do you think he dislikes me?"

"No, he told me you're cool," she said.

"High praise," Mickey said.

"Casey and Cheyenne and Derek like you also."

"Then what's the problem?" Mickey asked. "If you need more time, that's okay. If you want to think this over, it's okay too. I've waited this long. I can wait until you're ready to commit."

She held a napkin to her eyes for a moment. She whispered, "You mean it, don't you?"

"Of course I do. My life will never be complete without you in it." Mickey hadn't planned on saying that. But he realized as he said it that the statement was true.

She took away the napkin. It had mascara traces on it.

"Look, don't cry. If you--"

"When?" she interrupted.

"When what?" he smiled.

"When do you want to get married?"

"Whenever you want,"

"I wouldn't want a long engagement."

"How's ten minutes from now? I'll check the Yellow Pages for a justice of the peace. Are you finished with your burger?"

She gave a little smile. "I think we need a little more time than that."

"Why?"

"I'd like to have a real wedding. When I married Larry we

had a quick ceremony on the beach at Malibu. I wore a muumuu and he was in cut-offs. The minister had a flower in his hair."

"I see."

"This time I want a church, a gown, you in a tuxedo, Joey next to us in a little tux, my sisters and brother standing with us, flower girls, the organ playing *The Voice that Breathed O'er Eden-*"

"*The Voice that Breathed O'er Eden?*" he interrupted.

"I read it in a Wodehouse story. I think it's Victorian."

"Can you whistle it for me?"

"No. I don't know the tune."

"Why is it important?"

"Because L. M. Montgomery, the author of The *Anne of Green Gables* series, had it sung at her wedding."

"I see," he said.

"Right. My favorite series of books when I was a girl."

"So you've thought about this to some extent?" Mickey grinned.

"A little," she said. "Well, a lot."

"So assuming I acquiesce to these harsh conditions," Mickey said, "you'll agree to marry me."

"Oh, Mickey, do you really mean it?" she said, squeezing his hand.

He smiled and said, "Yes, but before you consent, you need to know a few things about me."

"Such as?" she asked, trying hard to look serious.

"I have not always been a good man."

"Oh?"

He swallowed, struggling not to laugh. "Often, on the golf course, when I've been practicing by myself, I have conceded myself ten or even twelve foot putts." Mickey made a show of being flustered and embarrassed. "I once found myself yet again in a huge sand trap on the fourteenth at Mill Creek. I'm in there so much there's been talk in the clubhouse of naming it after me. I--I lost my temper and failed to rake the sand trap after I flubbed several shots in a row. To my shame. Ah! You draw back! You are revolted!"

"I'm not revolted," she said. "I'm laughing at you."

He chuckled and grew serious. "But there is something you need to know."

"What is it?"

"You'd better let me show you." Mickey took her hand and looked into her eyes.

* * * * *

Rand Connor felt the world spin and dissolve into a sea of color and light. Then she was standing on the balcony of a hotel room, looking out over the ocean.

She looked to her left and found herself next to Logan. They were holding hands. "Where are we?" she asked.

"I brought you to Kaanapali, on the island of Maui. That," he said, pointing west over the ocean, "is the island of Lanai."

"How did we get here?"

"We aren't here. We're still in the restaurant. This is what I wanted to show you. I created this for you from one of my memories."

Rand felt like she was out of breath. "You're doing this in my mind?"

"Yes. It's like hypnosis, only a little more profound. I've done it to you before."

"When?" He turned and looked deep into her eyes. He showed her a few of the other times he'd done it to her. She saw herself in Tuscany reciting lines from Shakespeare. Then the scene shifted to an island in Stratford, Ontario, where she asked him to make love to her. Then they were walking on a beach on the shores of Lake Michigan, where he'd brought her to calm her before her dissertation defense.

"My gosh. I've dreamed about those places for years," she said.

"I tried to arrange it so you wouldn't remember," he said.

"Could you make it so I can remember this one?"

"Sure," Mickey said.

"Can we stay here forever?"

"No. We have to go back in a few moments. I have something to show you though."

He put an arm around her. "Look there for a minute," he said and pointed to the sunset above Lanai. The sky was ablaze with color: gold, red, purple, and colors for which she knew no words. A gentle trade wind stirred her hair, which she now realized was long, like it was when she'd first met Mickey.

For a few seconds the top of the sun turned a brilliant emerald green, beautiful beyond description. Then the sunset returned.

Rand gasped, her mouth open, at a loss for words.

"It's called the Green Flash," said Mickey. "It's rare. I've only seen it once."

Rand turned to him and put her arms around his neck. "Was that what you wanted me to see?"

"Yes," he said. "I wanted to share it with you."

And once again she was sitting in a restaurant holding a hamburger.

* * * * *

He released the vision with a gradual ease so she could remember.

Rand Connor stared at him.

"Mickey?" she said.

"Yes?" Mickey said, anxious about what she'd say.

"What did you just do?"

"I don't know what it is. Or why I can do it. Did I scare you?"

Rand drew back and furrowed her eyebrows, perplexed. "Why would you think that?"

"People tend to get scared when I do that to them."

"You take lots of girls to Hawaii?" she asked. Mickey watched her face twist into a scowl, indignation in every syllable.

"No, of course not. I. . ." then Mickey saw the little smile that told him she was teasing. "You're the only girl I ever want to take to Hawaii."

"Well, that's something at least." Now she gave him the brilliant smile.

"But I have tweaked other people's minds and given them visions. I don't even know what to call it."

"I wasn't scared. But--"

"But what?"

"Did you have the sense we weren't alone? Like someone was watching us?"

"I know what you mean. Whenever I go into someone's mind, three old women stand just beyond my vision, watching me. Then, that night I dream of them."

"Are you telling me that you have a recurring nightmare of three women?" she asked.

"Yeah," Mickey said, surprised at her reaction. "Why?"

"I do too. All my life. The nightmares were worse when I was going through the divorce."

"What do the old women look like?"

"I'm always reminded of the witches in *Macbeth*, I think. They've always scared me too."

"Do you ever dream about the Snake?" Mickey asked.

"Yes. I can't remember any of the dreams, though. Just being frightened."

They grew quiet for a few moments. "Does someone protect you in the dreams?" Mickey ventured.

"He used to," she said, "when I was little."

"He?"

She peered at him, studying his face. "Yes. He hasn't come to my dreams for years, though. Until the last little while."

He bit his lip. Mickey couldn't believe what he was hearing. "Have you seen him in the last couple of weeks?" Mickey asked.

"Yes," she said. "I'm sure I have."

"We need to talk more about this," Mickey said. "But are you accepting the proposal, then?"

"Of course I am," she affirmed. She slipped the ring on and admired it. "It's beautiful," she said. "It's the most beautiful ring I've ever seen."

He stood and tapped his beer glass with a fork. "What are you doing, Logan?" she hissed, as the people in the section near them grew quiet and turned to them.

"Excuse me," Mickey said. "This woman just agreed to marry me."

The people laughed and applauded. Rand, red-faced, stood. "You big dope," she said, and kissed him. "Anything for a round of applause."

CHAPTER 24

They drove back to Casey's house. Mickey saw the lights on and realized that Casey must be awake. Rand took Mickey's hand. "Come on in," she said.

"Hey Mickey," said Casey, rising and shaking hands.

"We have something to tell you," said Rand.

"You're getting married," said Casey. "Don't look so surprised. I knew this would happen from the first time you came over, Mickey."

"We want to have a civil ceremony as soon as possible," Mickey said. "Rand wants to have a large full scale wedding later on."

"I think that's super," said Casey, beaming. He walked over and hugged his sister. "Why don't you go up to see Aunt Julie and Uncle Earle in Lake Geneva?" said Casey. "He could have his judge friend perform the ceremony by the lake in a couple of days."

* * * * *

The midnight sky was black and the ocean was calm as two Zodiac inflatable boats came ashore in a cove at White Island. No one was around. Ten people surged ashore.

Armed with metal detectors, they walked back and forth on the island, crossing and re-crossing and crossing again the lonely rock.

At about three A. M., Asherah and Milcom walked to the southeast edge of the island. They found a path and walked up and down, the metal detectors waving. The clouds parted, and the full moon rose.

"Anything?" said the leader from above.

"Nothing. Nothing of any value whatever," said Asherah.

The leader walked away toward the north end of the island. The two people continued to search.

"He will return," said a voice behind them. They whirled.

"He will return," said the voice again. They saw a pretty young woman with red hair walking down the path toward them.

"Stop right there," hissed Milcom. The girl ignored them. She walked past them and stood on a promontory, looking to the southeast.

Asherah drew her gun in the same moment as Milcom. They fired in unison at the girl.

"What on earth?" screamed Baal, running back. They turned.

"The girl," said Milcom.

"What girl?" said Baal.

They pointed at her. "No one is there, you idiots," Baal said.

They looked and their mouths dropped open. He was right. Asherah screamed. Milcom choked. "But. . ." he said.

"What is the matter with you?" demanded Baal, harsh and angry.

The group returned to the rafts. They had found nothing.

"Now what?" said Dagon.

"I cannot find a descendant of McClelland," Baal admitted. "However, I do know where to find someone related to his friend Levin. We shall go after them next."

They decided to be patient for a few months before moving on the descendant of Sholem Levin. He was a rabbinical student named Steven Levin, who lived in New York. They shoved the rubber boats out to sea and sped back to the yacht.

It would take some time, however, before Asherah and Milcom would recover from their experience of seeing the Ghost of White Island. They were terrified to insensibility.

CHAPTER 25

Rand and Mickey loaded Joey and Mickey's dog Bogey into his car and drove north toward the town of Lake Geneva, Wisconsin. Mickey followed Rand's directions to a beautiful property with a large fine-looking house. It sat on eight acres framed by magnificent oak and pine trees with a commanding view of a small lake. The lake was terrific for fishing in the summer, Rand told him, and winter sports were great here too: snowmobiling and ice-fishing on the lake, ice-skating, cross-country skiing and even downhill at a couple of small mountains not too far away.

"Downhill in the Midwest, huh?" sneered Mickey.

"Of course. Oh, sure, it's crazy expensive, freezing cold, icy, windy, with real short runs. Other than that it's great."

"Uh, huh."

"And there's no need for that sarcastic 'uh-huh'. What a no-fun gloop you are."

"A what?"

"A gloop."

Silence. Then, "Rand?"

"Yes?"

"What's a gloop?"

"I don't know. I just made it up."

"I see."

"But that's what you are. A big gloop."

At this point, Joey began to laugh at them.

When Mickey pulled into Rand's aunt and uncle's home, Joey hit the ground running and took off with Bogey at his side. He threw her tennis ball for her to chase, then headed off toward the woods, running with Bogey, face alive with a smile.

"I guess he likes it here," Mickey said.

"That's an understatement," said Rand, and yelled at Joey to stop. "You can come out after lunch," she told her son. "First we have to say hello."

After lunch, Mickey walked with Rand's uncle Earle near the lake. They chatted, getting to know one another.

"Do you know the circumstances of the divorce?" Mickey asked him as they looked out over the lake together.

"Oh yes," Earle Fixx said. "Rand is as close to us as a daughter. She drove up here right after she came to stay with Casey. She told us the whole story."

"The divorce devastated her," Mickey said.

"Yes," Earle agreed. The two men came to a little bench overlooking the lake. Earle and Mickey sat, looking out at the water. Mickey sat for a moment or two, trying to frame what he wanted to say.

"Earle," Mickey said, "something is screwy with this divorce."

"I know," Earle said.

"This divorce has been bothering me, kind of nagging at me. I just can't help feeling the whole thing makes no sense."

Earle didn't seem surprised at all. "What makes you say that?"

"For one thing, Rand was so far out of character."

"Hmm."

"Rand is beautiful, loyal, intelligent and a fine mother," Mickey said. "She'd broken the affair off. Nevertheless Larry just insisted from the first moment that they get a divorce. Nothing about trying to reconcile, working it out. No counselors, or anything."

"I know," said Earle.

"Then Joey," Mickey went on. "Rand pleaded with Larry, begged him to think of Joey and the effect a divorce might have on him. No effect. How could a guy *not* want to be a father to such a wonderful boy?"

Earle shrugged. "I can't imagine."

Mickey went on. "I can certainly understand him being hurt by the affair, no doubt. It must have killed him. But I can't understand why he would jettison everything just to get back at her. Would a divorce make him feel better?"

Earle shook his head. "I agree this whole thing is puzzling. I don't know what to say about my former nephew-in-law," he said. "But when she married him, we thought Larry would be a good complement to her. He made a very good first impression. As time went on, though, he began treating Rand like she was rubbish. He seemed to want to get out of the marriage. We stopped receiving invitations to come to see them. Rand didn't confide in us. Still we couldn't help but be aware of the marriage problems."

"How could anyone treat her like that?"

"I wish I had some insights to offer, Mickey," he said. "I admit I was as puzzled as you. Julie and I asked ourselves many times: Why was his first reaction to the problem to seek a divorce? When you have a home, and a child, you try to preserve things if you can. This affair was an aberration, that's all."

"He wanted out of the marriage, that's obvious," Mickey said.

"Yeah, sure. But why did he choose to humiliate her, try to destroy her spirit?"

"Hmm," Mickey said. "That's been bothering me, too."

"On the other hand," Earle said, "I can see how much she loves you. I'm delighted."

"I've loved her since I met her at Madison." Earle glanced at him. Mickey nodded. "She told me so."

Earle snickered. They rose and strolled back in.

CHAPTER 26

John Morinec, the chief adjuster for the Alliance Insurance company and a vice president of the company, threw his pencil down on his desk. He glared at the file in front of him.

The claim he was reviewing seemed to be legitimate, at least at first glance. A sailboat named *Cool the Mark* had been docked at Long Beach near Los Angeles. The sailboat had hit a log off the coast off LaJolla, split and then sank beyond salvageability into the Pacific Ocean. One man had died in the wreck, drowned and mangled by sharks.

The man who had been lost had been named Mohammed Awad. He had rented the boat from its owner. The only way the police had been able to identify him was by a wallet containing several pieces of identification. The description on the license and the picture on the passport seemed consistent with the mangled body that washed ashore at Shell Beach near La Jolla, California.

John had thought at first that this claim was legitimate. The facts of the case seemed to match the parameters for accidental loss. *So why doesn't this make sense?* He asked himself.

He yanked up his telephone and called the adjuster, Darlene Meyer, who had sent him the claim.

"Yeah," she agreed. "The circumstances are questionable. In fact I lost sleep thinking about it."

"Darlene. Has this claim has been paid?"

"No. I just couldn't pay it without having you review it, John."

After he hung up, John stood and paced. Half a million bucks for a yacht the guy built himself. He'd taken plans to the bank and borrowed the money. He'd taken out the policy as soon as he'd finished it.

Then, a few months later, the boat sank.

What's wrong here?

He called Jane Leaf, his fellow adjuster and good friend, and asked her to come over to his office. John and Jane had been partners on a number of claim investigations. She was tough, smart, and determined. He trusted her instincts and valued her experience and insight. Carrying a cup of coffee, she strolled into his office and sat down.

"Let me bounce something off you?" he said. She nodded. He handed her the file and brought her up to date.

"What are you upset about?" she asked.

"I guess the big thing is: Why would this Awad sail alone from Los Angeles down to San Diego on a night when storm warnings were posted? I mean, if he *had* to get to San Diego, he could have driven down there in a lot less time. Why would he risk his life and property in a sailboat?"

"Hmmm," Jane nodded as she skimmed through the file. "Have you run Awad's name through immigration?"

John looked up. "Why?"

"French passport," she said. "Maybe you should contact Homeland Security."

"Now that's a thought," said John.

Jane sipped at her coffee. "What do you plan to do?"

"I want to talk to the boat's owner. But I can't find him."

"Can't find him?"

"Nope. The address is at one of those Mailbox places."

"Is he married?" Jane asked.

"No," John said. "Divorced. One child."

"I imagine he's paying alimony, maybe even child support. Why not talk to the ex-wife? I imagine she knows where he is."

He considered. "I guess I could," John said. "I've got an address for her, I think. At least she could tell me if her husband was in the habit of leasing out his sailboat."

"What's her name?"

"Miranda Connor."

CHAPTER 27

Julie and Earle staged a grand supper for Mickey and Rand at their house the night before the wedding: steak, potatoes, and fresh vegetables. Mickey cooked the steaks on a gas grill with Rand standing next to him on the back deck. The lake view and the woods made the place a paradise. Rand almost had to be sedated when she saw the dessert, a rum cheesecake with raspberry sauce.

The family went to bed early. Mickey took the living room pullout couch in front of the fireplace.

He lay on the bed, enjoying a final glass of the Chianti which had complemented the steaks. Mickey saw out the window that a storm had come up, with lightning and thunder. Rand came out of her bedroom and stood next to the bed.

"Hi," she whispered. Mickey could see in the firelight that she wore a long tee shirt.

"What's wrong?" Mickey asked.

"The storm looks serious. I'm a little scared of thunderstorms, you know."

"If I did know, I'd forgotten," Mickey said with a chuckle.

"Yep," she said. "So you get to be the adult. Everyone else is asleep."

He rose up on an elbow. "Nice jammies," Mickey teased.

"Bugs Bunny," she said, stroking the front of the shirt, where Bugs stood holding a carrot, smirking at him. Now Rand sat on the bed next to him.

"Are we getting married tomorrow?" she said.

"Unless we die in a nuclear attack," Mickey asserted.

She pulled the t-shirt over her head and tossed it aside. "I'm a big believer in dress rehearsals," she smiled. "Move over."

* * * * *

State Police Lieutenant Rusty Ivers stood over the body of a disreputable looking man. The body had stopped smoking, though his nails and long greasy hair had turned color. Rusty saw that the man was shirtless, wearing torn jeans and construction boots that had seen far better days. It was a rainy turbulent night, too dark to see a lot of detail.

"Electrocution?" he said to the medical examiner.

"Looks like the best bet, for obvious reasons. I'll get him on the table and let you know."

The rain fell around Rusty as he knelt next to the body. "I'm guessing the vic was drunk," said the ME. "A power line went down in the electrical storm. For some reason, he came out here and grabbed it."

"Strange. Who doesn't know that's fatal?" mused Rusty.

"That's why I'm saying he was drunk," said the ME. "Nobody would do something that stupid unless he was impaired."

Rusty nodded. "I don't suppose there's much to see out here," he said, glancing around the yard.

"Yeah. The rain will wash anything away, if there's anything to see in the first place."

"Okay," said Rusty. "Your guys can haul him away."

He stood and looked around the yard. It was a cold rain, and he shivered inside his slicker. He thought about his new wife Paula, at home, warm and comfortable in their snug bed. He sighed.

"Lieutenant Ivers?" said a voice at his right hand. Rusty turned to the voice and saw a tall man with thinning gray hair.

"Yes?" he said.

The man put out his hand and Rusty shook with him. "My name is John Morinec," he said. John held out a business card. It identified him as a vice-president of a large insurance company. "I'd appreciate it if I could talk to you. Do you need to stay out here?"

"No, I'm free," said Rusty. "There's not too much to see. My guys will work the area. Why?"

"Your wife called me," John said. Rusty's eyebrows shot up.

"You know my wife?" he smiled.

"Yes, we went to high school together," said John. "I interviewed her about a couple of strange deaths to people we went to high school with."

"Yes?" said Rusty.

"To be specific, Albert Thomas, and Paula's first husband Frank Capriatti."

"Ah, yes. Accidental deaths," said Rusty, his expression grim.

"Lieutenant--" John began.

"Please, John. You're a good friend of my wife. Call me Rusty," said Ivers with a grin. "Did you know this guy, too?"

"Oh yes. Bill Kidd, as nasty and worthless a piece of human filth as I've had the misfortune to know," said John. "Paula called me because she knew him also. I'm surprised he didn't screw up his own death."

"Come on," said Rusty. "I'm done here. Let's go to my house."

* * * * *

Rand lay next to Mickey in the silent house, embracing him.

"Your uncle seems pleased that we're getting married," Mickey whispered.

"Yeah," she said. "He and Aunt Julie are crazy about you. I know he'd like more children in the family."

"Are we going to have kids?" Mickey asked, and then felt idiotic. That aspect of marriage, for some reason, had never occurred to him.

"Why wouldn't we?"

He hedged. "Can we talk this over another time when I'm not so sleepy?" Mickey hedged.

"Sure. Just so we do."

Mickey had closed his eyes and just about dozed off when Rand said, "Oh, just one quick thing. My sister Cinnamon called while you were out walking with Uncle Tom. They're coming for the wedding tomorrow. After lunch she's going to take Joey to the Milwaukee Zoo."

"I haven't met this sister, have I?"

"No," she said. "She was in Florida when you came at Thanksgiving that year we were at Madison. She's a bit of a character."

"I see."

"She's bringing her boyfriend. I haven't met him. Don't worry; I'll get up early so no one catches us here."

She snuggled into him and they fell asleep together a few moments later. Mickey noted in a dim way that she got up sometime in the night, put on her Bugs Bunny t-shirt and went back to her bed.

* * * * *

John followed Rusty to his house, about fifteen minutes away. Paula greeted them and offered some coffee. "No, thanks," said John. "I'm so cold and wet I just want to warm up a bit."

"Perhaps a little Dewar's?" grinned Rusty.

"That'd sure help," said John, chuckling.

They sat in the living room and sipped at the scotch.

"What do you remember about this guy Kidd?" Rusty asked.

"Kidd was a loudmouthed, obnoxious little jerk," said John. "He went to our school but wasn't on the sports teams with us."

"Looked like a little runt," said Rusty.

"Yeah, he was small," agreed John. "He curried the favor of much bigger guys so that they'd protect him with his big mouth. Once I saw him sitting with a couple of other bozos in the bleachers in the main gym. He was taunting some black kids with racist cracks that he knew they could hear. He mocked them, made vicious remarks that the black kids, to their credit, ignored."

"He was counting on the bigger guys to protect him, huh?" said Rusty. Paula came in from the kitchen with some pound cake. The men helped themselves.

"I had left the group as soon as he had started," added John. "Some others stayed, encouraging him with their laughter. I'm ashamed now that I didn't apologize at the time to the black kids for his oafish behavior."

"Well, that's consistent with the other guys," said Rusty.

"Very much social outcasts."

"Uh, huh. Did Paula tell you about this Kidd guy?"

"Did you know him well?" Rusty said, turning to his wife.

She thought a moment, and shook her head. "No, but I remember a couple of incidents. One time—I think we were juniors-- a little freshman guy bumped into me while I was walking with Frankie and Kidd, just outside the field house."

"Were you hurt?" John asked.

She shook her head. "I wasn't hurt or bothered at all. The boy came around a corner and brushed against me, a simple accident. The boy asked if he'd hurt me, and begged my pardon. I told him don't be silly, I'm fine. Frankie grabbed him and pushed him to Kidd. Kidd looked around for any teachers or adults. He didn't see any. Frankie shoved his face right into the little guy's face. He asked him what he thought he was doing. The little guy was so scared he couldn't answer. It had just been an accident, I know. Frankie told him they needed to teach him some manners. He began slapping the kid while Kidd held his arms behind him. The boy cried and wet himself."

"Oh jeez," said Rusty, shaking his head.

"I hadn't heard this story," said John.

"I know," said Paula. "They howled with laughter at the kid. I screamed at them to let him go. Frankie had just told me to shut up—it wasn't that polite--when Mr. Jacobeit came out of the field house. You remember him, John."

John nodded. "Fred Jacobeit was one of the football coaches," he told Rusty. "One hell of a man. I got to know him man-to-man after college."

"He saw what was happening," said Paula. "He grabbed both Frankie and Kidd and made them let the freshman guy go.

He marched them to the dean's office. They laughed all the way. I think they got suspended for a few days. I sat with the little guy—what was his name?—until Mr. Jacobeit came back. He took the boy home in his car, I remember, so he could change clothes."

John nodded. "I would have expected that sort of kindness from Fred Jacobeit."

Paula thought for a moment, and said, "Kidd did something horrible to the boy, I think, later on. You know, in retaliation for him getting suspended."

"Would that be when he helped Albert kill the puppy?" John asked.

"What?" said Rusty, raising his eyebrows.

"Yes," said Paula. "What a dreadful thing to do. It appalls me to think of it even now."

"You agree that these aren't accidents, John?" asked Rusty.

John sipped at the scotch. "No," he said. "They're murders."

CHAPTER 28

Mickey woke up with a start and found someone standing next to the bed. The room was flooded with daylight. He focused on a face he thought at first was Rand's.

That idea faded away in a hurry when the person said, "Hey, Dude," since Rand didn't call him "Dude." Nor did she have pink spiked hair. Nor did she wear pink jeans and studded pink biking leathers adorned with chains, bells, whistles and other hardware, nor neon pink lipstick with matching nails.

Rand strolled in from the bedroom wearing her modest long t-shirt. She blinked. "Hi, Cinnamon," she said. Rand, it appeared, didn't remember that Mickey was naked. She sat down next to him and kissed him good morning. She said, "Cinnamon, what are you doing here now? Aren't you supposed to come later?"

"Like Rand?" said Cinnamon with no little asperity, "This is like later? It's like almost 8:30? Like where's the little dude?"

Rand consulted her watch. "Oh yuck," she said. "I'm on Pacific Coast Time. I'm thinking this is 6:30."

"Hello, Rand?" said Cinnamon. The word 'hello' seemed to have at least five syllables. She shook her head. "Is this like the lucky dude?" she asked, indicating Mickey.

"Sorry. You haven't met Logan. Mickey, meet my sister, Cinnamon."

He put out a weak hand. Cinnamon shook it and looked with disapproval at his unkempt hair. Mickey noticed now that he needed to use the washroom.

Cinnamon said, "This is like my boyfriend, Durango?"

"How you doin', man?" said a voice from behind her. "My real name's Eugene."

Durango seemed to be about seven and a half feet tall and only a little less wide. A dense zareba of black hair covered his face and arms. It matched his leather jacket, which covered an ill-fitting tee shirt, which in turn left a hairy navel exposed above a belt buckle, which read "Harley-Davidson" below a picture of an eagle. Mickey guessed that his facial expression was a smile.

"How do you do, Eugene?" Mickey said. Mickey offered his hand, which vanished into an enormous fur-covered paw.

"Call me Durango. Everybody does." He pulled up a chair and sat down next to the sofa bed. Cinnamon sat on his lap. Though she was as tall as Rand, she looked about the size of a two-year-old on Santa's lap.

"So you're from Colorado?" Mickey said, trying to make conversation, lying naked under a sheet, desperate to use the bathroom.

"No," said Cinnamon. "Durango like owns one of those like SUV's? and he like liked the name? so, like, well, he, like, changed his? We drove over in it? Like today?"

"Hey," said Durango. "I heard you two guys both have your doctors' degrees."

Rand and Mickey exchanged glances. They nodded.

"That is so cool," he said, shaking his shaggy head. "I'm, like, ABD on mine now," he resumed. "That means 'All But

Dissertation', you know." They knew. "About another six months, I think, and I'll be able to defend."

Mickey and Rand stared at him, thunderstruck. Rand recovered her wits before Mickey did. "Oh, that's great, Durango. What field?"

"Chemical engineering," he said.

Cinnamon beamed at him.

"Yeah," she snorted with contempt. "He'd be finished now? but he's, like, got a real prick? for like an advisor? He has to like rewrite his introduction? and his conclusion? The professors think his research? is brilliant, though."

Durango, resembling a horsehair mattress turned inside out, mumbled something like "Aw shucks" with fetching diffidence.

"You know," Mickey said, "I'm enjoying meeting you, but you see, I don't have any…"

Before Mickey could finish explaining his plight, Julie, Rand's smiling aunt, came in with a tray of coffee, croissants and bagels, a knitting bag slung over one arm. "Oh good, you woke the sleepyhead up." She beamed at Mickey.

Earle, Rand's uncle, entered right behind her carrying a tray adorned with cups and saucers, plates, and a pitcher of orange juice. Rand, Cinnamon, Julie, and Earle exchanged hugs and good mornings, smiling at him.

"I thought we'd have a quick bite in here this morning," Julie said. "Don't get up, Mickey. Just relax."

"Er," Mickey began, but then Casey, Cheyenne and Derek came in the French doors. Rand hugged her brother and sister and Derek, all of them laughing and excited. After enthusiastic welcomes, they drew up chairs around the sofa bed.

"Well, congratulations, you two." Casey looked with pride

at his sister Rand, then at Mickey. "You've got to be excited."

Rand agreed that she was indeed excited and beamed at Mickey, who wasn't, at least at that moment. He tried again. "Er--"

"Let me put on some clothes," said Rand. "I'll be right back." She sashayed off.

Joey came in with Bogey. Mickey saw that Joey had taken the dog out on her leash for her morning ablutions. She greeted everyone, wiggling and wagging her tail as she went from person to person.

"A trained killer, I see," said Casey, petting Bogey, who lay on the ground in front of him and held her feet in the air so Casey could pet her tummy.

"Uh-huh," Mickey muttered. "Look, I need--"

This time the dog interrupted. Bogey heard his voice and turned to him. The wagging grew more intense. She hopped onto the sofa bed, licked his face, and snuggled right in. She scratched at the blanket, bouncing the bed and pulling at the sheet. She turned in a circle three times, and then she plopped down, getting comfortable. Everyone laughed.

Except Mickey, who stifled a bellow of pain. Bogey had gotten to go out on the leash. Thinking about that made Mickey feel even more uncomfortable.

Joey removed his shoes and jumped on the side of the sofa bed, bouncing the bed. Rand came back, sweat suit on, hair and teeth brushed, smiling. The family set the trays at the foot of the bed and helped themselves, chatting, ignoring the fact that a naked man lay in the fold-out couch, covers pulled up to his neck.

"Careful, Rand," said her aunt, handing her a huge steaming

mug of coffee. It was poised right above his groin. "Here, take this quick, it's real hot. Take a sip; I got it way too full." Rand smiled at her aunt and took the coffee. She sipped it, the steaming cup one foot above his groin. She smiled at him. Mickey lay as still as possible, careful not to distract her.

Earle laughed about a joke he'd heard a couple of nights ago. It had been the showstopper at the local VFW.

"So a traveling salesman is driving through the Kentucky Horse country, see?" he began. "And his car breaks down. He looks under the hood and a voice behind him says, 'I think it's the carburetor.' So the salesman looks around but sees no one. He decides it must have been the car radio. He looks under the hood. The voice again says 'I'm telling you, look at the carburetor.'

"Wait a second," Mickey said, but Earle didn't hear.

"Well, this time when he looks up, he sees a sad looking horse standing there," Earle continued, to a few appreciative chuckles. "Sure enough the horse looks right at him. It says 'I'm telling you, it's the carburetor!' The salesman goes over and says to the horse, 'Can you talk?' The horse says, 'Yes, of course', and gives him expert directions for fixing the car. Sure enough the car starts right up. The salesman goes back over to the horse and thanks him. The horse nods but says 'Yeah, it isn't easy being ignored. Everybody loved me and wanted to be around me when I won the Kentucky Derby but now I just stand here all day long by myself.'"

"Er--" Mickey said, but no one looked at him. Mickey had begun to worry that the size of his bladder might cause that organ to interfere with his heartbeat.

"So," Earle went on to a rapt audience, "the salesman runs to the farm house and enters into negotiations for the horse. The farmer agrees to sell him for ten bucks. The salesman is amazed at his good fortune. He says to the farmer, 'You just sold a remarkable horse.' 'Uh-huh,' says the farmer. 'Well, just don't believe all that baloney about the Kentucky Derby.'"

The reaction to the joke was volcanic. Laughter. Glasses removed. Eyes wiped. Individual lines repeated. Guffaws. Coughing fits. Backs slapped. Even Bogey was smiling. The fact that Mickey lay in their midst naked under a sheet didn't seem to change the tenor.

Mickey, trying not to writhe in discomfort, didn't think the joke was all that damned funny. He remembered a line from Bertie Wooster. "Hoy!" Mickey yelled, quieting the cacophony.

They looked at him. "Yes, Mickey?" said Julie.

"Look," Mickey said, "the joy of this moment is diminished for me by the fact that I don't have any clothes on. Not only that, I have to use the washroom. And brush my teeth and hair. And I am suffering from near mortal embarrassment. If you all don't get out of this room for a few moments, I fear that I will need to take desperate measures that may end the party at once."

Making it clear that they were offended, they looked from one to another. They nodded and trooped from the room, giving him not a few suspicious and even resentful glances. Mickey wrapped a sheet around himself, toga style, and went down the hall to the washroom, carrying his clothes with what he hoped achieved impressive dignity.

Mickey felt them, rather than saw them, re-enter the living room as he entered the bathroom. Then Mickey heard the first chuckles. They started to shriek with laughter. *So much for dignity*, Mickey thought. *On the other hand, maybe they're still laughing at the joke. Sure, that has to be it.*

He got under the shower and tried to drown out the laughter. Mickey found himself wondering if anyone had ever drowned himself in the shower.

CHAPTER 29

L ater that morning, as Rand and the others started to get ready for the wedding, Mickey took Joey for a walk in the woods. They talked about baseball, then school, then what they were having for dinner, and how they were going to live together, Christmas, baseball, football, swimming, fishing and more topics than Mickey could remember.

When they returned to Earle and Julie's house, a lovely young woman opened the door. Mickey hadn't met her, but figured this had to be one of Rand's sisters or perhaps a cousin. Her hair was blond, cut short and elegant, her makeup was soft and attractive, and her nails were perfect red. She had on a blue business suit with a short, straight skirt, a formal blouse and high-heeled shoes.

"Hi, Aunt Cinnamon," Joey said.

Mickey looked at him, then back at her, staring like an idiot.

Cinnamon smiled and hugged them both. "It's about time you two got back," she said with a gentle voice. She walked into the house as Rand came out.

"Mickey, we need to go over some things with Cinnamon before the wedding, okay?

"Cinnamon?"

"Sure. She's my lawyer. Why do you look so surprised?"

* * * * *

The wedding started at noon. Cheyenne and Cinnamon stood next to their sister. Joey was the best man. He took great pride in handing Mickey the sapphire ring.

They had lunch in the house by way of an informal reception. Cinnamon and Durango put Joey in the huge SUV. Rand kissed him good-bye and told him they'd see him in a week. Cinnamon and Durango left for the Milwaukee Zoo with Joey, who was too excited to be upset.

Late that afternoon, Rand and Mickey left and drove to the northwest side of Chicago. They registered for the night in a beautiful suite at the Hyatt near O'Hare Airport.

They had a light sandwich dinner in the hotel restaurant. Mickey paid the dinner tab while Rand went to the room. Mickey walked in to discover that Rand had lit a few candles and turned out the other lights. She stood in the center of the room, wearing a terry cloth robe that the hotel supplied to the suite.

"I have a present for you," she said.

"You can't give me anything better than what you gave me this afternoon," Mickey assured her.

She loosened the tie and shrugged the robe off, revealing a tiny blue bikini.

"I found this a few days ago to wear in Hawaii," she said. "I decided, though, that it's something I'm only going to wear for you."

"Okay, so maybe I was wrong about the gift," Mickey said when he could manage it.

* * * * *

Rand Connor—*no, Rand Logan now*, she thought--sat on the bed in the hotel suite, too excited to fall asleep. She smiled as she looked down at her new husband, remembering the last hour or so in intimate and wonderful detail.

Sex with Larry had almost always made her feel as if she were nothing more than a receptacle. Climaxes came for her only with intense concentration and effort on her part, not because Larry had exerted any particular effort to please her. During the last several years of their marriage, she hadn't experienced them at all. She had sensed Larry's growing distance, something that sort of felt like jealousy becoming more and more pronounced as their unhappy marriage lurched along.

Mickey, from the first time they'd made love a few weeks before, always tried so hard to make her happy. He took care, making sure she was comfortable and enjoying herself, that she climaxed just before he did. He used the intimacy to deepen and to strengthen their love for one another

She had known the instant she saw Mickey on the golf course that he had never forgotten her, just like she hadn't forgotten him. For years she'd shoved his memory into a precious little knothole somewhere in her brain. Once in a while, though, this tall, tousle-haired redhead had shown up in her mind. Sometimes, he'd shown up in dreams.

After Larry had dumped her, Rand had been celibate by choice, despite some opportunities. She grimaced as she thought about some of the fantasies she'd entertained. But she hadn't pursued any of them.

She smiled as she thought of Mickey looking at her legs in

the golf cart that first afternoon. She of course had meant for him to do so, had even pulled the skirt a few inches higher.

She thought the story of the affair would appall him. Still, she couldn't let him fall back in love with her without knowing what she'd done.

All that was over now. She knew that no one would ever love her like Mickey did.

He woke from the little doze. He stretched a little and turned to see her watching him in the dim candlelight. "Hey," said Mickey with a grin. He held out his arms.

She pulled back the blanket and slid in next to him. He wrapped his arms around her. She put a finger to his mouth to make him pause. "Could you please take me to Hawaii?" she said.

"Now?"

"Yes, please."

"Okay. Look in my eyes."

CHAPTER 30

San Antonio, Texas
The Santa Lucia Medical Center
The next morning

John Morinec, the vice-president of claims for the Alliance Insurance company, chatted with Mrs. Thomas as she lay in her hospital bed, an oxygen tube under her nose. John wanted to talk about her son who had been crushed by a crane in a steel mill, but saw that the woman wanted to chat a little.

He learned that her husband had died some time ago. She'd come to Texas to visit relatives and fell in love with the area. With few ties to her old neighborhood, she wound up staying. She told him she loved the climate of South Texas, liked the people, the food, the medical care.

She didn't get too many visitors, but he saw that she was a peaceful person and her life had gone along okay. She liked to read, and write letters, and pray for others.

John liked her and admired her attitude. He hated to rush her into discussing the horrid events surrounding her son's death. He was also stunned at the contrast between this sweet gentle woman and the oafish thug he remembered from high school.

After a few moments, John drew the conversation around to Albert and his death. He told her he wanted to understand the circumstances if she could stand to tell the story.

Mrs. Thomas frowned, and her brow creased. She fidgeted with the satin hem of her cover for a few moments.

"I can't say anything bad about him now," she said. "He provided for me."

"How did he provide for you?" John asked.

"It became pretty clear in the months just before Albert died that I was going to be confined to a hospital soon and I would not be coming out. Of course long-term care is very expensive. My sister and I thought I could maybe go into a county home. I wasn't looking forward to that, I can tell you.

"After Albert died, I discovered that he'd taken out a big insurance policy with M and M Life." She told John the amount she'd received. He was thunderstruck. "It named me as the beneficiary. He also had some accident and life insurance through the company plan at work. Unless I live a long time, I have enough to take care of myself because of that."

That sort of thoughtfulness sounded nothing like the thug John had known in high school. John had imagined that Albert spending his life drinking, fighting, whoring and maybe being an abusive lout of a husband to some poor girl.

M and M Life has to be a small company I've never heard of, he thought. "Albert never married?" John asked.

She shook her head and he saw the faint look of regret. "My three other kids have turned out very well: good effort in school, nice families, solid jobs and so forth. But Albert . . ." She shook her head and her voice trailed off. Then she said, with a note of resolution in her voice, "He was a bully, always fighting, always causing trouble, and getting poor grades. I was thrilled when he managed to graduate from high school. I hoped he'd meet a nice girl."

She clutched at a tissue and wiped her eyes. "Then I learned that he'd been killed on the crane catwalk at work." Her voice grew soft and a tear leaked down her cheek. John murmured sympathy.

"He'd worked at the steel mill for several years and hadn't progressed in the company at all," Mrs. Thomas said. "When Albert was about twenty-five, he roughed up his boss."

"Roughed up?"

She nodded. She shook her head and frowned, gazing at the blanket. John saw that she was ashamed of the incident. "He pushed him against a wall." She sighed. "After work one hot summer day, he went to his locker to change clothes and shower but the millwrights had cut off the water. A pipe had broken somewhere and they hadn't been able to fix it by the end of the shift. So he went to the office and complained about the water."

Her cheeks flushed with embarrassment. "The superintendent told him what had happened with the pipe breaking. He offered Albert the shower in the mill next door. Albert began to bellow about his rights. At last the superintendent of the mill told him he had to leave." She motioned and John held a Styrofoam cup for her while she sipped a little water through a straw.

"He hollered at the superintendent. Yes, his boss. After a few moments the superintendent gave him five days off without pay. They went back and forth. Albert pushed him up against the wall. Three men heard the commotion. They ran into the office and pulled Albert off the superintendent."

"Did they call the police?" said John, thinking of how huge

Albert was and how frightened the superintendent must have been.

"No, they handled it in the mill. Albert lost ten days without pay. The union interceded so he could keep his job. It turned out the superintendent had had a couple of aggressive confrontations with other workers and had developed something of a nasty reputation also. I don't think Albert felt anything like regret about the incident except that he lost some pay."

She paused, and looked out the window. Then, with an effort not to cry: "Then about a year and a half later, his foreman found Albert crushed in a crane loft."

John murmured sympathy.

"He had both accident and life insurance with me as the beneficiary," Mrs. Thomas went on. Tears filled her eyes. A mother's love, John thought.

"Let me ask you something." She looked up and wiped at her eyes. "Wasn't he terrified of heights?" John asked.

She stared at him. "Yes. He couldn't even sit in the upper deck at baseball games. He would go white-knuckled if he had to drive over a bridge."

John took Mrs. Thomas's hand and said his good-byes. Then he hugged her. In the rental car, on the way to the airport, he couldn't stop thinking. *Why would someone who is terrified of heights go up to the crane loft to drink?*

CHAPTER 31

That morning, Rand and Mickey flew to Maui. The next day, they had pineapple, mango and other fruit for breakfast on the balcony of their hotel room. Mickey took Rand to Honolua Bay. She had never snorkeled but she was a fine swimmer and picked it up without difficulty.

They swam out to the coral reef and snorkeled together until about noon, when they went back to the towels on the beach.

Mickey held Rand's hand while she dozed in the sun.

She turned over and stretched. "Hi Hubby," she said.

"Hey," he responded.

She sat up on the blanket. She started to speak, then shut up. She said, "Can I ask you something?"

"Sure," he said. "Anything."

"How are we paying for this?"

"For what?"

"For Hawaii, for the clothes you bought me, the dinners. . ."

"Oh. There was something I didn't tell you."

"What? You're a mafia don?"

He laughed with her. "No. As a matter of fact I turn out to be rich."

She didn't speak for a few moments. "What?"

"I haven't always been of course. When I came to LA, I was comfortable but not rich. Now I'm rich." Mickey explained about his grandfather's legacy.

"So how much do you have?"

"Wait. The pronoun is 'we'." He gave her a rough estimate. "All of it's invested pretty well. I've got a lot of the land left too."

Her jaw was slack. "Why didn't you tell me?"

"Because I didn't want you to worry at some point that you'd married me for my money. I thought it was for the best."

She began to tear up. "So I'm not broke?"

"Nope. I'm planning on you and me devoting the rest of our lives to spending the money. You're the person I want to do it with."

A week later, Joey arrived at the airport. They spent a week with him on the beach, then they flew to Palm Springs, California, to a condo that Rand and her siblings had inherited from their grandparents.

* * * * *

Two days later, they'd just returned from a round of golf and were sitting on the porch with some iced tea when the doorbell rang. Mickey went to answer it.

He opened the door. John Morinec stood there. Both men stared at one another in surprise. "Mickey?" John said after a few moments.

"Johnny?" Mickey said. The two men shook hands, laughing and then hugged with pleasure of the reunion of two old friends.

"You're married to Miranda Connor?"

"Yes he is," said Rand, who had come up behind him. "Except it's Miranda Logan now."

"Honey, this is John Morinec," Mickey said. "He sat next to

me in Sophomore English when we were in high school. We played football together."

"Welcome, John," said Rand. "Please call me Rand."

"How do you do, Rand?" said John. "It's more like Mickey and I were best friends in high school. I'm sorry I look so surprised. I just wasn't prepared to see him."

"Please, come on in," said Rand.

John sat on the living room couch and Rand handed him some iced tea.

They chatted like old friends for some time. At last Mickey asked, "John, I haven't seen you for years. Why did you come to see me?"

"Like I say, you being here is a surprise. I came to see you, Rand."

"Me?" said Rand, a bit startled.

"Yeah. You were married to Larry, right?"

"For several years," she nodded.

"I want to know about his sailboat," John said.

The room became as silent as a mausoleum. Mickey had never seen Rand so taken aback.

"His sailboat?" she managed. "What sailboat is that?"

"The one named *Cool the Mark*. He docked it at Long Beach. . ." Johnny stopped, seeing how bewildered she was.

"I don't know about any sailboat," she said. "We've been separated for close to two years. Perhaps he bought it since then but. . ."

"No," John interrupted. "He built this thing three years ago. We insured it for about 13 months until it was lost at sea."

Again Rand couldn't respond.

"Honey," Mickey said. "What's wrong?"

"Larry never had a sailboat," said Rand. "In fact he's afraid of water. I don't think he can even swim. When we went to Cabo San Lucas for our honeymoon, he wouldn't even consider snorkeling with me."

John rubbed the tip of his nose, lost in thought for some time. He said, "Do you know where he is now?"

"No," said Rand. "I wouldn't even know how to contact him. He wanted no part of our son or me. I don't get child support or alimony from him."

Now it was John's turn to be surprised. "No child support? How did he. . ."

"Long story," Mickey said.

John realized that he'd overstepped the bounds of the conversation. "Oh. Okay. Anyhow I can't find him. I went to your condo in Santa Barbara, of course. I. . ." Again he broke off as he saw Rand staring at him.

"What condo in Santa Barbara?" she asked.

He gave her the address.

"What's wrong, Blondie?" Mickey asked.

"We never owned a home of any kind in Santa Barbara," she affirmed.

"What?" said John, with a double-take.

"No. I don't have any idea what you're talking about."

"But he's owned this place for several years," John said.

"John, you must have the wrong guy," Mickey said.

"Your maiden name *was* Miranda Fixx, right?" asked Johnny.

"Yes," said Rand.

"Born in Arlington Heights, Illinois? Brother named Casey?"

"Yes," said Rand.

"Married to Larry Connor from Harlan, Illinois? Graduated from--"

"Hold it," Mickey said. "Is this the Larry Connor you and I went to high school with?"

Johnny nodded. "Do you remember him?"

"Sort of. He was an artist and I was a jock."

"Now," said John, "he's pretty well known to the police in southern California too."

Rand stared at Mickey's friend open-mouthed. "The police?"

"A few years ago, he was arrested in L. A."

Rand couldn't frame the question. "What for?" Mickey asked.

"Forgery. They were never able to pin anything on him. He's been questioned and released by the LA cops several times. Each time they cut him loose for lack of evidence."

"Forgery?" said Mickey.

"Yeah, it's no surprise to me, anyhow," said John. "In high school, he was an expert in copying teachers' names onto hall passes. Ran a tidy business selling tardy slips."

Rand stood and walked to the picture window. Mickey rose and went to her. "Are you okay?" he asked.

"Mickey, what is this?" she asked.

John came over. "Please forgive me. I didn't mean to upset you--" she waved aside the apology, white as a sheet. Mickey took her arm and led her back to the couch.

Mickey handed her a glass of tea, and she drank, composing herself. John asked permission to continue, concerned. Rand nodded. "I think he's trying to defraud my company," said John. "The Alliance Insurance Company."

"Huh?"

"I work in a division of the claims department," he said. "We investigate suspicious claims. We haven't paid this one yet. I smell fraud. I just can't figure out how he did it."

"How can we help?" Mickey asked.

"I want you to help me check out the story," John said.

"Me?" Mickey said, surprised.

"Rand too, if you will," he said, turning to her.

Rand and Mickey shrugged. Mickey said, "I guess so. But John, isn't this a lot of trouble for a sailboat? What's it worth, a couple grand?"

"We're talking about half a million bucks," John said. Rand stood. Her jaw dropped, her eyes grew wide. John nodded. "And we want to toss the bastard in jail. Excuse my language, Rand."

She waved off the apology, her mouth open. "What do you mean, half a million?"

"That's what the boat was insured for."

"Half a million?" said Rand, stammering a little.

"Yeah. As his ex-wife, you might be able to kick a few doors open for me, huh?"

Rand agreed to help. John spent the night in the guest bedroom.

In the morning they dropped John's rental car off at the Palm Springs airport before driving to Los Angeles.

They went to Evangeline Trust, the bank that had held the note on Larry's boat. Rand produced identification and her marriage license. The banker, a Mr. Winfield, turned to his computer. "The accounts are intact," he said. "They hold a lot of money."

The banker asked for her signature. Although the name was

the same, her signature didn't match the writing on the record card. But Larry's signature was correct. No transactions had occurred for some time.

"Do you get it, Mickey?" she asked, when they were on the street. Mickey could see the anger in her eyes.

"He set up a separate account with some other woman," Mickey said. "He must have planned to divorce you and hitch up with the other woman."

CHAPTER 32

The marina in Long Beach was full of elegant sailboats with tall masts, generous cabins and colorful pennants.

They stopped at the leasing office and asked for details about *Cool the Mark*. The men in the office stared at them. No one knew anything about the boat.

Mickey mentioned the name of Larry Connor. One of the guys turned to his computer, examined the database, and said, "A guy named Connor rented a space here for a season three years ago."

They got the slip number and walked out on the pier to the slip. They talked with the people who were out on their boats. Several thought they remembered the slip in question had been vacant for the season maybe two or three years ago. A few remembered the shipwreck off LaJolla, but none remembered much detail.

He couldn't doubt their sincerity. The people were genuine in their bewilderment at their questions.

They walked back to their car. "Okay," Mickey said. "Now what?"

"I want to see this condo in Santa Barbara," said Rand. That morning Mickey had printed out a map on the computer to Larry's Santa Barbara home. They headed over to the 710 freeway, then took the 405 north to I-10 and followed it into Santa Barbara.

The condo, located in an exclusive development, boasted a stunning view of the ocean. They went to the condo office. Rand identified herself and asked to be let into Larry's condo. A manager agreed to walk with them over to the unit.

Rand's mouth hung slack when they walked in and she saw the gracious interior: high cathedral ceilings, oak hardwood floors, granite countertops, a marble fireplace and other luxury items.

The manager told them that the condo association had been taking care of the unit, at least the outside, because the mortgage and association fees had been kept current. The air was somewhat stale inside the condo, indicating that it hadn't been used for quite a while. The closets were well stocked with men's and women's clothes. The drawers brimmed full of underclothing and shirts. The bathrooms had ample towels and toiletries.

Rand's mouth hung slack, her eyes dull. She looked from side to side, her hand to her mouth, more disorientated than angry. Parked in the garage they found a thirty thousand-dollar Chrysler, about four years old, covered with dust. Rand asked, "Where did *this* come from?"

They left and headed to a coffee shop in a local mall.

"Here's what I think happened," said John. "Larry bought some plans for a sailboat. He took the plans to the bank where he and his business had several big accounts, Evangeline Savings and Loan. They loaned him the money to build the thing. They wanted to accommodate a good customer." Rand stared at her coffee cup.

"He bought lumber and supplies and then sent copies of the receipts to the bank. Then he returned the materials. He took a picture of another sailboat and sent it to the bank." Rand nodded and sipped at the coffee.

"Then he contacted our agent and bought a replacement insurance policy. He had a lot of policies with them, including life and a plan for the employees. The agent didn't hesitate to sell it to him. The commission was terrific."

"He told the Coast Guard he'd rented the boat to this Awad guy and it sank. Then he tried to collect the insurance money. Once he got it, he could pay off Evangeline and still find himself $500,000 ahead."

Rand sighed. "That fits with what we discovered, all right."

"Rand," John said. "I'm sorry I put you through this today. But you helped save my company $500,000. I'm grateful." She was still too stunned and upset to do much aside from nod.

Rand and Mickey dropped Johnny off at LAX, where he would hop a plane back to Chicago. They promised to stay in touch.

They drove in silence back toward the Coachella Valley. Rand didn't speak for a while. She said at last, "Do you get it, Mickey?"

"Yeah. I think Larry scammed you, too. He knew you'd never go along with insurance fraud, to say nothing of murder. I'm guessing he encouraged Mitch to seduce you so he could accuse you of adultery. He scored a terrific divorce settlement and freedom to spend the money he swindled."

"You may be right," she said.

"Do you have any idea where he might have gone?"

Rand shook her head and lapsed into silence.

They flew back to their house in the Chicago area a few days later. Mickey called John. "Hey, Bud. We're home."

"Yeah. I've been working on this thing on this end," said John. "We've assigned some of our company investigators to start looking for Larry. Nobody's had much luck. He seems to have vanished."

* * * * *

A few days later, Casey called them. "Hi, Sis," he said. "Tell Mickey to pick up the extension."

"I'm here, Casey," said Mickey. "Everything okay?"

"What's up, bro?" Rand said.

"Well, I've had quite an adventure while you were gone. I'll tell you about it. I've also managed to be married."

"What!" said Rand. Mickey, on the extension, laughed and offered congratulations.

"Look," said Casey. "I'm taking the family on a cruise to the Caribbean. I want you to come along."

Mickey was committed to direct a commercial, so they couldn't make the sailing date. They arranged to meet the ship in St. Maarten, Dutch West Indies. They couldn't wait to meet Casey's new wife, a widow named Anna, and her eighteen-year-old daughter McKenna.

Part III

CHAPTER 33
White Island
Summer

The beautiful cruise ship *Galaxy* had just left her berth in Charleston, South Carolina. Mohammed Awad stood with two other men on the top deck watching a young man on the deck below them. He stood alone near a group of young people.

"When can we move?" said the man on Awad's left.

"Not now," Awad said. "Wait until we arrive at St. Thomas. The yacht will rendezvous with us there."

"You think he knows where the treasure is?" said the other man.

Awad nodded. "I am certain," he affirmed.

"He's watching that girl," said the third man. He pointed out a young woman with copper colored hair. The other men grinned.

McKenna DiBiasi sipped at her iced tea on the top deck of the cruise ship, watching the harbor slip by as the huge boat made its way out to open sea. The sea breeze added to the exhilaration she was feeling. Seagulls wheeled around the ship, screaming for scraps of food. She laughed at the pelicans sitting on top of pilings.

"What's our first stop?" she asked her aunt, Cheyenne

Robbins, who stood next to her sipping a drink with an umbrella in it. Eighteen-year-old McKenna had not been aware this aunt's existence until a few weeks before. They had become fast friends, as close as sisters.

"St. Maarten, Dutch West Indies," said Cheyenne. "In two days."

"I think the days at sea are the most fun," said Cheyenne's husband Derek.

"Listen to him. The big cruise expert," grinned Cheyenne. The two young women giggled.

"I'll have you know that I grew up next to the sea," said Derek, looking amused. "The men in my family have always been seafarers."

"Right. The sea. Wolf Lake, Calumet City, Illinois," said Cheyenne. Derek grabbed her and the two wrestled, giggling and teasing.

Cinnamon, another aunt of McKenna's, came up behind her and hugged the girl's shoulders. "So when we get to Tortolla, how about going with us to snorkel over at Norman Island?"

"I've never snorkeled before," said McKenna. "I imagine I can learn though."

"Sure," said Cinnamon.

"Where's Durango?" McKenna asked Cinnamon.

"I left him and Mini and Rush waiting for the casino to open," said Cinnamon. "He's all excited to play blackjack."

McKenna laughed. Derek and Cheyenne trooped off to their cabin, claiming they needed to change for dinner. Cinnamon said she wanted to check on her boyfriend Durango and his good friends.

McKenna sipped her drink, watching the ocean slip by. This

was her first cruise.

"Are those women your sisters?" said a voice at her right. She looked up into the face of a dark-haired man about her age.

"My aunts," she smiled.

"Wow," said the man. "You sure have beautiful aunts."

"Thank you," she grinned. "You should see my Mom, too."

"My name is Steven. Steven Levin, from New York."

"I'm glad to meet you, Steven. I'm McKenna, from Chicago."

"I thought so. I saw you in the story on *Sixty Minutes* and *National Geographic*. You found Blackbeard's treasure in North Carolina a little while ago, didn't you?"

She nodded. "I was part of the team, anyhow. My grandpa Daniel figured out the riddle. My dad and I helped dig it up."

"Would you tell me about it?"

"Sure," said McKenna. The two young people sat on some deck chairs as she related the story. Over the next half hour McKenna related how she'd been kidnapped and held for ransom. The man she'd thought was her father, Alan DiBiasi, had come up with a plan to defraud his insurance company. After establishing a phony identity, he had arranged for McKenna to be kidnapped and held for ransom. She had escaped from her captors and come to North Carolina.

"So," she went on, "when we arrived at this St. Margaret's island in North Carolina, I learned that the man I thought was my father had set up a scam. He faked his death on a golf course in Puerto Rico."

"Faked his death!" said Steven. McKenna nodded.

"Right. An insurance scam. Then, I met my father, Casey Fixx."

"Oh. That part is kind of personal, I guess."

"Well, anyway, Alan DiBiasi is in prison. I've tried to talk to him, but he refuses to see me," said McKenna.

"That must be pretty difficult. I mean, you trusted him all those years--"

"And I did," said McKenna.

"And then he was willing to have you killed to collect some money."

"Yeah. That hurts." They sat and stared at the ocean.

"Do you think we could kind of hang out together on this cruise?" said Steven, after a pause of a few moments. "I came with my parents, and I like them a lot, but. . ."

"Sure," she grinned. "I know what you mean. That would be great."

Steven escorted McKenna to dinner that night. At the end of the meal she introduced Stephen and his parents to Casey and Anna Fixx, who had just been married. Then, she introduced the other members of the family.

The next day, McKenna found Steven at breakfast. "Hey," she said, and showed him the list of shipboard activities. "I want to take ballroom dance lessons this morning."

"I don't know how to dance," Steven protested.

"Well, that's why you take lessons, right?"

Steven shrugged and agreed. She met him thirty minutes later and they made their way to a cocktail lounge to take ballroom dance instruction.

Steven felt awkward at first. Still, he managed to giggle at himself and within a few moments, he fell into step. The enthusiasm of the two young people impressed their instructors, Tim and Suzie.

That night Steven and McKenna tried out the dances they'd

learned that day in front of their parents. "Classy," said Casey, holding his wife's hand and smiling up at his daughter and her friend when they returned to the table.

"Astounding," teased Micah Levin. "My son has never demonstrated any penchant for dancing."

* * * * *

Later McKenna and Steven walked along the top deck and stared at the moonlight that flooded the ocean. He took her hand and squeezed it. They sat on deck chairs and watched the full moon and the dramatic star field.

"This is so beautiful," she said. "I love the ocean."

"My great-great something-grandfather came to America somewhere around 1720," Steven said. "He was a rabbi. The boat he was on was the size of a teacup by comparison to this ship. The family legend says he was seasick all the time."

He related the story of Sholem Levin, kidnapped by pirates, sold into slavery, and later a leader of the Jewish faith in colonial America.

When he finished the story, McKenna DiBiasi and Steven Levin stared at the full moon, the light reflecting off the calm ocean. "Somehow, he escaped, and made it to America. That's all I know of Sholem's history."

"Good grief, what a story," said McKenna to her new friend, then shivered. She wrapped her arms around herself.

"Cold?" he asked.

"A little. Let's go dance."

CHAPTER 34

Two days later, *Galaxy* anchored in the harbor at Philipsburg, St. Maarten, an island in the Netherlands Antilles. McKenna looked up as Steven joined her at breakfast. "Want to go sailing?" he asked.

"I've never sailed before," she said.

"That's okay. Mom and Dad and I are going on a shore excursion. They told me to invite you. We race in an America's Cup boat. The crew will show us how."

McKenna agreed, excited. She hurried through breakfast and hustled back to her cabin to yank on her swim suit. Pulling on a pair of cut-offs and a sweatshirt as she went, she dashed to the third deck, where she boarded a tender to the dock in Phillipsburg. Steven and his parents had gone ahead to confirm the reservations and pay for the trip.

On the way down the dock, she saw a couple walking a few steps ahead of her. The woman, tall and blond, had a lovely figure. McKenna knew the woman at once.

"Rand?" she said.

The woman turned and McKenna saw the deep blue eyes of the Fixx clan. The woman's smile widened and McKenna sensed an aura of absolute joy. This woman looked so *happy*.

"You have to be McKenna," Rand said and hugged her new niece. She introduced her husband Mickey to McKenna.

"We flew into St. Maarten last night," said Mickey. He

jerked his thumb at the big ship anchored out in the harbor. "We just went aboard and found our cabin."

"We put our six-year-old into the youth program on the ship," Aunt Rand said. "We may not see him for the duration of the cruise." All three laughed.

"This is great," McKenna told them. "I'm anxious for you to meet my mom and Grandpa Daniel."

"Where are you going now?" asked Rand.

McKenna told them about the sailing trip. "Great," said Mickey. "We're going to the same place." Rand and Mickey accompanied McKenna to the pier and found Steven's parents waiting for them.

"I bought you a ticket," said Micah Levin, Steven's dad. McKenna offered to repay him but Mr. Levin refused. "Not a chance. I've never seen Steven happier than he's been since he started hanging around with you."

McKenna gripped Steven's hand as a tour director divided the excursion group into two teams. Steven's parents were assigned to another group. Then a launch took them out to the racing yacht. "Steven," she said. "That's the *Stars and Stripes*."

"That's what I meant. It's one of Dennis Connor's yachts. The other team sails that boat," said Steven. He pointed to another yacht thirty or so yards away. "It's a Canadian boat, *Far North IV*. We're going to be racing against them."

Logan volunteered to give the crew a pep talk. To the laughter of the team on *Stars and Stripes*, he delivered the St. Crispin's Day speech from Shakespeare's *Henry V*.

The crew assigned McKenna to the position of Winch Wench, showing her how to crank the boom. Steven sat a few feet away, opposite Mickey Logan.

McKenna had liked Mickey at once. His hug had been warm and kind, his smile genuine. McKenna saw his overwhelming devotion to her aunt Rand.

Now in the bright sunlight, she noticed that he had green eyes and copper red hair. He bore a surprising resemblance to McKenna's mother.

She was about to question him, but the gun sounded and the race began.

McKenna couldn't remember when she'd enjoyed anything more. Steven and Logan operated the main winch, which, the captain said, made them "grinders." The boat heeled under the force of the wind, knifing through waves, splashing the group aboard with cool salty water.

When the race ended, Steven took her hand and they climbed into the tender. He tried hard to smile, but his face was a little green. "You okay?" she asked him.

"I will be as soon as soon as we go ashore," he said. "A bit of seasickness. I'm telling you, the last leg of that race, you know, when we kept rocking back and forth, going up and down over the waves. . ." His voice faded.

"No kidding." she giggled. "But you haven't been sick on the cruise ship."

"No," he said. "It must have to do with the size of the ship."

"Yeah, I imagine," she said. "I've never been seasick."

"Jews should never go to sea," he said.

* * * * *

John Morinec sat in his office at Alliance Insurance. He rubbed his face, worried, as he hung up the phone.

Where the hell is Mickey? He put his head in his hands. *Oh*

God, please let him and Rand be okay. . .

His colleague Jane Leaf, tall and elegant, knocked and strolled into John's office. "Excuse me, John, I need. . ." She saw his face and her face took on an expression of some alarm. "What's the matter?"

John looked up. "I can't find the Logans." She sat down across the desk from him. "I've called their house, his cell, hers. Damn it! If anything has happened to them. . ."

"Bring me up to speed," suggested Jane.

He handed her three police reports. "This first case is an accidental death." Jane glanced at the file he handed her. "Albert Thomas," said John. As always when he thought about Albert, he became conscious of a bad taste in his mouth. "A punk. I doubt that anyone other than his mother grieved much for him."

"What do you mean?" Jane asked.

"He was cruel to animals. He and another guy killed a puppy once."

"Excuse me?" said Jane, drawing back in disgust.

"Yeah," said John. "Senseless brutality. The family who owned the dog had him arrested. The police and the school got him into some counseling. He also paid for the puppy, did community service rather than jail time. I don't think it helped. He was a brutal thug all his life."

"And he died a violent death."

"Yeah," said John. "I remember Albert tried to humiliate a freshman kid on the first day of football practice. He called the kid over after practice and said he wanted to show him something. Then he spat in the kid's face and laughed.

"The kid gave him an upper cut with his helmet right to the

groin. Albert bent over in pain and the little guy went after him, swinging his helmet like a club and screaming. Thomas had his nose bloodied, maybe broken, by the time the coaches broke it up. He stood there crying, clutching his groin. Albert never bothered that particular freshman again."

Jane looked at the next file. "What's this?" she asked.

"A guy named Frank Capriatti. Logan and I went to high school with him too. A bully, a thug, nasty as an infected big toe."

Jane glanced through the file. "What's his story?"

"Frank died in a hunting accident. Blew half his head off with a shotgun."

"Yuck," she shuddered in an expression of disgust.

"But here's the problem. Frankie hated guns. His dad became involved with some very bad guys when Frankie was in grade school. The old man got way over his head with gambling. At the age of nine, Frankie found his dad's very dead body in a freezer with five bullets in his corpse. Frankie would never touch a gun of any kind."

"Huh," said Jane, peering at her coffee cup. She frowned. "So it makes no sense for him to go hunting with a rifle."

John's facial expression said you see what I mean? "The state police investigated. The accident—if that's what it was--happened not too far from Kankakee. The farmer who owned the field found his body by a creek bed after a winter thaw. No other tracks or indications anyone else had been there, of course. The snow covered everything up. The cops concluded his gun went off by accident when he stumbled while going after a bird. But his wife says he never owned a gun. She also says he would never go hunting either."

"Hmmm," said Jane.

"I called his widow and made an appointment to see her. Mickey knew her in high school, too."

"What happened?"

* * * * *

John related his conversation with Paula Capriatti at her house near Harlan, Illinois. She was a quiet, graceful woman. Her voice was soft and silky, and she sat very upright as she talked. For some time, she related what had happened with her marriage to the abusive lout named Frankie, then Frankie's death.

How could anyone be unkind to this woman? he thought. She had long brown hair, a graceful figure and a gentle smile. He struggled not to stare at her, thinking of how her beauty had matured since she graduated from high school. He had to make an effort to concentrate on her story.

"Frank had been gone several weeks when the state troopers found him," said Paula. "Of course when he didn't come home, I notified the police. A farmer's son found him in a cornfield west of Kankakee. The shot tore his head to pieces—" She choked up for a second and John handed her a glass of water. She sipped a little and took a moment or two to compose herself and speak again. "The state policeman who came to the house said Frank's rifle had been impounded. The trooper told me it was a real expensive shotgun. I think he called it a Remington twelve gauge, does that sound right?"

John nodded. Paula resumed the story. "Rusty said that--"

"Rusty?" asked John. When she said the name, a blush came to her cheek and a gentle smile crossed her face.

"The state trooper," said Paula. She cleared her throat. "I began seeing him quite a bit." She held out her left hand. An exquisite diamond graced her ring finger. "We were married not long ago."

"He's a lucky man."

Paula blushed. "Thank you." She fluttered her hands in front of her face and giggled a little. She told him the police theory of the death was that Frank shot himself by accident. "The police think he must've tripped and shot himself. Rusty brought the gun back to me. But…" she paused.

"But?" John asked after a few moments.

She leaned forward and looked John in the eye. "I keep wondering some things," she said. "Isn't hunting usually a group thing, sort of like golf? I mean, don't people usually hunt together with a few other people? So who did he go with? Wouldn't you take along a dog to flush the birds? If so, whose dog did he use? We've never owned a dog and I can't think of anyone we know who has a hunting dog. And there's this: why would he go that far south? We have lots of fields around here. For another thing, when they found him he was wearing hunting clothes that I'd never seen him wear. Yes, the state police took me to identify his body." She shuddered at the memory.

"I don't know what happened to the work clothes that he had on when he left the house the last time I saw him," she said. "Lots of strange things like that keep occurring to me."

"You should be a cop," said John. "I'm an insurance investigator. You looking for a gig?"

She thanked him for the compliment. She told him she had started working on a college degree at the local community college. John told her how pleased he was to hear it.

"I'd never even seen the rifle," Paula said, returning to the story. "The police told me he owned it. I can't imagine him buying a rifle. He must've borrowed it." She went to a closet and came back with the shotgun. She let John look it over. "It still had several shells in the magazine when Rusty returned it to me, though he unloaded it for me. I'd like to return it but I don't know who owns it. I sure don't like having it around the house."

* * * * *

Jane tapped the rim of her coffee cup with a fashionable nail as John finished the story. Her brow wrinkled as she pondered.

"Then, there's this character," John said, tossing her the file on Bill Kidd. "Another loser." He told his colleague about the electrocution of Kidd in his back yard.

At last she asked, "Here's what I don't get, John. Why are you so disturbed about these three crumbs?"

"Well, let me show you this, too. You know this guy Larry Connor we've been looking for? The sailboat fiasco?"

"Uh-huh," she said, leaning forward, elbows on her knees, wrapping her fingers around her coffee cup.

He tossed her a fax from the Texas State Police. "Police think they found him. A house caught fire in Dallas not long ago. They found a man's body inside. His description seemed to be consistent with the description of Larry Connor. They found a driver's license that identified him."

"Yes?"

"His cousin collected a bundle on insurance for the house and the death."

"So. . ."

"Larry was friends in high school with Capriatti, Thomas and Kidd."

"Oh," said Jane, drawing out the syllable as the light went on. "You think someone is trying to get rid of some creeps?"

"Maybe. But one more thing is consistent."

"Yes?"

"They all had huge life insurance policies."

"What did they do for their livings?"

"Capriatti was a laborer in a shoe factory. Thomas worked as a janitor in a steel mill. Kidd mowed lawns for a lawn service."

"How about Connor?"

"Sort of well off, from what I can tell. Co-owner of a graphic arts studio."

"Your point is. . ."

"I can't figure why any of these guys bought life insurance policies this big. Look."

Jane's mouth dropped at the dollar amount of the policies. "Cripes. A laborer? A janitor?"

"Yeah. And the settlements were all paid to cousins."

"Not closest relative? Spouse? Parent?"

"Nope. But Paula Capriatti, now Ivers, received a nice settlement from a policy that she didn't know about. Had no idea it existed. Same with Thomas's mother. Had no idea her son had a life insurance policy. The company was named M and M Life. And guess what?" She raised an eyebrow. "I can't find an insurance company by that name."

"Have you talked to Connor's ex-wife? His son?"

"That's what I'm saying. I can't find either Connor's son or his ex-wife."

Jane ran a finger around the rim of her cup, her lips pursed.

"Then I found this," said John, handing her a slip of paper. "Some years ago, someone bought a policy for my friend Mickey Logan--"

"The guy who married the former Mrs. Connor?" asked Jane.

"Right. Look at the amount."

Jane looked. "Oh my," she said, stunned. "Doesn't he have a good estate without insurance?"

"Yeah. If he died Rand would be set for life even without this policy."

"How did you find out about this?" Jane asked. "These policies all come from different companies."

"I used the national database. I knew what to look for, so it wasn't too hard."

"So let me get this straight. You're thinking your friend Mickey is in danger?"

"And maybe Rand and their little boy," said John. "I think we're dealing with a serial killer. Or, more likely, a gang of serial killers." Jane nodded.

CHAPTER 35

After dinner on the *Galaxy* that evening, Steven and McKenna found Rand and Mickey strolling with their son by the swimming pool. "Mom, can I go now?" Joey asked, with a quick nod to McKenna and Steven.

"I guess so," sighed Rand and the boy sped off toward the front of the ship.

"He's so excited," said Mickey to McKenna and Steven. "He bolted his dinner. The kids' group is doing some sort of a special craft tonight."

Steven and Mickey chatted as they walked into the bar and found Casey and Anna Fixx. Casey introduced his wife to Mickey and Rand. "Anna," said Casey, "this is uncanny. Mickey could be your brother. He looks just like you."

"I don't know if we're related," said Anna Fixx. "But you're right about the resemblance." She invited Rand and Mickey to sit with them.

"Mom, Dad," said McKenna, "did you know that Mickey's first name is McClelland?"

* * * * *

The reaction of Anna Fixx to his name startled Mickey. Her mouth dropped open and she peered at him with some intensity. She turned to her husband who looked just as surprised. She took his hand and looked into his eyes.

"Okay," he said a moment later, as if Anna had said something to him. "Hey Sis, may I have this dance?" Rand agreed, delighted.

"In that case, Mickey," said Anna in a charming southern accent, "would you dance with me?"

"Sure," Mickey said.

Anna made light chitchat with him as they moved around the floor. The band—two people playing a synthesizer and guitar—performed a slow foxtrot.

A few moments passed, during which Mickey led her through the dance. She followed his leading with grace. "Mickey," Anna said, drawing back to look deep into his eyes.

"Yes?" Mickey said, continuing to be mystified by the way she looked at him. Not romantic, but curious and puzzled.

"You know Myrthynne, don't you?"

The name was familiar. Mickey couldn't identify who Myrthynne was, however. "Who?"

"Has anyone ever talked to you about the Cymreig?"

"I don't think so." His mind was whirling. He'd been stunned, also, at the resemblance between him and Anna.

Anna continued to question him as they danced. Then she bit her lip. She asked, "Will you trust me for a moment?"

He shrugged. "Sure."

"Look into my eyes."

"Okay. . ."

Lights and colors swirled, and a moment later, Mickey wasn't dancing in the bar of the cruise ship anymore. Mickey found himself standing with Anna in a beautiful cave with gentle sounds, lovely scents, and warmth in the air that was

altogether pleasant.

"Mickey," she said. "This is our great grandfather."

He turned and saw a huge man towering over him. The man had a gray beard that was tinged with a copper color like his hair and that of Anna. He also had stunning emerald eyes.

"Mickey," said the man. "At last. Thank God you met Viviane."

"That's my name when I'm here," Anna explained.

"You are familiar, sir. Have we met?" Mickey asked.

The giant gave him a sad wan grin. "My real name is Myrthynne. Let me show you when we first met." He looked into Mickey's eyes.

At once, Mickey saw the scene at the time he had been attacked at the University of Wisconsin. He recalled meeting Myrthynne and some of the man's enigmatic statements.

"I've been here before," Mickey said. "I remember now."

"Yes, when you were injured, several years ago," replied Myrthynne. He turned to Anna. "Mickey's life has been plagued by Nehushtan. Nehushtan haunts him with witches."

"Let him see," said Anna. She looked into his eyes for a few seconds. Again Mickey felt the warm comfort of the Paik as she examined his thoughts. "Yes," she said after a few moments. "I understand."

"Why am I here?" asked Mickey.

"We need your help," said Myrthynne.

"You need me?" Mickey stammered. "What on earth do you need me for?"

"Come with me," said Myrthynne, looking into his eyes.

The cave dissolved and the three of them stood on top of an island. The moon was full above the horizon. The sea was glittering with moonlight but winter winds screamed and waves crashed against the rugged shoreline, sending spray high into the air. Mickey saw a lighthouse standing about one hundred yards away. "Where are we?"

"On White Island," said Anna, taking his elbow, "about ten miles out from Portsmouth, New Hampshire."

"Right," Mickey said. "Now I recognize it. I've read about the lighthouse and the island. The island is famous for its legends, I remember."

"Here is one of those legends," said Myrthynne, nodding over his shoulder.

He turned and saw a figure walking toward them, bathed in moonlight, wearing a long cloak, copper hair blowing. "Who is that?" Mickey asked.

"Your great-grandmother," said Myrthynne.

Mickey's jaw dropped. "What?"

"Yes. Her name is Martha Herring. She saved your ancestor, a man named Owen McClelland, from slavery. When I heard your name, I suspected that you must be related to him."

"I studied Owen's story in college," Mickey said. "I even wrote some papers about him. He's always been one of my personal heroes."

"Martha married Owen," Myrthynne went on, "and you are their offspring through her son John, who was born with the Cymreig. But only one person in your family, your grandfather, has inherited the Cymreig since her son. The skill has been all but forgotten. Now it has emerged in you."

Mickey remembered his parents screaming at him to stay out of their minds, forbidding him to use the gift.

"Martha died and Owen and her sons buried her on Star Island, Mickey," said Myrthynne, pointing to the southeast. Mickey saw the dark hulk of an island in the distance, rocky and forbidding, like this one. "She was brave and good. But she cannot be at rest."

"She's been dead since the eighteenth century," said Anna. "My daughter saw her some years ago, when I brought her here on a vacation."

"You mean, this is a ghost?" Mickey said. The red hair of the beautiful young woman blew around her head.

"Yes," said Myrthynne. "She is being faithful to a promise."

"What do you mean?"

"She made a promise to a man named Sholem Levin who was Owen's best friend."

The name struck him and Mickey turned to Anna. "Levin?"

"That's right," said Anna. "The young man with my daughter is also named Levin."

"Steven is Sholem's descendant," said Myrthynne.

"My gosh," Mickey said. "It never occurred to me."

"Right," said Anna. "Martha promised Sholem that she would stay with and care for the great treasures until the rightful owner came for them."

"Yes," said Myrthynne. "Martha does this by choice. She believes in her charge."

"I'm proud to be her grandson," Mickey said, with some reverence.

"As you should be," Myrthynne nodded. "We want you to set her free."

"What can I do?"

"You must find the High Priest," said Anna. "He needs to come here and recover the treasure."

"Does treasure still remain? From what I remember of the legend, Martha used the treasure to find and rescue Owen, then for his education at Harvard."

"That's the legend, yes," said Myrthynne. "But Owen left instructions. You must find the instructions, and then come to the islands and find the real treasure."

He cast his eyes around the bleak landscape of the deserted island. Martha's specter stood some feet away, not looking at them. "The real treasure? Not gold and silver and precious stones?"

"No," said Myrthynne. "This treasure is worth far more than any gold."

"Why don't we ask Martha where it is?"

"She cannot talk to anyone. She cannot see us, nor is she aware of our presence."

Mickey walked to the ghost. Anna and Myrthynne followed him. She appeared to be seventeen years old. The ghost stood at the low point of the island, staring out to sea. "He will return," she said in a faint voice.

"Martha," Mickey said.

The ghost didn't respond. It continued to stare to the southeast. "All right, Grandmother," Mickey said. "You can't hear me. But I promise I'll save you."

"Good-bye, Mickey," said Myrthynne. "I will see you soon."

In the next instant Anna and Mickey were dancing in the lounge on the cruise ship. No time whatever seemed to have elapsed. The band was playing the same song, and the same people were dancing next to them.

"I've always considered myself a freak," Mickey said. "Like I'm something strange, out of place."

"No, you are not a freak," said Anna. "You are blessed. The Cymreig is a gift you and I have. So does my grandfather. He came along on the cruise with us. You'll meet him later."

"I'll look forward to it."

"You must learn to see the Cymreig in other ways," she said. She went into his mind and taught him a few things about how to Paik another person. She showed him the story of the Cymreig, of Myrthynne, of Gareth, of Nehushtan.

"Nehushtan?" Mickey said.

"That's the name of the Snake. It wants to destroy us. That's why you have the nightmares."

"Why is the Snake afraid of the Cymreig?"

Anna sighed. "The Cymreig is truth, wisdom, courage. The Snake, Nehushtan, is fear, doubt, envy and guilt. He can use guilt to destroy you."

He pondered this, still wondering if this was one of his vivid dreams. "Is the Crystal Cave real?"

"Yes," she affirmed. "It's been well hidden for centuries."

"Where is the Crystal Cave? I mean, can we go there without the Cymreig?"

"I don't know where it is. Wales, I think. I've been there many times. It is a sanctuary where we can be recharged, energized, and encouraged. From now on you also can go there when things are difficult."

"Does anyone besides us and your grandfather know about the cave?"

"A few people. Casey has been taken there on a couple of occasions. But he only has vague, undefined memories of the cave and of Myrthynne. As he should. It is not a place for most people to go."

"How about McKenna?"

"Myrthynne brought her there once to encourage her when she'd been kidnapped. She remembers it. Also, Casey's sister Cinnamon remembers a dream of the Cave, a gift when she helped rescue McKenna from kidnappers."

"Have you taken McKenna back?"

"No. I don't want Nehushtan to know anything more about her."

He thought for a few moments about all the dreams he'd had for years. "What does the Snake look like in your dreams?" Mickey asked.

"Mud colored. Red eyes. Huge. Always rearing."

"That's what I see too. Then three old women join it and chant terrible things to me."

"In my dreams the Snake turns into a man," she said. "Someone tall, with a black beard and red eyes. I've never seen his face. I'm not afraid of him in the dreams now because I'm married to Casey. He always protects me."

"I have only a vague memory of some of the dreams," said Mickey. "I think I remember dreaming of Rand before I met her. I know I had dreams of her when we were separated. But now she seems to be with me in the dreams all the time."

"Casey and I face Nehushtan together. That makes the dreams bearable."

He agreed. "The dreams haven't been so bad since I married Rand."

"I understand. Having someone to love eases the pain." The song ended and she took his arm as they returned to the table.

"Anna," Mickey said, "do you ever see three old women?"

"No," she said. "But Nehushtan can take many forms. And he has many helpers."

"Can you teach me more about how to Paik? I've just been doing it on instinct."

"Of course. But not tonight. We'll do some tomorrow."

"I'll look forward to it."

Rand and Casey came back to the table. "Casey's a terrific dancer," she said, and poked Mickey in the chest with a finger. "You could learn a lot."

He glanced at Anna who smiled at him. "I've learned quite a bit tonight."

The conversation turned to a discussion of McKenna, and her school work, her talents and abilities. The pride that Casey Fixx took in his daughter impressed Mickey.

Sometime later Anna and Casey excused themselves. Mickey stood and shook hands with Casey. Then Anna came over and hugged him. The hug was full of affection.

CHAPTER 36

Mickey Logan lay on the bed in his cabin on the *Galaxy* next to his wife, snuggled against her, thinking of how his life had changed that evening. Anna Fixx, so lovely, so gracious, understood him in a way that few other people ever had.

"Did you like the people we met today?" Mickey asked Rand.

"Yes, very much," she said. "Anna could be your sister. She looks just like you."

"You're not upset that she hugged me, are you?"

She snickered. "You mean, am I jealous?"

"Well, yeah."

"Anyone can see she's crazy about her husband. Besides, I know you," she said.

He leaned up and looked down into her face, trying to read her expression. "What does that mean?"

"I know that you couldn't be duplicitous."

He hugged her, and stroked her hair. Mickey kissed the tip of her nose. "Thanks."

They dozed off. Mickey dreamed of White Island, rock bound and pelted by huge waves. Rain pelted the island and soaked Mickey to the skin. He stood on top of the Island looking out to sea and feeling terrified. Mickey sensed the presence of the snake.

His grandfather appeared and walked toward him. His expression reflected fear and concern. "Mickey," said Papa. He looked strong, vigorous and handsome.

"Papa," Mickey said, using the name he had called his grandfather when he was a little boy. Mickey realized that he hadn't thought about his grandfather for some time. When he was awake Mickey couldn't even remember what the man had looked like.

"Do you remember that you made a promise?"

"I remember that I promised something. But I don't remember what. Can you remind me?"

"Yes, when the time is right."

"Why have you come to me now?"

"Because you are near to the High Priest. You have also met someone who can teach you to use the Cymreig. I died before we could work together on how to use your gift."

The presence of the man who had been the kindest person in his life made him feel lonely. Mickey began to cry. "I miss you, Papa."

"Find the High Priest, little Green Eyes. We will see each other again when you do. I love you, dear little boy. . ." Papa turned and walked away. Mickey called to him, trying to stop him. Then Papa turned to a breath of vapor and vanished. A huge snake appeared where Papa had just stood. It opened its mouth, ready to swallow him.

"Mickey." Mickey heard the gentle voice of the girl who protected him. Mickey turned and saw three old women, who snarled curses at him, telling him they couldn't wait to kill him.

"Mickey!" said Rand's smoky voice.

He opened his eyes. A candle burned, giving a gentle light to their cabin on the ship. Rand leaned over him, shaking him.

"Wake up, Mickey. You're having a nightmare." She embraced him.

"Rand," Mickey said, tears running down his cheek. "I was just with my grandfather. He died when I was a little boy. He came to warn me to prepare me for what we have to do."

She pulled back, her brow wrinkled, mouth open a little. "What do we have to do?"

"I can't explain right now," Mickey said. "We'll talk in the morning."

The blonde hair fell around her face. "You're being weird." She laughed. The candlelight made her look so beautiful that Mickey began to tear up again. Mickey thought about his great-great grandmother's spirit, who walked a lonely rock in the cold north Atlantic.

"Why are you crying?" she asked with a gentle smile. She stroked his hair and wiped away his tears, comforting him.

"I don't want us to be apart ever."

"Why would we have to be apart?" she said, running her fingers through his hair.

"I don't know. I . . . I guess we don't."

"Of course we don't. You're not getting rid of me."

"I never want to."

"Well, then," she said, her hand caressing his chest, "I think we ought to do something about it."

"What did you have in mind?" Mickey noticed that the pain of the dream had begun to ease. Her fingers soothed every fiber of his soul.

She slid her hand along his body. "How's this for a start?"

"Great start," Mickey agreed, and they began to kiss.

Sometime later, she wrapped her arms around him and laid her head on his chest. They fell asleep again. The Snake didn't return to his dreams.

* * * * *

The next morning Mickey put on some workout clothes and took Joey up to the buffet breakfast to allow Rand to sleep in a little. Joey wolfed the food, and then dashed off to his playgroup, blathering something about a scavenger hunt.

Mickey worked out for a little while before returning to the cabin to shower and shave. Rand had awakened and left the room, to his disappointment.

He found her sunning herself by the pool. Mickey leaned and kissed her. She smiled, stretched, and pulled him down for a deeper kiss.

They went in to the buffet. They each took a plateful of fresh fruit and went out to a table on the aft deck, where they sat at a table with an umbrella to shield them, enjoying the warmth of the Caribbean sun.

Rand and Mickey looked up as an elderly man approached their table carrying a tray. He seemed about eighty years old. The man asked permission to sit with them.

"Sure," said Rand. "We'd be pleased."

"Beautiful day," said the man as he sat.

"My name is Rand and this is my husband Mickey."

"I know," said the man.

"You do?" Rand said, surprised.

"Yes." He gave them a smile. "My name is Daniel Oakley. You know my granddaughter Anna."

"Oh, yes, Grandpa Daniel." Mickey smiled and shook his

hand. Rand rose, embraced him, and then shook hands with the gentleman. Like Anna, the man had vivid green eyes.

"Do you know Myrthynne also, Mr. Oakley?" Mickey asked.

"Yes, I do."

Rand shifted her glances back and forth at the two of them. "What are you guys talking about?" she asked, mystified.

They didn't answer. Mickey didn't know where to begin to explain.

"I don't want to be rude," said Rand. "But why are you here, Mr. Oakley?"

"You mean on the cruise? Well, Casey, my grandson-in-law, invited me--"

"No. I mean here, eating breakfast with us on the aft deck."

Mr. Oakley hesitated, and gave Mickey a glance. He turned back to her. "I came to take your husband away with me. But you can come too. Ah, here's Anna."

Anna sat down and squeezed Mickey's hand. "Are you all right?"

"What do you mean?" Mickey asked.

"Did you sleep last night?"

He swallowed. "I had a nightmare. The same one as always."

"The Snake," said Anna, nodding. Mr. Oakley looked grim. Rand glanced from person to person, her mouth open, blue eyes wide with bewilderment.

"Are you ready to go?" Anna asked.

Mickey took a bite of pineapple and gave Rand a little nod to reassure her. Mickey took her hand and said, "Okay."

Anna took his other hand and looked into his eyes. Daniel did the same to Rand.

In the next moment Mickey stood on a beach with Anna, her grandfather, and his wife.

"Where are we?" Mickey asked.

"This is Okracoke Island on the Outer Banks of North Carolina. Lieutenant Robert Maynard of the British Navy beheaded Blackbeard about a hundred yards out there." Anna pointed out toward the Atlantic. "His bones are at the bottom of the ocean."

"Blackbeard the pirate?" asked Rand.

"Yes. His real name was Edward Teach. He was a vicious murderer and criminal," said Daniel Oakley.

Now Rand began to look a little panicky. "How did we get here?" asked Rand. "Aren't we on the ship?"

"Why. . ." Mickey broke off the question when he saw a young man coming toward him. He recognized the man from pictures in an old family album. It was his grandfather.

"Hello, Mickey," said Papa. "You've come at last."

"Yes, Papa, I have," Mickey said. Mickey embraced Papa, feeling tears of joy rising in his delight to see his grandfather.

"It's all right now," said Papa. "You can remember."

Mickey stood back and held Papa's hand. He introduced Anna and Daniel. "Papa," Mickey said. "This is my wife Rand."

"Hello, beloved daughter," said Papa, embracing Rand.

"Hi Papa," said Rand, kissing his cheek.

"But Papa," Mickey said. "You're . . . dead."

"I know. This is a memory I left with you when you were a little boy and I was near death," said Papa. "Come, Little Green Eyes." Papa walked Mickey and Rand to the ocean and waded in a few inches of water. Papa held Mickey's arm at the elbow and put an arm around Rand's waist.

"Mickey, the book I gave you is called the *Tanach*, the Hebrew testament. Inside the book is a letter from Grandfather Owen. The letter will tell you how to find a treasure."

"What is the treasure?"

"The staff of the High Priest of ancient Israel and a stone called the Urim and Thummin. Both can do amazing things, but they only work in the hands of the High Priest."

"You mean, like magic?"

"Not magic the way you think. But the High Priest will be able to use these objects."

"Why is this important now?"

Papa held his gaze, then turned and squeezed his arm in affection. Mickey remembered that his grandfather would use that little gesture when Mickey was little. They looked out to sea. "Nobody knows where the treasures are," he said. "Nor does anyone know how to find the directions in the book. But something has changed that may help.

"In 1948 Israel re-emerged as a state in the world community," Papa said. "The heart of Israel is its identity as the people of God. They are the priest nation, the nation that is meant to serve as the intermediary between men and God. Now they have again emerged as a nation. It is vital that they have a spiritual leader."

"Why?" Mickey asked.

Papa stared out to sea, his lips moving a little. Mickey remembered that he did that when he was thinking, trying to compose a reply to one of his grandson's childish questions. "A book in the New Testament, called the Letter to the Ephesians, says that the struggle of the world is not against flesh and blood, though most people believe it is. Paul, the author of the letter, claimed that mankind's struggle is against the powers of supernatural evil."

Mickey's skin crawled. "Who is Israel's spiritual leader now?"

"I don't know his name but he's the one who is meant to be the High Priest. The time is right. The High Priest needs the staff of Aaron, as well as the Urim and Thummin."

"What is that?"

"A stone from the ancient priesthood of Israel that Great-Grandfather Owen learned to use."

Mickey shook his head, looking at his feet, considering what he knew about Owen. "But Owen couldn't have been the High Priest. We aren't even Jewish."

"Somehow he was given the grace to use the stone to protect him and to ease his heart," said Papa. "It's strange, I agree, but King David wasn't the High Priest either. Yet he also was given the power to use the stone."

"What should I do?" Mickey found himself feeling a little shelled by all this. He'd faced some challenges in life, but nothing like a treasure hunt for two of the greatest treasures of a nation.

"Take your wife and go to the island with the High Priest. Find the staff. When you do, you will find the stone. The High Priest will know what to do with them."

"Papa. Tell me how to find the High Priest."

"You will know him when you see him, little Green Eyes." Grandfather hugged him. "I don't think I can stay any longer. Learn to use the Cymreig. Your new friends will help you." Papa hugged Mickey, smiled at Rand, and then turned and began to walk away.

"Papa?" Mickey said. Then they were sitting at a table on the aft deck of the cruise ship *Galaxy*.

"Are you all right, Mickey?" asked Rand. Anna and her grandfather were staring at him, concerned.

"Yes," Mickey said. "That was a memory. He planted it in me when I was six years old, just before he died."

Anna's daughter came over to the table. She brought over her friend Steven, who shook hands with him.

Mickey looked through the young man's eyes into his mind and Paiked—

Moses stood before him. "Eliazar," said Moses. "The Eternal has commanded me to make you the new High Priest. You must take the place of your father Aaron, who now rests with his fathers. You will be the High Priest. . ."

Then the scene shifted and he was staring into eyes of a king. "Zadok," said the king. "You are the High Priest. Take the staff and the breastplate."

He put on the breastplate and said "King Solomon. I will serve you and God well, I pledge."

He turned and walked forward, the bells attached to his garment ringing, a rope tied around his left ankle. If the bells stopped ringing, the priests would realize that he had come under fatal judgement from the Eternal and pull him from the Most Holy Place.

Sholem—who had now changed into the great High Priest, Zadok--pushed aside the veil of the Most Holy Place carrying a bowl of goat's blood drained from a sacrificed animal. Awestruck, he entered and saw the Shekinah cloud. The chamber was dim but he could see the Ark of the Covenant with its two kneeling cherubim on the atonement cover. The workmanship was exquisite. The chest was covered with hammered gold, the work of the ancient craftsman Bezalel during the time of Moses. He paused to touch the beautiful ark. Then as he had been taught, he began the task of scattering the blood of the sacrifice.

He set the bowl by the heavy curtain, then came and sat on top of the Ark in the place known as the Mercy Seat. He kept his legs moving so that the bells continued to ring. He began to chant, listing all the sins of the people of Israel—

* * * * *

Mickey released the Paik as Anna had shown him to do. Steven and he again stood on the aft deck of *Galaxy*. The young man staggered a step or two but Mickey held him so he didn't fall. "What. . ." Steven gasped. Then fear began to creep into his eyes.

Mickey smiled to reassure him. He shushed him by putting a finger to his lips and nodding reassurance. "Let's talk later," Mickey said.

"What's with you two guys?" said McKenna, looking puzzled.

"Nothing," Mickey assured her. "It turns out Steven and I know each other."

"How. . ." began McKenna.

"I'll explain another time," Mickey told her.

McKenna and Steven pulled over chairs from another table and began to chat with Rand. Mickey touched Anna's hand under the table. She looked at him and locked eyes. Mickey Paiked her.

They stood together on White Island in the next second. The moon illuminated the waves which crashed against the rocks.

"Why are we here?" Anna asked.

He told her what Grandpa McClelland had told him. "That's him, Anna," Mickey said. "McKenna's friend Steven is the High Priest."

She lifted an eyebrow. "You're sure, aren't you?"

"I am, yes," Mickey affirmed with a nod. "I know he's young but he has the archetypes. Can you Paik him too? You know, confirm it?"

"I will," she said. "But now what?"

He thought for a second. "We need someone who reads Hebrew," Mickey said. "My grandfather told me that my *Tanach* holds the key, but the writing and the notes are in Hebrew."

She waved a hand, dismissing the problem. "Steven is fluent, so that's fine."

"Okay," Mickey said. He turned and looked around, searching for Nehushtan or the old women. "Meanwhile, I'm a little scared."

"Scared?" asked Anna, drawing back, looking puzzled.

"Yes," Mickey said with a nod. "I had the sense when I was with him that Steven is in danger on this voyage."

"Okay, I'll check and see if I react the same way." Anna shivered. "Nehushtan is here watching us. Do you sense him too?"

"Yes I do. We should go back."

They again found themselves sitting at the table on the aft deck. Less than two seconds had transpired. Rand was laughing with Steven and McKenna about the boat race the previous day.

Daniel turned and looked at his granddaughter Anna and at

Mickey. "Are you all right?" he asked in an undertone.

He nodded. "Paik me," Mickey said to Daniel.

He felt Daniel slide into his mind. As always, colors and lights swirled around him.

In a moment, Mickey stood with Anna's grandfather on Ocracoke Island, looking out to sea. Mickey explained what had happened with Steven. "Yes," said Daniel. "I thought he was something special."

"But he's in danger here on the ship, I think."

Daniel explored Mickey's mind, and watched Steven's reaction to what had happened when Mickey Paiked him. "Yes. I sense it also."

"We have to protect him."

"The Snake always wants to destroy us," said Daniel. "We have to protect ourselves against him. I'll try to help Steven." He released the Paik. Again colors swirled, lights sparkled, and Mickey heard a rushing of wind.

They came back to the table and rejoined the conversation.

CHAPTER 37

McKenna DiBiasi watched what was happening with interest. Knowing her mother and great-grandfather as she did, she could sense that tensions had mounted. Mom pushed back her chair, excusing herself to get some fruit and other breakfast goodies. "I'll go with you," McKenna said.

Steven rose but McKenna waved him back down and told him to enjoy his coffee. She followed her mother into the buffet area and caught her elbow. She pulled her mom to a table by a window.

"Okay," said McKenna, as they sat and turned to look out the window. "What's going on here?"

Mom picked at the tablecloth and pushed around some silverware. She sighed, "I can't pretend that there isn't an issue, honey. It has to do with your friend Steven and with Mickey."

"What?" said her daughter.

"It seems that Steven is much more important than I thought at first. Mickey is too. " They paused as a waiter poured them some coffee, making a little chitchat with them.

"Mickey has the Cymreig too, doesn't he?" asked McKenna.

"Yes, but Steven also has something he has to do."

"Steven? What do you mean?"

Anna stared out at the ocean. It was a gorgeous day. The sun shining from a brilliant blue sky sparkled on the calm seas.

Anna pushed her hair away from her eyes. "Do you remember much about the Old Testament?"

"I know the famous stories, I guess, but I'm not an expert."

"In ancient Israel, from the time of Moses until after the time of Jesus, a single man stood between God and man. He was called the High Priest. He was the spiritual leader of all Israel."

"Like Caiaphas, the High Priest who dealt with Jesus?"

"Not exactly. Caiaphas was apostate, put in place by a corrupt Sanhedrin. The office of High Priest was always hereditary through Zadok, Solomon's High Priest."

McKenna thought for a moment. Her mother was looking out to sea. "What does the High Priest have to do with us?"

"I'll try to explain, honey," said Anna after a little hesitation. "No one has served as the High Priest for almost two thousand years. In order to receive the office a man had to prove his lineage to Zadok, a descendant of Aaron, the first high priest. The Romans destroyed the temple in A. D. 70, as you know."

"I remember. At the time they kicked the Jews out of Israel."

"Right," said Anna. "The destruction included the hall of records and genealogy in the temple. So today no one can prove that he is the rightful High Priest unless. . ." Anna paused. She adjusted a fork, pushing it next to a knife.

"Unless?" said McKenna after a wait.

"The implements of the High Priest could prove the priest's right to the office."

"Like what?"

"One thing would be the staff of the High Priest."

"The staff that Aaron used before Pharaoh?" said McKenna.

"Yes," said Anna. "It is the same staff that turned into a Snake at the burning bush, and became a monster before

Pharaoh, that turned the Nile to blood, that parted the Red Sea."

"What does this have to do with Steven? I mean he's not. . ." McKenna stopped and stared at her mother. She knew her mom's expression. Anna nodded. "Mom? Could Steven be the High Priest?"

"Mickey and Grandpa and I think it's plausible, honey," said Anna. "If he is, he has to recover the staff and the rest of the treasure. At some point he'll have to enter Jerusalem and take his place in the temple."

"Does he know?"

"Not yet. And we can't be certain until he finds the staff. If he's the High Priest, he'll know how to use the staff when he finds it."

"How?"

"We don't know. But Mickey's great-great grandmother needs him," said Anna. "You met her when we went out to White Island. Her name was Martha Herring. She is waiting for the return of the High Priest. . ." Anna reminded her daughter about the legend of the ghost of White Island. McKenna sat gaping at her mother.

CHAPTER 38

The next day, Rand and Mickey met Anna and Casey in an outdoor café on St. Thomas, Virgin Islands. McKenna came in accompanied by her friend Steven.

McKenna looked around the group. "Where are Derek and Cheyenne?" asked McKenna. Her mother shot her a look. "Oh," she said. "Again?"

Everyone laughed. Anna gave Rand a look. Casey rose. "Rand, come with Anna and me," he said. "Let's go to the café table outside."

"Is something up?" said Rand as she squeezed Mickey's hand. Anna nodded.

* * * * *

The three Arab men sat at the back of the café and watched young Steven Levin laughing and joking with the American girl. They were not used to seeing women dressed as she was. The girl's sundress lay well above her knee, revealing athletic, trim legs. Her arms were bare and her face was not covered.

Inappropriate in their county, of course. Even sinful. But they weren't as interested in her as in Levin.

They looked in surprise at the man who sat with them. He and the girl were both tall and had hair that was thick and the color of copper. They exchanged glances. Brother and sister perhaps?

The three Americans were laughing and joking. The three men smiled with anticipation.

They were patient. They would wait until the right moment.

They planned to kill the young Jew today. First, however, they would take the information they needed from him.

In addition, they had been assigned to kill the man with the red hair. They had to make it look like a street mugging.

* * * * *

Mickey shifted in his chair and said, "Steven. Have you ever heard of the Urim and Thummin?"

"Sure, I've read about them," said the young man, his eyes widening in surprise.

"I think I know where the stone might be."

Steven opened his mouth to reply, shut it, and stared at Mickey in surprise. "You what?" he managed.

"Yes. I believe that my great-grandfather may have found it and even used the Urim stone. I might know where the staff of the High Priest is too."

"Aaron's staff?" Steven asked. Mickey nodded. Steven gaped at his new friend open-mouthed. "That would be. . ." He turned toward McKenna. "Did you know this?"

"Mom told me yesterday," she said, laying a gentle hand on his arm. "She asked me not to say anything until Mickey had a chance to talk to you."

Steven nodded and put a hand to his forehead. Again, he struggled to speak.

"How is this possible?" Steven asked.

"I told McKenna that we'd met before," Mickey said. McKenna took Steven's hand and squeezed. "It wasn't quite true. However, I'm pretty sure that one of your ancestors was my great-great-grandfather's best friend."

Steven looked from his friend McKenna to Mickey and back again. "What do you mean?" he asked Mickey.

Mickey took a deep breath. "This is quite a story, Steven. My ancestor was named Owen McClelland. He was eighteen years old when he left home in New Hampshire.

"Pirates hijacked him," said Mickey. "He wouldn't return for several years." He began the narrative of his ancestor.

* * * * *

Rand sat across from Anna and Casey at a small table. "If you're correct," Rand said, "this would be one of the greatest finds in archeological history."

"Yes, it would," Casey agreed.

Rand leaned back in her chair. She bit at a fingernail, thinking it over. "Did you know about this treasure before?"

"It's a famous legend. People have scoured White Island for years looking for the treasure of Sandy Gordon. The ghost of Martha Herring is supposed to haunt it as well."

"Ghosts? Legends?"

"Mickey has something that might hold a secret," said Anna. "It's in an old copy of the Jewish Testament which belonged to his great-great grandfather."

"He's shown me the book," Rand murmured. She stared at her brother and his wife, fumbling for words.

"Mickey is going to talk to Steven about going to the island today," said Anna.

"Yes, and McKenna wants to go with Steven to help him look," said Casey. "Would you and Mickey go with them? We'll be glad to take care of Joey."

"Yes," said Rand. "We would be honored." She hesitated for a few moments before she asked, "Do you think there's danger?"

"We don't know," said Anna. "The danger could be very serious, yes. If they were searching for mere gold and silver and jewels, we wouldn't go along with it. However the treasure that they would be looking for is far more significant than any wealth."

Rand had to agree.

CHAPTER 39

When Mickey reached the part of the story where Owen met Sholem, Steven Levin interrupted. "Was that my great-great-grandfather?"

"Yes," Mickey said. "Our ancestors were lifelong friends. They first met on a pirate ship."

Steven gave a low whistle. McKenna took his hand and squeezed it. They exchanged smiles.

Mickey continued the story up to Martha's death, and related a little about Owen's ministry and teaching career in the early colonies.

Steven's mouth was agape for most of the story. "Owen and Sholem were remarkable men, weren't they?"

"Oh yes," Mickey said. "They wrote about the need to fashion a reunion between the Jewish faith and Christianity. Both were brilliant spiritual leaders in early America."

"I didn't know the story of how Sholem escaped from slavery," said Steven, his face glowing with delight.

"He was a brave man," said McKenna.

"The best," Mickey agreed.

Steven extended his hand to him. "I'm honored to meet you, Mickey."

Mickey grinned as he shook Steven's hand. McKenna leaned over and kissed Mickey's cheek. Then she turned to Steven and squeezed his hand.

Mickey watched her, thinking about what a lovely young woman she was. He'd become fond of McKenna and found himself thinking of her as a favorite little sister.

He shifted in his seat and glanced toward three Arab men who sat on the other side of the cafe.

He saw one of the men stand and walk out the door at the back of cafe. The other two rose. They walked over to them. *What on earth?* Mickey thought.

One of them leaned over. "You three. On your feet. Come with us."

Steven turned. "Excuse me?"

The first man drew back his coat. The handle of a large knife protruded from his belt.

"What is this?" demanded McKenna.

The man spoke in a low voice. "This is an order, not a request."

Mickey put his arms around McKenna and Steven. They followed one of the men while the other brought up the rear. The group walked out the door. They walked along until they found an alleyway. The man in the lead pushed them down the alley.

"We are going to kill you," said the first man. "You can either have this go well or you can die in pain and terror, all three of you." He drew his knife. "What will it be?"

"Why would you want to kill us?" McKenna asked. To Mickey's surprise, her voice projected more curiosity than fear.

"Shut up, child. Now, Jew," the second man spat the word, "if you want to spare your friends unnecessary pain, you will tell us where it is hidden. If you do not, we shall kill your parents next."

Steven's mouth hung open, his lips moving, trying to articulate some sort of a reply. "Where what is?" asked Steven.

The two thugs exchanged glances. "The treasure, you idiot," said the one with the knife.

Steven stared at him. "What treasure?" he asked.

"We shall start with you," the first man said, pointing to McKenna. "Last chance, Jew."

McKenna and Mickey moved in front of Steven. "You'll have to try to kill us the hard way," Mickey said.

"Very well," said the first man, drawing his finger along the blade of his knife, grinning. "You will be second, child." He started forward, raising the knife, looking right into Mickey's eyes.

Lights and colors swirled in the man's mind. He found himself standing on a scaffold surrounded by a crowd of jeering Americans. His hands were tied behind him. Someone seized him from behind and forced him to his knees. As he watched, a man with startling green eyes mounted the platform. To his horror, this man drew forth a large jeweled sword. Someone pushed his head onto a stump of oak. The man heard the blade whistling...

Mickey jerked out of the man's mind, leaving him in the beheading scene. In the next second the man started screaming.

The second man started forward, menacing with his knife. Mickey braced himself to deflect his attack. McKenna, though, took two fast steps and launched a blinding fast kick, which broke the man's wrist and knocked the knife from his hand. In almost the same motion she scissor-kicked him under the chin and snapped his head back so hard Mickey thought she might have decapitated him. The man fell backwards, stunned.

Then powerful hands seized both of the men and lifted them high into the air. The hands twisted them in midair and slammed them hard onto the asphalt of the alley.

The two Arabs looked up into the eyes of three gigantic men. "Stay right there, you son of a bitch," growled Durango, who'd burst into the alley followed by his two friends Mini and Rush.

Durango stepped forward and hugged McKenna. "Are you all right, Honey?"

"Yeah, Durango. Thank you."

"I saw you kick the knife away from this clown," said Durango. "Nice move."

"I'll say," Mickey said. He was still shocked at how well McKenna had handled herself. She grinned at him, then turned and hugged Steven, who was standing in an apparent daze.

Now three police officers rushed into the alley. They spun the men over and yanked their arms behind their backs. The officers twisted plastic ties onto their wrists. The second man screamed with the pain to his broken wrist.

The police hauled the two to their feet, both of them still shaking their heads. The impact of being slammed hard to the ground left them groggy.

Anna and Rand came down the alley. Anna ran to McKenna. Rand and Mickey turned to embrace Steven, who was trembling with the violence of the encounter. Casey joined them a minute or two later. He'd gone after the leader.

"I saw him until he reached the pier," said Casey. "Then he disappeared into the crowd."

The group returned to *Galaxy*. When their group went in to

dinner that night, Mickey could see that McKenna and Steven were still shaken. Nonetheless, Mickey grinned as he watched them eat a fair portion of rack of lamb.

The third man avoided capture.

* * * * *

The third Arab, Mohammed Awad, sprinted down the street when his henchmen took the girl and the two men out to kill them. He dodged into several crowds and cut through a couple of stores to make sure he hadn't been followed.

Reaching the main street, he sprinted east from the main harbor to the second harbor, about a half mile away.

He reached the dock and hurried to the third boat in line.

The crew cast off and the speedboat sped off toward a yacht which had been following *Galaxy* for two days, remaining just out of sight of the huge ship. An exceptionally wealthy business man owned the yacht. He sympathized with the need to rid the world of Western influence and had loaned it to Awad for this adventure.

As Awad came aboard, he spoke to the others in Arabic. "Well?"

"No word yet," came the reply.

Mohammed Awad cursed. The henchmen should have called by now. That they hadn't could mean only one thing.

Failure.

He gritted his teeth in fury. He went to the main salon of the yacht and reported to the Sheik. A little later, the yacht weighed anchor and headed toward Florida.

Two nights later, Awad rode the speedboat as it came into shore near Lantana Beach on the east coast of Florida, south of

Palm Beach. The quiet beach, bordered on the west by beautiful homes, was deserted except for a beautiful woman. She flashed a light twice when a man aboard the power boat flicked a powerful flashlight on and off.

Awad dropped overboard in the dark night and waded ashore. The boat departed, heading back to the yacht that waited a few miles off shore.

The woman met him and handed him a towel and a terry-cloth shirt which matched his swimming trunks. She gave him a small beach bag which contained a wallet and several other identifying papers for him. The two linked arms and walked toward the pier at Lake Worth. If anyone saw them, they would appear to be an attractive couple strolling on a moonlit beach after he had taken a swim in the warm summer waters.

Awad found he was having a hard time concentrating on the mission. Astarte, the young woman posing as his wife, was his cousin. She was disguised as an American, wearing a skimpy bathing suit and a wrapper. "How are things here?" he managed to ask.

"No problem," she said.

"He remains infatuated with you?" he asked.

"Obsessed." They laughed at the stupidity of the American. The news didn't surprise Awad. Two high-priced New York City prostitutes had instructed Astarte in sexual techniques. "He believes that I am traveling to sell computer software."

"When do you see him next?"

"Two days from now in Charleston. When the boat docks, he will follow the young Jew."

"Will he help?"

"Without doubt. He is greedy. He believes he is going to

come into fabulous wealth." They smiled. The two American henchmen would die as soon as the gang found the treasure.

She linked her arm through his, smiling and talking to him as if they were in love. At the pier they climbed into her car and headed inland.

Still no word from the men. Awad stroked his beard, considering. At least they didn't know the overall plan. If they'd been captured, they couldn't betray the mission.

CHAPTER 40

Rand and Mickey joined Steven and McKenna for breakfast the morning after the attack by the two Arab men. Durango and Mini sat near them at a deck table, playing gin rummy but also keeping an eye on McKenna and her friend as they ate breakfast.

"They still haven't found that one guy who ran off?" asked McKenna.

Mickey shook his head. "I doubt they will," Mickey said. He took a sip of coffee.

"How did he get away?" asked Steven. He forked a little egg into his mouth.

"Hard to say," Mickey said. "But these clowns never operate alone. There's an organization operating here."

"Why were they after us?" asked McKenna, biting at a piece of pineapple.

Mickey hesitated. "They were after you, Steven. I felt it in the man's mind. McKenna and I just happened to be there."

Steven's mouth dropped open. "Me?"

"Yeah. They think you know about a treasure. Also I do know something is special about you. I don't know how they would know it, though."

"Do you know why they wanted to kill you?" McKenna asked Steven.

"I'm a Jew," he shrugged. "For terrorists like those guys,

that is sufficient."

"There's more to it than that," Mickey said.

"Do you know what he meant by asking me about the treasure?" Steven asked him.

"I think so. He means the treasure of the pirate Sandy Gordon, hidden somewhere in the Isle of Shoals. I think they believe that you might know something about that."

"I don't know anything about it," asserted Steven.

"Sure," Mickey said. "If you knew where it was, you'd go get it."

"I do have Sholem's writings," said Steven. "They are prized possessions in our family, as you will imagine, and I've read them many times. He didn't mention any treasure."

* * * * *

McKenna invited Steven to accompany her and her family on a boat trip over to Norman Island after *Galaxy* docked in Tortolla. The Fixx family went ashore and found their tour.

"This is a famous island, even if no one has heard its name," said Mickey.

"What does that mean?" asked McKenna.

"Norman Island is the island that Robert Louis Stevenson used as the model island for his book, *Treasure Island*," said Mickey. The group grinned at him.

"Try to ignore him," teased Rand. "He can't help it. He's an English teacher."

The group laughed.

McKenna learned to snorkel in no time. Steven had some trouble with his mask at first but joined her in a few moments to explore a small cave. Rand and Mickey swam near them.

Later that morning McKenna and Steven sat together in a bus careening along the road from the snorkeling trip at Norman Island. "Those terrorists wanted to kill you," she said.

"It's nothing new," he said with a shrug.

"Why do Arabs hate Jews?" asked McKenna.

"The answer goes back farther into history than anyone remembers," he said. "And it hasn't improved since Israel declared statehood in 1948." He talked for a while about the conflict in the Middle East over the state of Israel.

"Life must be hard on the Palestinians," said McKenna.

"It's an example of how life shouldn't be led, I agree," said Steven.

"Wasn't the land owned by the Palestinians before Israel supplanted them?" asked McKenna.

"What do you mean?" asked Steven, puzzled.

"Well, they call Israel's presence an occupation," she said. "Israel refers to it as disputed territory."

"Right," he nodded.

"The Palestinians also refer to themselves as freedom fighters."

"I know," he said. "They also like to compare themselves to the American Founding Fathers like Jefferson, Thomas Paine, and Nathan Hale."

"Was the land ever owned by the Palestinians?"

"No," Steven assured her. "On the other hand, the land did belong to the Jews centuries ago. Archeology always bears out the Biblical records."

"It does?" she asked.

"Oh sure," Steven said. "For example: in January of 2003, a polished black stone was found on Temple Mount. It was inscribed by a Hebrew King named Jehoash. Some Arabs found it during some excavation on Temple Mount. They tried to destroy the stone."

"Why would they do that?" asked McKenna.

"The stone strengthens the basis of the claim of Israel to Jerusalem," said Steven. "The Palestinians, though, say that Israel has no claim to Jerusalem, let alone Mount Moria, where the Dome of the Rock stands."

"Was the stone for sure a relic?"

"Oh yes. It was inscribed with authentic Ancient Hebrew. It was similar to other writing used on Moabite stones."

"Who was this king?"

"In Hebrew, it's Jehoash," said Steven, pronouncing it in the ancient language. He told her about the king. "He came to the throne at the age of seven, reigned for 40 years and worked to rebuild the temple when the priests didn't follow through on the repairs. He was assassinated by two officials in his cabinet."

McKenna digested this for a while. "What do the Palestinians want?" asked McKenna.

"Most news sources believe that they want a homeland and control over holy sites in Jerusalem."

"Like that mosque on Temple Mount?"

"The Dome of the Rock, yes," Steven nodded. "Most Israelis, however, regard those reasons as phony excuses for rioting, trouble-making and land grabbing."

"Land grabbing?"

"Sure," said Steven. "Prior to the 1967 Arab-Israeli war there was no movement for a Palestinian homeland. During that war, Israel captured Judea, Samaria and East Jerusalem."

"From the Palestinians?"

"No. The land belonged to King Hussein of Jordan at that time."

McKenna thought. "Then before that time?"

"No. Palestine has never been an autonomous state. The term Palestine was first coined by the Romans. They took it from the term 'Philistine.'"

"Oh," said McKenna. "As in David and Goliath."

"Right, and the story of Samson and Delilah and a hundred others, I guess," said her friend. "In 70 A. D., the Romans began their genocide against the Jews. You know the story. They crucified Jews until they ran out of wood for crosses."

"Yuck," McKenna shuddered.

"The Romans also smashed the Temple and declared that Israel was no more. Nonetheless, never in all of history did Palestine exist as autonomous. Beginning in the first century the land was ruled by the Romans, then Islamic and Christian Crusaders, then the Ottoman Empire, then after World War I, the British. There is no Palestinian language, nor has there ever been a Palestinian state governed by the Palestinians."

"What are they then?" asked McKenna.

"The Palestinians are Arabs like the Jordanians, Syrians, Lebanese, and the Iraqis. The Arabs control more than 99% of the land in the Mideast. Israel comprises about 1/10 of one percent of the landmass."

"The Arabs want it all though."

"Yes," said Steven. "The fighting is about greed, pride, envy and covetousness. Israel could never concede enough land."

* * * * *

Galaxy docked on Saturday morning. McKenna and her

family were among the first of the groups to disembark. Their luggage sat waiting for them.

McKenna hugged her parents and promised to be careful. She was elated to spend some more time with her friend Steven. Also, she looked forward to getting to know her new Aunt Rand and Uncle Mickey.

Casey and Anna departed for the airport along with Cheyenne and her husband as well as Cinnamon and the three bikers who were moaning about how much money they'd dropped in the casino. Durango hugged McKenna.

"Watch yourself," he said. "I don't think we've seen the last of that one guy."

"We took care of his buddies anyhow," shrugged McKenna. "Besides no one knows where we're going."

"Uh huh," said Durango. He exchanged glances with Rush and Mini.

Rand and Mickey agreed that they would meet Steven and McKenna in a few days. They were going home to Geneva to pick up Mickey's car and settle their son in with Anna and Casey. Joey was excited to stay with them, to the relief of Rand and Mickey.

McKenna hugged them goodbye. Then she joined Steven and his family for the drive north to their apartment in New York City.

CHAPTER 41

Rand and Mickey stayed busy packing the next afternoon. Mickey hoped to leave for New York in a day or two, depending on how Joey adjusted to the idea of his parents being gone. As far as either one of them could tell, the boy seemed ecstatic about spending time with Anna and Casey.

Anna's kindness to her new nephew impressed both Rand and Mickey. She read to Joey, took him for walks, fussed over him and spoke to him with kindness and love. He responded in kind.

Mickey mentioned how impressed he was with her gift with children. She shrugged. "I don't know that it's a gift. My father once told me that people are attracted to you if they feel safe with you. I just try to make him feel safe."

"It's working," Mickey said.

They had arranged for Joey to stay overnight with Anna and Casey so they could see how he handled the situation. Early in the afternoon, Mickey and Rand worked to pack for New Hampshire. Mickey had just picked up a couple of sweatshirts and was folding them into a duffel bag when the phone rang.

"Mickey. Thank God." John Morinec, his high school buddy and insurance man.

"Hey, John," Mickey said, puzzled at the obvious relief in his voice.

"I've been worried sick about you. Is everything okay?

Rand? The boy?"

"Yeah, sure it is," smiled Mickey. "What's up?"

"Where in hell have you been?"

"We went with Rand's family to the Caribbean on a cruise. Everything's okay. What's wrong?"

John paused. "I need to see you. Could we have dinner tonight?"

Mickey covered the mouthpiece and asked Rand.

"Sure," she shrugged. "We have to eat, you know."

Mickey suggested the Tribella restaurant in Batavia, not far from their home. Mickey gave John directions and they agreed to meet at seven. "Get a table for five," said John.

"Five? Why five?" said Mickey, but his friend had hung up.

* * * * *

Rand and Mickey were sitting in the bar with cocktails when John blew in. He had a beautiful woman with him. Another guy followed them.

"Hi, Mickey," the woman said, shy. "Do you remember me?"

Mickey recognized the voice. He'd heard it first when he was fourteen years old and in a study hall in the library at Harlan High School. She had been one of his best friends through high school.

"Paula?" He asked. She giggled and hugged him.

"I was afraid you'd forgotten me," she said. "It's been a while."

He gawked like a yokel at her. "Paula?" Mickey said again, stunned with surprise. "What are you doing here?"

"John asked us to come. I was thrilled to see you again." She turned and took the hand of the handsome, crew-cut guy. "I want you to meet my husband, Rusty Ivers."

Mickey shook hands with Rusty. From his posture and military look, Mickey guessed that he was a cop.

"Yeah," Rusty said. "I met Paula not long after her husband died."

"Frank died?" Mickey asked.

Paula nodded. She didn't seem too distressed. She held out her left hand. Mickey saw the diamond on her ring finger. "Terrific," Mickey said, and meant it. Rusty seemed like a perfect guy for her.

Lauren, the Tribella hostess, came over. "Are you ready, Mickey?"

"Yes," he said. Lauren showed them to their table. Mickey kept an eye on Rusty fussing over Paula. He treated her with kindness and gentleness, holding her chair and offering his arm. Though Mickey could tell that she liked him a great deal, Mickey thought Rusty looked smitten with her. Not that Mickey blamed him. Paula was exquisite.

John grew serious. "Mickey, Rand," he said. "You have no idea how glad I am to see you." He began to tell his story. Frankie's death. The murder of Albert Thomas. Kidd's electrocution. The interviews with Paula and with Mrs. Thomas.

"Now," he said, turning to Rand. He took her hand. He bit his lip, struggling for words. "There's something else."

"What?" she said, growing tense.

"I'm sorry," he said. "I heard from the Texas State Police. They told me that your ex-husband had been killed in a house fire in Dallas."

Rand sat motionless, folding and refolding her napkin as

John filled in some details.

"Honey?" Mickey said stroking her arm. "You okay?"

She gave him a blank stare. "Mickey?" she said. "What do I say to Joey?"

"We'll tell him together, I promise."

She hugged him. "Thank you." She turned back to John. Despite her distress, she mumbled, "Do you have any other details?"

"He had a huge insurance policy," said John, consulting a notebook. "The beneficiary was someone named Marisa Mitchell. She also went to high school with us."

Rand squeezed Mickey's arm hard. Mickey shot her a glance. She'd flushed with what Mickey thought was anger. John asked him, "Do you remember her?"

"Oh, yeah, I think so," Mickey nodded. "Sort of quiet and mousey? In all kinds of art classes and a good student."

"That's her," said John. "I don't think they were married. Marisa used to work with Larry at his graphics arts studio in LaJolla."

"Did she have a brother?" Mickey asked.

"I don't know," John said. "Why?"

"Rand?" Mickey said.

"Some time ago I was--" she swallowed and considered her napkin "--involved with someone named Martin Mitchell."

"Martin Mitchell?" said Rusty, narrowing his eyes a bit. "Tall guy, dark hair with blond tips, thin, good muscles, pretty good with women?"

Rand shot him a quick look. "Yes."

"A man named Martin Mitchell used to play golf at my club. Good athlete, pretty fair golfer. Word got around that he'd cheat anytime he could. Most of the regular guys at the course wouldn't get into a money game with him."

"Did he go by the name of Mitch?" Rand asked.

"Yeah," said Rusty. "I haven't seen him for maybe five years. I heard he'd skipped town." Rand and Mickey again exchanged glances.

"Do you know why?" Mickey asked.

Rusty waved his hand. "I don't know for sure," Rusty said. "I heard some rumors he'd gotten in trouble with some big gambling debts."

Rand looked distressed at hearing about a man with whom she'd been intimate. She bit her lip. Mickey squeezed her hand.

"Do you know if this Mitch had any family?" Mickey asked.

Rusty gnawed at his lower lip, and furrowed his brow. "I think he did mention that he had a sister. Something about the West Coast." He turned to Paula to make sure she was comfortable. She gave him a radiant smile.

As the waiter distributed their dinners, Mickey mused a bit about Paula, who had remained a friend with him through graduation. Mickey couldn't get over how beautiful she'd become now. She had a gentle softness in her features, a glow. Mickey could tell Rand liked her too.

Rand and Mickey slid the conversation to happier topics. Paula sat forward in her chair, excited and bubbly. She loved this social occasion with another couple, having fun, laughing.

Mickey sighed. Thinking about what her life had been like with that creep Frankie touched him. This outgoing, happy person had been submerged in a miserable existence for so long.

CHAPTER 42

After dinner Paula and Rusty made their excuses. They had about a forty-five minute drive to get home. Mickey hugged her good-bye and agreed to try to stay in touch. Rand promised.

"Well?" John asked when the couple had left the restaurant. "What did you think of Paula?"

"I've never seen her happier," Mickey said.

"Yeah. Frankie treated her like hell. I think he beat her sometimes, though she doesn't talk about it."

"Figures," said Mickey. "He was a bum in high school. I never understood why she wanted anything to do with him."

"Her parents pushed her into the marriage," said John. "They thought she'd never amount to anything, didn't want to pay for college, wanted her out of the house, all that They were idiots."

Mickey snorted with contempt.

"Anyhow, Frankie left her a life insurance policy that left her fixed pretty well for finances. Still Frankie's death feels real strange."

"Strange?" Rand said.

John nodded. "I think someone is killing people we went to high school with."

Mickey and Rand stared for a moment. "Said what?" said Mickey.

John shrugged now. "That's why I was so worried about

you. Tell me. Do you have a large life insurance policy with Nebraska Life?"

Mickey blinked in surprise. "No, I don't. I've never heard of the company."

"Look at this." John flipped a piece of paper to him.

Mickey and Rand stared in shock at the paper. It related that he owned a life insurance policy worth $500,000. The beneficiary was someone named Martin Scarletti, a cousin.

"Who is Martin Scarletti?" Rand asked. Mickey shook his head, baffled.

"I don't have a cousin, as far as I know," said Mickey. "Certainly, no one named Martin Scarletti."

"We tried to run this guy down," said John. "His address is a mailbox franchise in Boulder, Colorado."

Mickey was stunned. "I don't know anyone who lives anywhere near Boulder," said Mickey. "I've never heard of this company."

"Right," said John. "I spoke to our agent who wrote the life insurance policy for Frankie. He took the information over the phone. Frankie sent him a money order. The agent never met him, but a guy who looked like Frankie, same build, size, eye color and hair showed up for the physical. But the doctor couldn't swear that Frankie himself had showed up when I showed him the picture.

"Besides agents don't ask real serious probing questions when they're writing policies this big. Oh sure, they do routine checks for identification. But the checks are mostly superficial. They also ask about some health issues: say cancer, AIDS, or heart conditions. But Mickey, the premium was gigantic and therefore so was the agent's commission. I'm sure the agent was spending the commission as he was writing the policy. Frankie—well, whoever appeared at the physical and said claimed to be Frankie—seemed to be healthy, and besides, who's going to buy a policy for someone else?"

John sipped at a liqueur. "The scene showed no sign of suicide," he continued. "No note, no warning behaviors, anything. Guys at his office said they never saw anything different in him. Then one day he went hunting—something he never did before--and didn't come back. He carried an expensive rifle—a Remington .12 gauge-- and they can't figure where he got it. He didn't ask the farmer who owns the field for permission to hunt there. He parked his car off the road, hidden from view. The police found no fingerprints in the car but his, and of course Paula's too.

"The state cops called it a simple hunting accident in the absence of any other true evidence to the contrary. Frankie knew zilch about guns. They figured the most probable explanation was that he had an accident and blew his head off."

Mickey looked John in the eye. "Johnny, Paula didn't kill Frankie."

John waved a dismissive hand. "No one suspects her. She's covered for the day he disappeared. A girlfriend from her church came over for dinner, and Paula was at least an hour away from the death scene when Frankie bought it."

"I'm glad she's in the clear," Mickey said.

"We don't have a thing to go on here except my suspicions. I've developed a sense for fraud. I just don't know how it's working here. Three deaths, or four with Larry, with no common denominator except that the guys knew each other in high school."

Rand said, "You don't think Paula wants to defraud you, do you? I mean, she's too smart to take out an insurance policy on her husband and then have him killed to collect."

John shook his head. "I'm sure she didn't come up with the plan. Besides she's married to a state cop. I checked him out too. He's sharp. If she's committed insurance fraud, she wouldn't marry someone like him who could find out."

The waitress came over. Johnny grabbed the check and gave her his Visa card. She retreated.

"The guy who was killed in the supposed boat accident was a guy named Mohammed Awad," John said. "Homeland Security sent me a picture."

"They know about him?" Mickey asked.

"Oh, yeah. He was a known terrorist. They'd been looking for him for a long time. Rumors had him living in this country under an assumed name." He reached into his briefcase and pulled out a photograph, which he handed it to them.

Mickey stared at the picture. Mickey remembered sitting in the café on St. Thomas. He'd just told McKenna and Steven the story of Owen and Martha and Sholem. Three Arab guys were sitting across from them. . .

"John," Mickey said. "This guy didn't die in the Pacific Ocean."

"What do you mean?"

"He just hired two guys to kill me and my niece and her friend on St. Thomas." He told John the story of the incident in the alley in the Virgin Islands.

"That explains the insurance policy," said John, his face grim.

John promised he was going to call Homeland Security and

give them a heads-up on Awad. Rand and Mickey said goodnight and headed for home.

"I'm scared, Mickey," said Rand.

"Yeah. Me too."

"If that guy and Larry staged this boat accident with this Marisa, why wouldn't Larry stage his death? Collect the life insurance there too?"

CHAPTER 43

McKenna stood with Steven in the window of the World Financial Center, gazing out on the crater that had once been the World Trade Center.

After the confrontation with the Arab men on the boat, she felt she needed to understand the Muslim anger against the US and Israel. She'd asked Steven to bring her to Lower Manhattan.

Steven put an arm around her. "You okay?" he asked, seeing her eyes moisten.

"Steven, it's so big," said McKenna. "I couldn't begin to imagine how big it was from the pictures."

"On 9/11, a friend of our family was trapped on the subway for about eight hours on the other side of Manhattan," Steven told her. "They didn't know what was happening. Cell phones didn't work down there, transistor radios weren't working. A lot of them thought that New York had been hit with a nuclear attack."

"This is almost as bad as a nuclear attack," said McKenna.

"Yeah," said Steven. "One fire company sent their guys down here. They all died."

"All of them?" said McKenna.

"Not only that," said Steven. "Lots of people saw bodies falling and heard them hitting the ground. Many of the witnesses haven't recovered from the horror of that day."

The friends walked down to a plywood wall at the north of

the crater. McKenna read some of the graffiti.

"Have you been to Pearl Harbor?" asked Steven with reverence.

"No," said McKenna. "My mom went there with my father once. I saw the pictures."

"I've been there," said Steven. "It's very different than it is here."

"Why?" asked McKenna.

"At Pearl Harbor, the Japanese had a very specific purpose. Don't get me wrong, now. I don't condone it, much less endorse it, but I do understand it. Do you follow me?"

McKenna thought for a moment. She said, "Go on. I think I know what you mean."

"The Japanese wanted to neutralize the influence of the U. S. in the Pacific," said Steven. "They wanted control of Guam and the Mariana Islands as well as other places including Manchuria in China. They thought that if they could annihilate the American Pacific fleet, they could take over in the Western Pacific and get so entrenched that they couldn't be ousted."

"I studied that in American History in high school," McKenna nodded.

"They carried out a vicious, well-planned and well-executed attack," Steven went on. "However the Japanese underestimated the way that America would respond, as did the Muslim fanatics who were behind the attack here."

They walked along a chain-link fence to a gate. Ten yards away was a makeshift shrine with flowers, pictures and other memorials. As they watched, a woman with two teenaged men walked to the gate. A uniformed security man unlocked the gate from the inside and bowed her out.

The woman didn't speak to them. She held her sons' hands and walked past them without a glance. McKenna spoke to the guard. "What is that place?"

"It's private for the families of those who died in the towers," he said.

"Oh," said McKenna. She turned and looked at the retreating figure of the woman and her sons. "Oh my," she said. The guard nodded, then closed and locked the gate.

McKenna and Steven walked around the perimeter of the World Trade Center. Two men followed several yards behind them. McKenna didn't notice that they were watching them with intense care.

* * * * *

Mickey and Rand arrived at the Levins' apartment later that day. That evening they drove with McKenna, Steven and his parents to the Levins' summer home on Long Island. The cozy town of Southhold on the North Fork featured lovely walks, shops and restaurants.

After dinner, Mickey joined Steven and McKenna on the front porch of the house. He held out an antique copy of the *Tanach*. "Steven, I want you to look at my book," Mickey said. "It's supposed to tell us where to look. But if Owen wrote directions in it, I haven't seen it. It has some marginal notes in Hebrew, which I can't read."

Steven took the old book with some reverence. It was leather bound, the pages brown and brittle with age. He opened it and leafed through it, being as gentle as possible. "What am I looking for?" Steven asked, turning the pages.

"A note from my great grandfather Owen. Something about

where the treasure is buried. But nobody's ever found a note or a clue."

"Huh," said Steven. "I need to spend some more time with this."

"According to the family legend the treasure was buried on White Island at first," Mickey said. "That's where Martha hid it when she came to the mainland after the British Navy executed Gordon. When Martha saved Owen from slavery, they came back and moved it to a safer location. No one knows where," Mickey admitted.

CHAPTER 44

McKenna woke up early the next day and found her uncle in the kitchen drinking coffee. "Genetic," he said. "I always wake up earlier than I need to." McKenna smiled, and she and Mickey changed into sweats. They ran a few miles together through the quiet streets of Southold.

Later, she and the rest of the group drove to the ferry. From there, they went over to Shelter Island. On the south side of Shelter they took another ferry to the Hamptons. Rand and Mickey left McKenna and Steven in the Hamptons and went off to shop and sightsee.

Steven drove McKenna to the lighthouse at Montauk. They parked in the lot and walked to the beach.

"How beautiful," said McKenna. "It's so poetic here." The waves were gentle, and a breeze off the ocean invigorated the two of them. The rocky beach lay at the bottom of a path from the parking lot.

"I know," said Steven. "The waves are high and furious in the winter. The snow and the ice give way to the beauty of the spring and summer."

Steven took her hand and they walked together along to the rocky beach. The rocky shore forced them to be careful where they stepped.

Steven spread a blanket. They took out a couple of sandwiches and enjoyed a picnic. They watched several small fishing boats offshore and listened to the call of the gulls.

McKenna took his face in her hands. She kissed him. "I've wanted to do that since we met," she told him.

The next kiss also went well. When she backed up, she could see how delighted he was. She grinned at him.

Two men leered at them from a distance. One of them turned to the other and made a pumping motion with his hand. They laughed. The laughter provided a nice break from the tedium of following the two young people.

* * * * *

The next day Mickey drove the group to Orient Point at the northeast end of the upper fork of Long Island. They took the ferry across to Connecticut. Resisting the impulse to spend time in New London and Mystic, they focused on driving on I-95 up through Rhode Island, past Boston and into New Hampshire. They found a hotel in Portsmouth.

They took a suite with two bedrooms, and a fold-out couch. Rand and Mickey took one bedroom and McKenna took the other. Steven agreed to sleep in the living room on the foldout couch. Before dinner, they visited a local Sears store and purchased shovels, picks and assorted digging supplies.

Two men watched them, staying out of sight.

* * * * *

Rand shook him awake. Mickey heard the banging on the door to their room. Groggy, Mickey fumbled for his glasses on the bedside table. He looked at the alarm clock on the table. 2:00 A. M.

Rand slipped into pajamas and a robe. She shuffled over and

opened the door. Mickey saw Steven standing there, wearing a T shirt and pajama bottoms, holding the *Tanach* and a magnifying glass.

"Steven," she groaned. "It's two A. M."

"I know. But this can't wait. Get Mickey."

"I'm here, Steven," Mickey said, tugging a robe on over his Tee shirt and boxers as he walked to the door. "Is the hotel on fire?"

"I don't think so," grinned Steven, all but dancing into their bedroom. "I think I know where the treasure is," he said. "Or at least where Owen's note is. Look here," said Steven. He sat at the table and opened the *Tanach*.

He pointed to an underlined passage. "It's from Exodus," Steven said. "The first reference to the staff." He walked to Rand's side of the bed and opened the drawer in the bedside table. He pulled out the Gideon Bible and leafed through it. "In the Christian text it's called Exodus chapter 4, verse 2. Moses is at the Burning Bush."

"I remember the passage," Mickey said, adjusting his glasses. He looked where Steven was pointing in the Hebrew text. In the margin Mickey saw a couple of characters written in Hebrew. They tried not to laugh at Steven's enthusiasm.

"What does it mean?"

"It says 'under front'," said Steven.

"Well?" said Rand.

"Well, look," said the young man.

He turned to the cover of the book and saw the usual binding paper glued to the cover. "Still not tracking," Mickey said. "Better spell it out."

"Here," said Steven, handing him a glass and pointing to the bottom of the page. "See that?" A small stain was visible at the bottom.

"So what?"

"It's a tiny bit of glue."

Mickey's brain began to function now. "I get it. You think Owen pulled up the binding paper and--"

"Yeah. It's your book, Mickey. You ought to open it up."

Mickey was as excited as Steven was at this point. Mickey crossed the room to their luggage. He took a razor knife out of his camping gear and came back.

Steven jerked a floor lamp over next to the table. "Wait," said Steven. "Let me get McKenna. . ." he said as he ducked to the bedroom next door in the suite. He banged hard on McKenna's door.

He was back in less than a minute with the bleary-eyed redhead, who was pulling on a bathrobe over her nightgown. While the others watched and chatted, Mickey went to work cutting away the glue that held the paper to the cover. It took him several moments.

At last the page was free. Mickey pulled it back, being careful and going slow. Under the endpaper, Mickey found a thin sheet of old onionskin paper. Mickey recognized the characters as Hebrew, and saw Owen's now familiar signature at the bottom of the page. "Yep," Mickey said. "There's writing on it."

Steven took the paper and adjusted his glasses on his nose. He looked over the Hebrew characters.

He looked up and smiled. "It's a letter from Owen, all right. He greets you, Mickey. He writes that Grandfather Sholem and Martha helped him move the treasures to Sugar Island. We have to find the pine tree."

"There must be lots of pine trees out there," said Rand.

"I didn't say it made sense. Below the pine tree we'll find your grandfather's initials. We have to dig below the initials. Then we look into the light."

"It sure doesn't make sense," McKenna said.

Mickey shrugged. "Let's hope we figure it out when we get over there," he said.

CHAPTER 45

In the morning, they decided to go out to the Isle of Shoals to look around for a clue. They headed to the dock.

Mickey rented a small cabin cruiser, which negotiated the ten miles to the Isle of Shoals without difficulty. They anchored at Sugar Island and walked to the top of the uninhabited rock.

In the distance they could see Star Island, the largest of the islands in the chain where a hotel and retreat center stood. White Island with its famous lighthouse stood to the east. "I'll have to go to Star Island," he said. "Martha is buried there. I'd like to see her grave." Rand nodded.

As they approached Sugar Island, they saw no sign of a pine tree or even a place with enough soil where one could grow. They took a few seconds to organize a search. Steven and McKenna started to walk around the north side of the Island. Rand and Mickey strolled in the opposite direction.

They realized that they weren't seeing any signs of life or even human visitation to the island. Nothing loomed up at all. "Are we going to have to scour this rock on our hands and knees?" asked Rand.

"Maybe," Mickey frowned. "I think maybe the clue would have to be somewhat obscure to keep people from finding it by accident."

After about twenty minutes McKenna called out. "Hey.

Here's a big hole."

Rand and Mickey marked their location and came across to her. The hole was about five feet across. Steven knelt and shone a flashlight inside. "I can see down to the bottom," he said. "No water. Looks like sand on the floor of a cave."

"How deep?" said Rand.

"Hard to say," Steven said. "Perhaps fifteen, twenty feet or more."

"Does anyone see any point in investigating the hole?" Mickey asked. No one did.

Rand and Mickey went back to their mark and resumed their search.

* * * * *

McKenna, still kneeling by the hole, looked up. She saw a small cliff several yards away and walked over. The tide was full and gentle waves broke against the rocks below. A ledge lay several feet below her with a large pile of rocks of various sizes. The rocks were the size of softballs and basketballs.

Something struck her as strange about the pile of rocks. She didn't know what it was.

She turned around and walked back toward the hole. Some grooves cut into the rock at her feet attracted her attention. She knelt down to look closer at the marks. The grooves were old and well weather worn. But. . .

She saw that these were not natural marks. Though the marks were obviously extremely old, she could see that someone had chiseled them into the rock.

They resembled like a pine tree.

She jogged back to the cliff and peered over at the ledge

again. The ledge was about eight feet wide and extended several feet in both directions. But only the one place had a pile of rocks.

"Steven," she called.

"Ayuh?" he said as he trotted over. She giggled at his use of the local dialect.

"I'm going to climb down to that ledge," she told him.

"Why?"

"Look at the pile of rocks."

Steven studied it for a few moments. The light went on. "You think someone stacked them there?"

"They don't look like a natural formation." She took his hand and pulled him to the mark on the ground. "Does that look like it was chiseled into the ground?"

He knelt and looked. "Hm," he nodded. He jogged a few yards away and brought back a handful of sand. He poured it into the marks and smoothed it. A picture emerged.

"Well?" he said.

She peered over his shoulder at the marks. "It sure looks like a pine tree to me."

"Me, too." He pointed at the little cliff. "And the tip of the tree points toward that cliff where the rocks are piled. Let's climb down to the ledge."

The little cliff had plenty of handholds and they had an easy climb to the ledge. The two friends dropped onto the ledge and approached the pile of rocks.

"Well?" said McKenna.

"Okay," said Steven. "I have a funny feeling."

"What do you mean?"

"I can't explain. Like an excitement. Let's pull the rocks

away."

They tugged at the rocks and let them fall over the side, where they bounced away and into the surf. Removing the rocks proved to be easy. In a few minutes they felt air blowing against their faces from behind the pile.

"A cave?" asked McKenna.

"I'd guess it leads to the hole we shined the light in."

Ten minutes later they had cleared an opening.

"What are you two doing down there?" came Rand's voice from above.

They looked up. "We found a cave," said McKenna. "The opening is about five feet high, maybe three feet wide."

Mickey and Rand clambered down the side of the cliff and joined them. McKenna wiped her hands on her jeans and turned to look out to sea.

She saw a beautiful yacht cruising by the island.

A little bell went off somewhere in her mind.

They hadn't seen any other boats out here. So what was this yacht doing here?

Her uncle interrupted her thoughts. "If nothing else," said Mickey, "it would be a good place to put our stuff if we decide we want to camp out here. . ."

"Yuck," said McKenna.

"No way," said Rand. "We're going back to the hotel. Hot showers, real bathrooms, restaurants. . ."

". . . Or to take shelter," finished Mickey with a grin. "Seems to be out of the wind."

CHAPTER 46

The four of them soon had the opening cleared. Steven seemed to be trembling with excitement. He climbed in first with Mickey right behind. The two women followed. The cave enlarged as they walked back into it, and in a few steps the four of them could walk side by side.

Steven took a flashlight from his backpack. He pointed it at the sand on the floor of the cave. "Look," he said. "Could those have been footprints?"

"It doesn't look like anyone has been in this cave for a long time," said Rand.

They walked down the passageway to where sunlight shone down on a pit of sand about twelve feet across. They found themselves in a circular room perhaps thirty feet in diameter.

Steven walked around the room. The cave continued back into the island beyond the room. "Hey," he said. He pointed to a crack in the floor. "When rainwater or waves crash in, the water drains into the crack and out to the sea."

"Let's get the supplies," Mickey said. Steven and Mickey retreated down the passageway to the mouth of the cave.

* * * * *

Within a few moments McKenna heard them yell down from the hole at the top. Down came all the shovels and picks, along with some canned foods and juices and bottled water.

One can rolled to the side of the cave. McKenna walked over to pick it up. She shone her flashlight on it.

She stopped and stared for a moment.

"Rand, come here."

"What?" said Rand, joining her.

"Look," said McKenna.

Rand followed the beam of light. "I see them," she said. Two letters had been chiseled into the cave wall about a foot above a pile of rocks. O. M.

"Owen McClelland," said McKenna.

"Mickey. Steven," Rand yelled. "We found something!"

* * * * *

Mickey and Steven clambered down to the cave and joined them. "The treasure is supposed to be below the initials," said Steven.

A small pile of rocks lay below the initials. They removed the stones, which took a fair amount of time. In the small pit below the rocks, the sand was dry and they excavated it without difficulty. A foot or so down, they found water-proofed canvas, which might once have been white.

They used their hands to remove the rest of the sand around the canvas and pulled up the cloth. The canvas covered a leather case about four-and-a-half-feet long.

"What is it?" asked McKenna.

"I'm pretty sure the staff is inside," Mickey said.

"Open it, Steven," urged McKenna.

Steven, his hands trembling, pulled away the rotten canvas and opened the leather case. He drew forth the polished almond wood.

"We're looking at history, aren't we?" said Rand.

Mickey embraced Rand and McKenna as Steven stroked the wood. "This has been lost for centuries," Steven said.

"And now it goes into the fire," said a gravelly voice behind them, startling them all.

They turned to see three men and a woman standing at the entrance to the cave. The intruders pointed guns at them as they walked forward. Mickey recognized the first man from his picture.

"Hello, Awad," Mickey said.

Rand stared at one of the men. He was a little shorter than Mickey, with dark hair and a beard. "Larry?" she asked.

"Yes, hello, Rand," he sneered. "Hello, Logan. It's been a long time."

"Nowhere near long enough, Connor," said Mickey, stifling a desire to beat the hell out of his wife's ex-husband.

Larry waved a hand. "Of course, Rand, you'll recognize this man."

Rand choked as the other man came forward. He was about six-two, with short blond tipped hair. "Mitch," she said.

"Yes," said Mitch. "This is my sister," he said, indicating the woman.

"Marisa Mitchell," Mickey said.

"How sweet of you to remember, Logan," sneered Marisa. She had dyed red hair and an olive complexion. Her blue jeans and a leather jacket accentuated her striking figure. "I'm surprised you haven't forgotten all about me."

"No such luck," Mickey said. "You have changed, I will admit."

"Marisa," said Rand. "Yes. Of course. From the office party."

Mickey remembered the story of the night that Rand had first been intimate with Mitch. Her husband Larry had taken Marisa into his office.

"Enough of this. Tell us where the treasure is now. If you do, you will receive bullets to the head and be at peace," said Awad.

"And if we don't?" said McKenna.

"The alternative is slow torture," said Awad. "We will shoot individual body parts and let the agony work on you."

"You'd torture me, Larry?" said Rand. "You'd leave your son an orphan?" Larry didn't answer. He shifted his weight from foot-to-foot and avoided looking in her eyes.

"Now," said Awad, raising the pistol, "where is the treasure?"

"This is the treasure," Mickey said, pointing to the staff in Steven's hand.

"A stick?" said Awad with a thin smile. The cave was too dark for Mickey to see his eyes to Paik him. Mickey had to try to pull him into the light.

Awad fired the pistol in the general direction of McKenna. She screamed as the bullet whizzed by her head. "The next one will be aimed at the child's shoulder."

Mickey grabbed McKenna and Rand and shoved them behind him. "The staff is the treasure!" Mickey yelled. "There are no jewels! No gold! No silver! This is what we were looking for!"

Awad snorted with disgust. He turned to the other men. He pointed with his guns at the wall on the other side of the cavern. "Line them up over there. We shall start to kill them and continue to search ourselves." Larry and Mitch prodded them to the wall and backed away.

"Shoot the girl in the blue coat first," said Awad. "Perhaps that will loosen their tongues."

Larry and Mitch stepped back. They were looking to the right of the group. Mickey turned and followed their gaze. He saw nothing but the tunnel of the cave extending back into the darkness.

"Shoot," said Awad.

The rifles crashed in the enclosed cave. The smoke took several seconds to dissipate.

"Where did she go?" said Mitch. His mouth was open and his eyebrows raised. "I know we hit her." Mitch and Larry and Marisa stared down the cave. Their faces shadowed with fear.

"What are they looking at?" whispered Rand, holding his hand. Mickey put his arms around her.

"Shhh," muttered Steven. "Everything's going to be okay."

Mickey turned to him. Steven appeared taller, unafraid, and confident.

Awad shook his head, clearing his thoughts. He blinked several times. He drew himself up and seemed to recover. "Never mind. A trick of the light."

His cohorts didn't respond. Awad fired his pistol down the cave. At the noise, Larry and Mitch and Marisa jerked as if waking from a nap. "Shoot that girl," he said, pointing at McKenna.

The two men turned their rifles to McKenna. She drew herself up and stared at them without flinching.

"Last chance," said Awad. "Tell us where the treasure is."

"Shoot, you miserable excuse for a human," snarled McKenna. "At least I won't have to breathe the same air as you."

"Why are you protecting it?" said Awad. "Give us the treasure."

"You'll kill us anyway," said McKenna. "We aren't afraid of you. Get it over with."

Awad flipped a hand. "I tried to be merciful."

"Wait," Steven stepped in front of McKenna. He held up the staff. "Shoot me, cowards," he snarled. "I'm the Jew. I'm your enemy. Shoot me."

The three men and Marisa stared at the staff, their mouths agape, eyes wide, in apparent terror. They didn't move. Awad again managed to recover and shouted at them. They stirred and looked at Awad. He nodded. "Shoot the Jew," he sneered. The two men aimed their rifles at Steven and pulled the triggers.

Several clicks echoed in the cave as the men depressed their triggers. The guns didn't go off.

Awad turned to them, his face a mask of fury. "What are you waiting for?"

Larry and Mitch held their rifles, examining them. They shook them and whacked them with their hands. They tried again. Again clicks. "What the hell?" said Larry.

Awad seized the rifle from Mitch. He pointed the rifle at Steven, who didn't flinch in the least. Awad pulled the trigger.

Click.

Awad racked the slide and examined the weapon, turning it up and down. "Give me yours," he said to Larry. He pointed it at Steven and pulled the trigger.

Click.

Awad lifted his pistol. He aimed it at Steven and pulled the trigger.

Click.

"Strange, isn't it," said Steven. He held the staff before him. All four of them froze, staring at the almond wood staff. Steven tossed it toward Awad.

When the staff hit the ground, it clattered and then lay still.

The staff dissolved into a puddle. Then it reformed itself into a huge creature.

Chapter 47

For the rest of his life, Mickey could never describe the being to anyone else. He had a hard time looking at it. It burned with a light that filled the cave. About ten feet long, it seemed to have three pairs of wings. The creature had eyes in front and on its back and sides.

"What is it?" said McKenna, her voice hushed.

"It's a seraph," said Steven. "A creature of absolute purity. This is the creature that terrified Pharaoh and his court."

Marisa screamed as the seraph fixed some of its eyes on her. Mitch and Larry dropped their rifles and stood frozen against the wall.

Awad alone seemed able to talk, though his face turned the color of cold gravy. "What sorcery is this?" he mumbled, his back against the cave wall. He pointed his pistol and pulled the trigger.

Click.

The seraph lifted its front pair of wings and moved toward Marisa. She screamed and turned to run toward the mouth of the cave.

The seraph moved a fraction of an inch. A beam of red light shot from a pair of its eyes. The red light struck her in the back. An aura of ruby light enveloped her. She disappeared.

Now the creature turned toward Mitch. He backed away, screaming and holding up his hands. The red light lashed out again.

In a moment Mitch had vanished as well. The creature turned to Larry.

Steven strode forward and spoke to the creature. Mickey realized that he was speaking Hebrew. The seraph paused, waiting. Steven approached Awad and Larry, who crouched, trembling, against the wall. He took their guns away and handed them to Rand and Mickey.

Mickey pulled McKenna and Rand to him and hugged them.

Steven grasped one of the seraph's wings. The seraph stiffened and transformed again into a staff of almond wood. The glow in the cave faded. Rand and Mickey raised the rifles at the two cowering men. "On your feet, guys," Mickey snapped.

Awad looked into Steven's eyes. "A marvelous magic trick, Jew." He reached behind his back and yanked another gun from his belt.

He pulled the trigger four times. This time it went off.

The bullets stopped in front of Steven's face and hovered a moment in midair. Then they turned to the staff. The bullets smacked into the staff and dropped to the ground.

As Awad squeezed off his fourth shot, Mickey pulled the trigger on his rifle. A stream of bullets tore into Awad's knee. Awad collapsed, screaming as the bullets all but severed his leg. He dropped the gun and shrieked with agony. Steven came forward and picked the gun up.

Rand snapped. She rushed to Larry. She dragged him to his feet and pummeled him, screaming, out of control. Larry, too stunned to respond, tried to cover up his head and began to cry. By the time Mickey and Steven pulled her away, Larry's face was bloody and he sobbed with fear and pain and confusion, almost unconscious.

Mickey held her and whispered comfort to her until she regained her composure. Rand pulled out her cell phone from its little holster on her belt and called the Coast Guard.

* * * * *

They waited to come out of the cave until they heard the Coast Guard helicopter overhead about ten minutes later. They couldn't be sure that Awad hadn't stationed other thugs outside the cave. Mickey sure didn't want a gun battle.

When the chopper approached, they emerged and saw the yacht speeding away to the east. It had fled the scene when the choppers appeared. Another Coast Guard helicopter, a Sikorsky gunship, sped off in pursuit off the yacht. A cutter had set out and would take over the massive vessel.

The Coast Guard helicopter took off with Larry and Awad in custody, leaving the four of them. They told the crew that they would come back to Portsmouth in the rented cabin cruiser.

"Awad will lose his leg, I imagine," said Rand.

Mickey shivered, still a little shocky at having shot another person. Mickey hugged her. "That's all right," Mickey said. "He can ride a wheelchair to the execution chamber. But. . ." Mickey paused. "Something's troubling me, Honey," Mickey said.

"What?"

"Who were they shooting at?"

"That surprised me too," she said. "They shot down the tunnel of the cave. But they seemed to think they were shooting at someone, not just trying to scare us."

"Right, and something else just occurred to me" Mickey said.

Rand drew back. "What's that?"

"We stopped digging when we found the staff. Maybe the Urim and Thummin are still in the hole."

"Or maybe it's hidden somewhere else? Perhaps another island?"

"Or maybe--" Mickey got to his feet. "Steven," Mickey called. Steven and McKenna came over to them. "Would you know the Urim and Thummin if you saw it?" Mickey asked.

Steven pushed his glasses up, thinking. "I don't know. No one knows what it looks like."

"Come on," Mickey said.

The four of them climbed back down to the ledge and entered the cave. Steven hurried to the excavation where they'd found the staff. He peered in. "I think I see something else in there." He reached in the hole and began to clear sand away. In a few moments he withdrew a package, perhaps six inches wide and eight inches tall, wrapped in waterproofed canvas.

With great care, he removed the canvas. He uncovered an old book and examined it. "It's a Bible," said Steven.

"Why would Owen bury a Bible?" asked McKenna.

Steven opened the book. "There's writing inside the cover," he said. "It's a note written in Hebrew."

"Read it," urged Rand.

Steven cleared his throat. His hands again trembled with excitement. "'To whoever reads this: I pray this letter is in good hands and that you who read it are the one to whom the staff and the stone belong. I believe that all men will see Jerusalem as the City of Peace again and that the High Priest will return.'"

"I think that's you, Steven," said McKenna, taking his arm in hers.

"I'm just a kid," he said, and squeezed McKenna's hand on

his arm.

"How did you know how to use the staff?" Rand smiled.

"I don't . . . I mean, I just knew," he said, with a hand at his forehead. "There's more," he said.

"Keep reading," urged Rand, tapping the old Bible.

He adjusted his glasses and looked back down at the book. "'My wife promised to guard the treasure. My friend Sholem bound her with an oath to protect the staff and the Urim Stone until the High Priest frees her. The Son of Zadok will return when the time is right. Go to her on White Island. Set her free, Zadok.'"

"That's the legend of the ghost then," Mickey realized. "The ghost is supposed to say 'He will return.' Everyone has always thought that meant the pirate Sandy Gordon. But she's talking about the High Priest, the rightful owner of the staff and the Urim and Thummin. My grandmother. . ."

Steven put a comforting arm around his shoulders. Mickey felt confidence surge through him. "We'll go to her now," Steven said. "She can be at peace."

Now as Steven embraced him, a little light went on in Mickey's mind. "She was here, wasn't she?" Mickey said.

"Yes," said Steven, removing his glasses and wiping at his eyes. He rubbed the bridge of his nose. "Martha came to protect us and the treasure. She stood right there"—he pointed to the sand pit, which was bathed in sunlight—"and they aimed their first shots at her. She scared them to distraction. The Seraph was the final touch."

"Does the letter say anything else?" Mickey asked.

"There's a bit more," Steven said, putting his glasses back on. He resumed. "'We have hidden the remainder of the pirate treasure and the stone. Look into the light. You will see where it lies. Go with God who delivered me from the hand of slavery. Sincerely, Owen McClelland.'"

"Look into the light?" said McKenna.

They looked at the light that shone through the hole and illuminated the sand pit. "Could something be buried in there?" asked Rand, pointing to the sand that lay beneath the opening in the cave's roof.

Mickey rubbed his chin and thought it over. "I don't think so. Rain and surf would come in," he said.

They stepped into the pit and looked up into the light. A foot or so above their heads, Mickey saw a ledge. He leaped, caught the edge of the ledge and chinned himself. He saw a small opening stretching into blackness.

"There's a cave back in there," Mickey said. He let go and dropped to the sand.

McKenna said, "Boost me up there, guys."

Steven and Mickey cupped their hands. McKenna stepped into them, and they lifted her up. She pulled herself onto the ledge. "Flash," she said. Steven handed her a flashlight.

"I'm coming up too," called Rand. In a minute McKenna pulled her aunt next to her. They switched on their flashlights.

"We'll be right back," McKenna said. "We're going to crawl back into the cave."

A few moments later McKenna yelled down. "Watch out, guys. We found a block and tackle. The rope crumbled under our fingers."

They brought it back to the ledge and dropped the antique block and tackle over to Steven and Mickey. Then the two women went back into the cave.

In a few moments Rand came back, breathless with excitement. "We found it."

Mickey gave Steven a boost. Then he leaped and pulled himself up. They crawled into the small cave.

A seaman's chest sat against the back wall of the cave. A rusty lock sealed it shut.

CHAPTER 48

Rand and Mickey waded to the cabin cruiser. They grabbed a come-along and a block and tackle. Mickey carried a four-wheeled dolly ashore and to the hole. They carried the tools back to the cave.

It took about an hour to haul the heavy old chest up through the hole. They dragged it to the boat and hoisted it aboard.

Mickey started the engines and sped the cabin cruiser back to Portsmouth. Rand telephoned the Coast Guard, who said they'd be waiting.

Back in Portsmouth, the Coast Guard escorted them to a bank where they put the old chest into the main vault.

At six o'clock that evening, with local TV cameras watching, they cut the rusty old lock away. With some difficulty Steven and Mickey turned back the lid.

Gold and silver and jewels filled the chest about halfway. On top of the loot was an old leather case. Steven opened the case and extracted a translucent red stone.

"The Urim and Thummin," said Steven, lifting it with reverence.

* * * * *

Martha woke and felt The Dream begin again. She had experienced The Dream before. It seemed always to be the same. Had she had The Dream once? Or a million times? She couldn't remember.

Before she found herself here in the cabin on White Island, she recalled holding Owen's hand, with young John and David at her bedside. Sholem and his wife stood at the foot of her bed.

A coughing spasm took her breath away. Owen clutched her hand tight, tears on his cheeks. She saw wracking grief in his eyes.

"Owen," she gasped. "Please do not grieve. We will be together again, I promise."

"I know we will," her husband sobbed. "But this is too soon for you to leave."

"Dear ones," she struggled to speak a final blessing. "Walk in love as I have loved you. . ."

Then everything went dark, as if all the candles in the room had been extinguished at once. She knew she had fallen asleep, for The Dream came.

Once again she was on White Island, in the little cottage where her first husband, Gordon, had imprisoned her. She rose, feeling cold, but without pain.

She thought it strange that by no exertion of her will could she wake up from The Dream.

Martha walked out of the cottage. She didn't remember opening the door.

Making her way down the rocky path, she headed toward the lowest spot of the island.

As she went along, she realized that she remembered another dream. She had found herself in the cave on Sugar Island where the great treasures were hidden. Three men and a woman, dressed in peculiar clothing made of leather and blue cloth, faced her, holding strange devices that seemed to be weapons, like guns. But she had never seen guns shaped like these. The people spoke words, English she thought, but with a strange accent.

Martha recalled thinking in this dream that she had to act. In the next second, however, she heard a sound that she had come to know all too well during her life on *The Flying Scot.*

Gunshots.

Then she was in the cottage again, waking up.

She strolled toward the spot on White Island where she had last seen *The Flying Scot,* sailing off into oblivion with Owen, the love of her life, bound to the grate at the foremast. She suffered again from that pain, knowing that the pirates were beating and humiliating the man she loved.

To her great surprise, she saw the ruby light that emanated from the Urim stone. It surrounded two men who looked familiar. To her delight, she thought she recognized Owen and Sholem. "He will return," said Martha, turning and hurrying toward the light.

"Martha," one of the men said.

"Hello, Husband," she said, delighted to see him.

"No. Not your husband," the man said. "I'm sure I look like him, because I'm your grandson."

"Oh," she said, disappointed that it wasn't Owen. Why hadn't he come? She felt a little fear. Was he all right? "You are John's son?"

"Yes," he said. "Hello, Grandmother."

Martha stood for a moment, relishing the welcome warmth of the Urim light. "What is your name?" she asked the man.

"My name is McClelland Logan," the man said. He turned to the younger man. "This is the High Priest of all Israel. His name is Steven Levin, Sholem's grandson."

"Hello, Martha," said Steven, his voice gentle and kind. "It is time for you to rest at last."

"Are you really Zadok's son?" said Martha.

He lifted his eyebrows and gave her a big grin of joy. "Yes, I am," he said.

"I have been waiting for you." She felt her red hair stir around her head as if in a high wind. She lifted a hand and tucked the hair behind her ears.

"I know," Zadok's son said. "Here is Owen's stone."

He pointed to the Urim and Thummin and extended his hand toward her.

Martha took his hand. The red light extended to envelop her. She looked around and realized that two young women stood there also. She studied their faces. She beamed at McClelland. "You have the Cymreig, grandson."

"Yes, Grandmother," he said. "This is my wife, Miranda. My niece, McKenna." His voice choked with tears. She overflowed with compassion for the man.

She stepped over and hugged him. He returned the embrace. "You have been faithful beyond all hope," said McClelland. "You came to help us yesterday. Now you can be at peace. Look into the light and find Owen. He is waiting for you."

She released him and turned to Sholem's grandson. "Zadok," she said, "Forgive me my promise."

"It is forgotten," said Steven. "I have the great treasures and they will be safe now. Thank you, Martha. I know your great sacrifice. You will suffer no more. You are free to be with my grandfather's best friend."

Martha heard a familiar voice say, "Beloved." She turned

and saw that another person had joined the group. He was tall, with a blond beard and blue eyes. She was so glad to see him that she began to cry. She reached out her hand. He took it and squeezed.

She said, "Owen. Oh, dear Owen. Thank God you've come for me."

"As you came to save me," her husband said in his familiar, gentle voice. "Come to be with me now. John and David are waiting."

Martha looked at the four friends. She turned back and again embraced her grandson. "Goodbye, Grandson and all of you," she said in her gentle and loving voice. "Walk in love, as I loved Owen and my sons."

"We promise," they replied.

Martha turned to her husband. He pointed to a white horse, waiting for them four or five yards away. They walked together to the lovely creature. Owen lifted her and seated her on the horse's back. In the distance, she saw a beautiful golden gate. As she watched, the gates opened to her. Her father, John Herring, hurried from the city to greet her. Behind him, people in beautiful garments sang a welcome to her.

* * * * *

Mickey watched Steven close his hand over the glass. The red glow faded and disappeared. The four of them stood in the moonlight on White Island, listening to the eternal surf crash against the shore.

McKenna crossed to Steven in the moonlight. She put her arms around him and kissed his cheek. "Good job," she said. "Bravo."

Trembling with emotion, Steven stroked his friend's hair and hugged her. He leaned down and kissed her.

Rand embraced Mickey. His tears wouldn't permit him to speak.

CHAPTER 49

A few days later, Mickey pulled up in front of Casey's house about nine o'clock in the evening. Joey ran out and leapt into Mickey's arms, then hugged his mom. Mickey carried him into Casey's house while Bogey barked and greeted them.

Joey told them everything that had transpired while they were gone, yakking at a breakneck pace. At last Rand and Mickey put him in bed and came back to the family room. They called for a pizza, which arrived a half hour later.

Casey couldn't take his eyes off his daughter. He glowed with pride. "So. Good job, McKenna," said Casey to his daughter who sat next to him, hugging her father's arm. Anna sat on the other side of her daughter, her arm around McKenna's shoulders.

Casey saw the tears in McKenna's eyes. "What's wrong, honey?"

"It's Steven," she said. "He's such a good friend. I don't know if I'll see him again."

"Oh, I think you will," said Rand. "The High Priest is scheduled to enter the great city soon."

"He is?"

"Oh yes. When the Fourth Night comes."

"You think he'll remember me?" McKenna asked her mom.

Anna handed her a slice of pizza. "Yes," said Anna. "I

imagine you'll always stay in touch."

"I hope I find someone like him I can love."

Rand took Mickey's arm. They smiled at each another. "I'm sure you will," Rand told her niece.

"You receive love to the extent that you give love, Honey," said Anna. Now she turned to Mickey. "Meanwhile," she said, "I've been given a new brother." She grinned at Mickey Logan.

"Me too," said McKenna.

Casey poured them a little scotch. "What happened to Larry the Creep and that Mitch guy?"

Mickey told them what had happened in the cave, and how Marisa and Mitch had vanished. He narrated what they'd learned from the police and Coast Guard in Portsmouth. "Larry met Marisa on a trip to New York not long after he married Rand. We don't have the details, but it seems that she and her brother Mitch arranged the meeting. Larry remembered her from high school. She had changed from a mousy little girl into a devastating beauty."

"With the help of several skilled surgeons," said Rand, with a dismissive wave.

"Bitter," Mickey said, unable to repress a grin.

She snorted. "Larry threw everything away for a fabrication."

"Larry became intoxicated with Marisa," Mickey resumed. "She pretended to return his infatuation. As soon as they began the affair, he told her about the insurance fraud ideas. She loved it. She and her cousin Awad had been looking for an opportunity to smuggle Awad into the U.S. from France. The first guy Larry went after was me. I didn't put it together until I realized how the scam worked. I was a trial case."

"Insurance fraud?" said Anna.

"Mitch sucker-punched me and almost killed me when I was leaving the University of Wisconsin," Mickey said. Mickey told Anna and Casey the story of the first time Rand and he said goodbye to one another.

"Why did he do that?" asked Anna.

"Mickey and I made no secret of being best friends," said Rand.

Mickey sipped at the scotch for a moment. "Larry learned that Rand and I were close friends and assumed that we were involved in a romance. He didn't know that Rand was too loyal to betray him."

"They investigated and found that Mickey is alienated from most of his family," noted Rand. "So they figured no one would miss him or insist on an investigation into his death."

"Larry bought an insurance policy when he learned that Rand and I were friends," Mickey said. "He used a false name to designate himself as my beneficiary. He took Mitch to Madison with him and let Mitch confront me. Larry guessed that I might be able to recognize him from high school. They beat me until they thought I was dead or couldn't survive."

"These weren't professional thugs though," said Rand. "They screwed it up. All they did was to put Mickey out of commission for a while."

"Larry and Mitch and Marisa realized that they could buy insurance policies on people," Mickey explained. "They just had to find someone who could pose as the individual to take the physical. They set up bank accounts to make the payments."

"Larry decided to kill a slob named Albert Thomas who also went to high school with us. A nice check for his mother kept her from asking too many questions. She was in the hospital and lacked the energy to insist on an investigation."

"Not long after they brought in Marisa, she and Larry set up a real loser named Frankie Capriatti. A little research showed that he was an abusive bum with few friends. Nobody would give a damn if he died, not even his wife," Mickey said.

"These people are patient," Mickey went on. "They set up the policy, paid the premiums until the right time, and staged a convincing hunting accident."

"Marisa was the bait," said Rand. "They drugged Frankie and shot him in a corn field during a miserable snow storm. Snow covered the body and Frankie wasn't found until their trail was long gone."

"When the police found Frankie's body, the crime scene was months old," Mickey said, sipping the scotch. "Despite his wife's misgivings, the most likely explanation of his death was a hunting accident." Casey shook his head in disbelief at the malevolence of the plan.

"Larry set up a dummy corporation called M and M Life and paid out what was tantamount to hush money to the families of the victims," Mickey told them. "When she got a nice settlement from life insurance--which was a fraction of what the policy paid to Larry and Marisa--Paula didn't encourage any further investigation. Not that the police had any evidence to go on anyhow. I'm pretty sure Larry's gang killed several more people in this scheme and were going to kill many more."

Anna rose and picked up a blanket from the couch, which she draped around McKenna's shoulders. The young woman grinned at her mother and snuggled against her dad.

"Then," Mickey said, "they threw a poor Arab guy to the sharks so Awad could assume his identification and identity and sneak into the country."

"He and Marisa ran three or four other ingenious insurance scams--"

"While he was still married to me," said Rand, and Mickey saw her cheeks burning.

"--that netted them a lot of working funds," Mickey said, taking Rand's hand. "One fraud was a house fire. Another was a jewel theft. Marisa was Awad's cousin and a member of his terrorist cabal. She was also a graphic artist. Larry arranged a job for her at his firm and took her with him to his business when he set it up in La Jolla. I don't think his partner knew anything. With the infatuation that came with the affair and the success they had with the scams, he decided he needed to divorce Rand." Rand's cheeks flushed, and she stood and walked to the window, staring out into the night.

"Larry may have loved Rand when they got married," Mickey said. "He thought that she fit the image of a good corporate wife, but he didn't want children because he thought they'd interfere with his life."

"He knew his wife well enough to know that if Rand learned that he'd been withholding affection because he was involved with another woman, she'd go after everything she had. So he maintained the fiction of marriage and began humiliating her, withholding affection, ridiculing her, and so on."

"Larry hired Mitch, Marisa's brother, to work for him at the L. A. office. He promised Mitch a big bonus if he'd seduce Rand. When Mitch saw her, he was quite willing to attempt a seduction. It worked. Larry let it go on for two months, but then Rand broke it off. Mitch, meanwhile, had taped some of their encounters. Larry sprung it on Rand."

Rand turned away from the window, pale with humiliation and fury. She muttered something about feeling stupid.

Casey crossed to his sister and embraced her, murmuring comfort to Rand. "So where does Awad come in here?" he asked.

"He had to find a way to get into the country. Immigration has gotten pretty tough for known Arab terrorists."

"So this is when they killed the Arab guy in the boat scam, right?" asked Anna.

"Sure. With a little disguising, Awad blended in well."

"Now how did they learn about Steven?" said Casey.

"I don't know if they knew about him being the High Priest. But Awad's ancestor was a desert sheik who owned Grandfather Owen almost three hundred years ago. This sheik was a scholar who wrote down and preserved the legend of White Island. He recorded the story and names, including Rabbi Sholem Levin, Owen's lifelong friend."

"An Arab scholar, huh?" said Casey.

"Oh, yes. The West owes a tremendous debt to the Arabs," Mickey said. "They preserved the great literature of Greece and Rome for posterity. They have a great sense of historicity. The library at Alexandria was one of the great ones in history.

"Grandfather McClelland had no reason not to tell him," Mickey continued. "After all he thought he'd die as he was, a slave in a far-off country, no one aware that he was alive nor that he'd even survived the pirate battles."

"Awad researched the legend of the treasure of White Island. He and his cabal went to White Island and sneaked ashore. They turned the island upside down looking for the treasure, when no one else was around, of course. When they didn't find it, they knew they needed some information. With some effort, he figured out that Steven was a descendant of Sholem."

"So," said McKenna, "they intended to beat the secret out of Steven and his parents. Awad lined up a couple of guys and they met the ship in Charleston, South Carolina, where they bought passage."

"On St. Thomas, they planned to kill McKenna and me," Mickey said. "They figured that would scare Steven into telling them the secret. If it didn't, they'd kill him and then go for his parents. They had a getaway all lined up."

"Awad escaped by motorboat to the yacht. The men were to signal when they had the secret and then they'd escape by small airplane to another island."

"Mitch and Larry picked Steven and me up in Charleston when the boat docked," said McKenna. "They followed us for several days and were right behind us when we got to Portsmouth. Awad and Marisa met Larry and Mitch in Portsmouth, where they saw us picking up camping supplies and tools for digging. They trailed us to the island on the sheik's yacht. When they saw us go into the cave, they decided this had to be it."

"They were right," Mickey said. "But their timing was lousy. We'd just found the staff. We would have kept digging if they hadn't come in to the cave at the wrong time."

"So they were screw-ups from one end to the other," said Casey.

"The only thing Larry ever did that made sense was marrying Rand," Mickey asserted. "He could have had a good life with a loyal, happy wife and a wonderful son. But he couldn't be content."

CHAPTER 50

Rand and Mickey decided it was too late to head home, and Casey and Anna offered them their guest bedroom. They accepted, delighted. After Rand and Mickey took Bogey for a late night walk, they came in and found McKenna waiting in the living room. She wore jeans and a sweatshirt, shoes on. "Hey," Mickey said. "What's up? Are you going out?"

"Mickey," said McKenna, "could I speak to you a moment?"

"Well, sure," Mickey said.

"I'm going to bed," said Rand. "Don't sit up too late, you guys."

Mickey sat down on the couch next to McKenna and took her hand. "What is it?" he asked. "You look distressed."

It took a few seconds. She stared at the floor as she framed the question. "Would you help me?"

"Of course," Mickey said.

"Would you take me to see my father?" she asked, turning to him and covering his hand with hers.

"DiBiasi?"

"Yeah."

"You need to confront him. Okay, I'll drive you to the prison in the morning," Mickey said.

She shook her head. "I've tried that. He won't see me."

"Then what can I. . ." It dawned. "The Cymreig?" Mickey asked.

"I can't ask Mom and Grandpa Daniel to take me there. Mom doesn't need her life confused by seeing him again and Grandpa hates him too much."

"Okay, I get it," Mickey said. "Now?"

"It's after midnight. He should be asleep."

He squeezed her hand and looked through her eyes. In the next moment they stood inside a cell at a minimum-security prison. A man slept on a bunk. Mickey walked over and kicked the bed.

The man stirred. "On your feet, DiBiasi," Mickey sneered.

Alan DiBiasi looked at Mickey, baffled and stupid with sleep. His hair was mussed and he was unshaven.

"Daddy," said McKenna. DiBiasi, blinking with confusion, turned to McKenna, who stood with her arms crossed, her eyes blazing with fury and sadness. "Why did you do it?"

"This is a dream," said DiBiasi, rubbing the sleep from his eyes. "You can't be here. It's ridiculous."

Mickey grabbed a couple of fistfuls of DiBiasi's gray pajamas. He yanked the stunned man off the bed and to his feet. Mickey pushed him toward a wall, and smacked him hard against it. "Does this feel like a dream?" Mickey asked.

"What the hell do you think you're doing?" gasped DiBiasi, struggling for breath, tugging at Mickey's arms.

Mickey backhanded DiBiasi, who began to cry. "Shut up and listen to McKenna," Mickey said.

Mickey held DiBiasi until the man calmed down. "What. . ." DiBiasi said, when he got his breath.

"Daddy," McKenna said, tears on her cheeks. "I was your daughter. How could you?"

¬ THE END ¬

Title: ACID

- Author: Jeff Lovell
- Publisher: TotalRecall Publications, Inc.
- HARD COVER ISBN: 978-1-59095-116-3
- PAPERBACK, ISBN: 978-1-59095-117-0
- EBOOK, Nook, Kindle, ISBN: 978-1-59095-118-7
- Number of pages: 352
- Publication Date: 2013

Rick Howell, living in the shadow of two women who have the power to change reality, must risk his life to stop the genocidal exploits of a desperate lunatic who wants to acquire their powers. The discovery of a mind controlling drug opens a pathway to frightening mental abilities for Rachel Farrell, who can move backward and forward in time at will, while Donna Riske, Rachel's best friend, can control the thoughts of others.

Title: The Coven of the Spring

- Author: Jeff Lovell
- Publisher: TotalRecall Publications, Inc.
- HARD COVER ISBN: 978-1-59095-113-2
- PAPERBACK, ISBN: 978-1-59095-114-9
- EBOOK, Nook, Kindle, ISBN: 978-1-59095-115-6
- Number of pages: 336
- Publication Date: 2013

An ancient secret, with frightening new powers, emerges to terrify and destroy.

Grace DeRosa, a gifted research chemist, lives with her husband Jim and their seventeen year old daughter Crissy. Grace finds a hidden spring in the woods near Salem, Massachusetts. She discovers that the consumed water imparts unique and fearful powers that lead to the ability to read minds, create terrifying mental pictures and force the user's will on others.

Title: Emerald

- Author: Jeff Lovell
- Publisher: TotalRecall Publications, Inc.
- HARD COVER ISBN: 9781590950807
- PAPERBACK, ISBN: 9781590950814
- EBOOK, ISBN: 9781590950821
- Number of pages: 348
- Publication Date: 2015

Emerald begins with a pirate assault on a merchant vessel. Blackbeard, or Edward Teach, terrorized the east coast of America from Nova Scotia down to the Virgin Islands. This book shows how people with a unique mental power called the Knack fight against the evil of pirates from 1715 to the present day, and even includes a long look at the court of King Arthur, and his chief advisor Myrthynne, who also had the most powerful manifestation of the Knack. This book, then, flows in several time periods and pulls together romance, villainy and a dramatic treasure, all of which frame a love story between a woman with the Knack and a man devoted to loving and protecting her.

Title: The Cape

- Author: Jeff Lovell
- Publisher: TotalRecall Publications, Inc.
- HARD COVER, ISBN: 9781590952078
- PAPERBACK, ISBN: 9781590952085
- EBOOK, ISBN: 9781590952092
- Number of pages: 228
- Publication Date: 2016

People say that *Der Fleigen Hollander*—*The Flying Dutchman*, as it is known in English—vanished with all hands in the sixteenth century off the Cape of Good Hope. Yet the ship has been by reliable, truthful people all over the world, suggesting that the ship is trapped in a time warp somewhere in the treacherous ocean south of the Cape. When her father is kidnapped by the ship, Therese goes to find him and rescue him from the self-imposed, Purgatorial imprisonment. In the search she is joined by her mother and a lifetime best friend, who seek to help Therese draw his soul back from the pit of Hell before he is lost for all eternity.

Title: Jazz and Ella

- Author: Jeff Lovell
- Publisher: TotalRecall Publications, Inc.
- PAPERBACK, ISBN: 9781590953006
- EBOOK, ISBN: 9781590953013
- Number of pages: 104
- Publication Date: 2015

Jazz and Ella tells the story of Jazz, a fourteen year old high school freshman, and his best friend, Ella, who meet on the way to Disney World. A supernatural being gives them each a magic amulet, which the children use to transport themselves to new and different worlds. They meet and deal many situations that cause them to face their fears and even terrors; that suggest ways that situations can be handled; and they see some of the choices that they will have to confront as they grow up.

Title: Gina and Colby

- Author: Jeff Lovell
- Publisher: TotalRecall Publications, Inc.
- PAPERBACK, ISBN: 9781590953259
- EBOOK, ISBN: 9781590953266
- Number of pages: 136
- Publication Date: 2016

A Magic Amulet Allows Two Teen-Agers to Discover how to Make a Difference in the World of Animal Poaching

Two teen-agers, different in every way, form an unshakeable friendship as a result of the adventures they share after meeting in Disney Springs. Transported through a magic amulet to a totally different culture and continent, they are offered an opportunity to make a difference in the lives of endangered animals.

Dangers abound as they face poachers and pirates in their attempts to rescue these creatures, and they discover a courage within themselves that leads each one to a positive change in how they view themselves and others.

Title: Marina and Dan

- Author: Jeff Lovell
- Publisher: TotalRecall Publications, Inc.
- PAPERBACK, ISBN: 9781590953228
- EBOOK, Nook, Kindle, ISBN: 9781590953235
- Number of pages: 128
- Publication Date: 2016

This ancient Egyptian Adventure, part of the Mousegate Series, traces the story of Marina and Dan, best friends since childhood, as they wrestle with the concept of heroism and how it applies to them. When offered a unique, but potentially dangerous opportunity by a spiritual being, they must make a decision that will stretch them in ways they never imagined. Able to experience first-hand the miraculous events that have been talked about for centuries, they witness the impossible become possible as they walk with Moses during the ancient biblical era where the crossing of the Red Sea took place. Both their friendship and their faith is strengthened through the adventures encountered together.

Title: The Third Day

- Author: Jeff Lovell
- Publisher: TotalRecall Publications, Inc.
- HARD COVER ISBN: 9781590959947
- PAPERBACK, ISBN: 9781590959954
- EBOOK, Nook, Kindle, ISBN: 9781590959961
- Number of pages: 288
- Publication Date: 2016

The Old, old man walks in all the countries of the world, tracing and retracing and tracing again his betrayal, unable to find peace or grace since his betrayal of the Nazarene some two thousand years ago. Two newlywed young people and their spouses find themselves called to help him and recover an incalculably valuable treasure, worth far more than any earthly price. The group must go to the Virgin Islands and recover the treasure to help the Old Man redeem his soul and save others from a disastrous fate at the hands of a desperate cult.

www.ingramcontent.com/pod-product-compliance
Lightning Source LLC
Chambersburg PA
CBHW020328120726
47904CB00002B/325